ACCLAIM ... AND
CINDY MARTINUSEN COLOMA

"Rich with symbolism and picturesque Texas landscape, *Song of the Brokenhearted* is a reminder that our plan for our life is often not in sync with God's. Readers will enjoy walking alongside Ava on her journey of self-discovery. Sometimes in the most broken places of life comes true transformation, setting us on the path that can only be seen through God's eyes. Highly recommended."

—BETH WISEMAN, BEST-SELLING AUTHOR OF *NEED YOU NOW* AND THE LAND OF CANAAN SERIES

"Lessons in grace abound in this heart-tugging story of broken pasts and futures filled with unexpected hope. In Ava's struggle to trust and in her eventual triumph, many readers will find pieces of their own stories."

—LISA WINGATE, NATIONAL BESTSELLING AND AWARD-WINNING AUTHOR OF *DANDELION SUMMER* AND *BLUE MOON BAY*

"This heartwarming tale comes from a talented duo. Cindy's gift of lush storytelling is an ideal match for Sheila's lovely insights into enduring relationships. *Sweet Sanctuary* beautifully portrays the complexities of a mother's heart."

—ROBIN JONES GUNN, BEST-SELLING AUTHOR OF THE SISTERCHICKS' NOVELS

"As a child I assumed that some families (not mine) were perfect. Eventually I grew up and figured out how wrong I was. That's probably why I appreciate *Sweet Sanctuary*. Peeling back layers of heartbreaks and secrets, Wren struggles to understand her family's old wounds and how they impact her own life . . . an important story of forgiveness, healing and hope."

—MELODY CARLSON, AUTHOR OF *HERE'S TO FRIENDS* AND *RIVER'S SONG*

Other Novels by
Sheila Walsh

Angel Song with Kathryn Cushman
Sweet Sanctuary with Cindy Martinusen Coloma

Other Novels by
Cindy Martinusen Coloma

Eventide

The Salt Garden

Orchid House

Young Adult Novels

Ruby Unscripted

Beautiful

Caleb + Kate

Song

OF THE
BROKENHEARTED

SHEILA WALSH

AND

CINDY MARTINUSEN COLOMA

THOMAS NELSON
Since 1798

NASHVILLE   DALLAS   MEXICO CITY   RIO DE JANEIRO

Published in Nashville, Tennessee, by Thomas Nelson. Thomas Nelson is a registered trademark of Thomas Nelson, Inc.

The author is represented by the literary agency of Alive Communications, Inc., 7680 Goddard Street, Suite 200, Colorado Springs, CO 80920. www.alivecommunications.com.

Thomas Nelson, Inc., titles may be purchased in bulk for educational, business, fund-raising, or sales promotional use. For information, please e-mail SpecialMarkets@ThomasNelson.com.

Scripture quotations are taken from *The Living Bible.* © 1971. Used by permission of Tyndale House Publishers, Inc., Wheaton, Illinois 60189. All rights reserved.

Publishers Note: This novel is a work of fiction. Names, characters, places, and incidents are either products of the author's imagination or used fictitiously. All characters are fictional, and any similarity to people living or dead is entirely coincidental.

Library of Congress Cataloging-in-Publication Data

Walsh, Sheila, 1956-
  Song of the brokenhearted / Sheila Walsh and Cindy Martinusen Coloma.
    p. cm.
  ISBN 978-1-59554-687-6 (trade paper)
1. Life change events--Fiction. I. Coloma, Cindy, 1970- II. Title.
  PS3623.A36615S56 2012
  813'.6--dc23

                    2012017522

Printed in the United States of America

12 13 14 15 16 QG 5 4 3 2 1

This book is dedicated to those like me who thought our lives were over only to discover that when we offer our brokenness to God, we have only just begun.

—Sheila

To Jenna Jane Benton—for your frendship, inspiration, and creativity that never fails to amaze me. And for making me pray out loud, often.

—Cindy

One

"YOU NEED TO WAKE UP," AVA TOLD HERSELF AS SHE GRIPPED THE steering wheel between quick gulps of the coffee she'd grabbed at an all-night gas station.

She turned onto Walnut Street and the directions to the Gibson residence became unnecessary. Her destination was obvious by the cars parked at awkward angles around the two-story stucco house.

Tonight was not the night for casseroles, sympathy cards, or flowers. That would come tomorrow, and in the days that followed. This was the time to arrive empty-handed and with as few words as possible.

She rose from her car into a warm autumn night, pausing to watch gray puffs of clouds drift across the nearly full moon. The moment gave her the strength to go toward the front door and to become the helpful stranger in a house of deep grief.

A bouquet of silver balloons hung unmoving from the lamppost at the end of the walkway. Jars lit by candles lined the path to the house; most had already burned themselves out. A large banner hung over the front door: *Congratulations, Joshua and Jessica!*

Ava wondered if she should suggest taking down the reminder that hours earlier this had been a house of celebration and joy. Perhaps she could do it herself a little later.

An older man answered her knock wearing rumpled clothing and a deep frown drawn in the corners of his mouth.

"Are you a friend of the family?" he said, studying her in her designer jeans and beige sweater.

"No, I'm Ava. Hannah called and asked me to come."

His frown softened slightly. "Come in. We had the media stop by already. Sharks. I don't know how they heard so fast. Most of the family is in the formal living room. I'm their neighbor across the street there. I've known Jessica since she was nine . . ." His voice trailed off.

"I'm sorry. It's very painful."

"It is," he muttered.

Ava followed the man beyond the foyer and sweeping staircase and toward a silent gathering of people who stood at different places around the room. A half-eaten cake rested on the table.

"Hannah? This lady said you called her."

The woman from her Bible study stared at Ava a moment, then recognition dawned on her face. She rose quickly from the chair.

"Ava. Thank you for coming."

"Of course," she said. As they embraced, Ava felt the woman

lean heavily against her. For a moment, she feared Hannah would collapse.

"She was my only niece, and more like a daughter to me," Hannah said within the sobs that shook her. "Such a beautiful girl, and such a lovely heart. They were so happy . . . How can they be gone, just like that?"

Ava offered no answers as she held the middle-aged woman while she cried. Ava felt the pain echo in her own heart. Though she often was around tragedies since starting the ministry at church, Ava had yet to become desensitized to the grief.

"I can't believe you came out this late at night," Hannah said, wiping the tears from her face. "I'd heard you talk about the Broken Hearts, but I had no idea . . . Do you come out in the night like this all the time? Your husband must hate it."

"It's not just me. Our team takes turns being on call. But nighttime seems to be when most people need help," Ava said, picking up several of the tissues that Hannah dropped on the floor. "Is there anything specific you need right now?"

"I don't know." Hannah stared at her with a blank look as many did when Ava asked the question. Still, she asked instead of taking over—that, too, would come later.

"My sister is upstairs, but she wanted to be alone. Joe, my brother-in-law, was trying to drive to the . . . the site."

"Oh no," Ava muttered. On the drive into Fort Worth, Ava had passed the remains of the wreck along a lonely stretch of highway. Red flares dotted the road, dividing drivers from the tragedy strewn in broken glass and bits of metal across the asphalt, off the shoulder, and into the darkened farmland.

Ambulances were gone, and a tow truck was loading a mangled twist of metal that had once been the car of this newly engaged couple who believed their entire lives stretched before them.

Ava shuddered to think if it were Sienna and Preston. Her daughter and fiancé had celebrated their engagement over the summer. Nothing would comfort these parents tonight or for many nights to come. Such a loss was unfathomable, and Ava's heart felt a physical ache for this family who was planning a wedding several hours earlier, but now would begin planning two funerals.

"Seems someone stopped him from going. But I don't know where he is."

Ava placed her hand on Hannah's shoulder.

"Well, I'm available for whatever you need. The team has helped make funeral arrangements, we can organize food, and we've started memorial funds in some cases. We can do a little or a lot, just let me know what's needed."

The woman cried again. "Thank you. I can't believe we're talking about this. Their engagement announcement was just five hours ago. It doesn't seem possible that they're both . . . gone."

"Hannah," a voice called.

Hannah hurried toward the entry and looked up the oak stairway.

"She's asking for you," a woman said, peering down from the top.

Hannah glanced at Ava as if asking permission.

"I'll be down here if you need me, or you can call me in the morning. Try to help her rest for now."

Hannah nodded and headed up the staircase with her jaw clenched and eyebrows rumpled.

Ava had an awkward moment of not knowing what to do with herself. Her eyes swept the rooms that veined off on both sides of the foyer. She moved quietly to pick up cups, plates, and half-empty champagne glasses left over from the engagement party. She found the kitchen still disheveled and set to work. It was obvious the people living here usually kept the house neat and tidy. Having the house clean might not be noticed tomorrow as shock slowly wore off, but a messy one would certainly add to the stress.

After cleaning as much as she could, Ava made coffee and set out mugs beside the cream and sugar on the long tile bar. A few people came in here and there, though none spoke to her. Some took cups of coffee with mumbled thank-yous.

As Ava swept the dining area, she saw a small face under the table staring up at her. She jumped in surprise, then bent down to meet the dark eyes staring back at her.

"Hello. What are you doing down *there*?" she said gently despite the racing in her chest. A child beneath a kitchen table—it touched a memory she'd tried to bury long ago. "Come here, sweetie. I won't hurt you."

The girl didn't move toward her, but she also didn't move away as Ava knelt on the floor and inched toward her.

"How long have you been there? Would you like something to drink or eat?"

The girl nodded. Ava reached for the little hands clenched around her knees. Finally she coaxed the child out.

The girl wrapped her arms around Ava's neck as she picked her up. Ava guessed she was about five years old, close to the age she'd been on a night when her childhood home had been the hub of a tragic gathering. No one had seen her hiding beneath a table as people talked about her mother's death.

"Oh no, I thought she was asleep," a woman said, flying toward the child. Ava handed her over, but the girl's dark eyes stared after Ava.

"Thank you," Hannah said, standing in the doorway with her hands hanging from her sides as if too heavy to do more than dangle there.

"I think she's thirsty or hungry," Ava said, scooping up the last of the dirt beside the table. She dumped it in the trash and returned the broom and dustpan to the pantry.

"Little Grace adored her Uncle Josh," Hannah said, sitting on a bar stool. She played with the rim of a coffee mug. "My sister isn't doing well."

Ava turned on the dishwasher and joined her at the bar.

"She won't for a long time. I'm sure none of you will. Would you like to pray?"

Hannah nodded. Ava took her hands and prayed quietly. When she finished, she opened her eyes to find Hannah gazing at her.

"Thank you for being here."

Ava paused after closing the front door. She stood on a patio chair and pulled down the banner over the door, then folded it up. She'd give it to Hannah at the right moment.

Two

THE NEXT MORNING, AS AVA WHIPPED EGGS IN A BOWL FOR BAKED French toast casserole, she caught something amiss in the green of the backyard through the kitchen window.

It was a rare Sunday morning with all three of them at home. They'd attended the Saturday service at church, Dane hadn't bustled off to the office as he'd done most weekends in the past months, Ava had said no to helping with an afternoon fund-raiser, and Jason didn't have any friends or football buddies staying over for once.

The pleasure of waking past seven to a quiet house sent Ava to the kitchen, following the scent of freshly brewed coffee—brewed by timer as usual—with her thoughts flipping through her aunt's old book of recipes.

She'd left the Gibsons' house after two a.m. with the promise to return later today. But the family remained heavy in her thoughts after she arrived home and slid into bed. Perhaps Sienna's engagement made the tragedy more poignant—a reminder to cherish what they had.

Now, between the cinnamon and heavy cream, Ava paused from savoring the morning light to focus harder through the clear glass window over the sink. Out beyond the shimmer of the swimming pool among the manicured lawn and hedges, the wispy branches of the weeping willow tree seemed jaundiced and more sparse than usual.

The door to the mudroom opened, and Dane's slippers padded across the tile floor. He carried a coffee cup and held up a newspaper. "Look what I found. An actual *Dallas Morning News* made with ink and paper. When was the last time I read one of these on a Sunday morning?"

"I can't even remember. It's like listening to music on our record player. I didn't know they made newspapers anymore," Ava joked as she poured in the heavy cream and stirred the batter. The cinnamon swirled through the white liquid.

Dane gave an approving grunt at the ingredients stretched across the granite counter. "I'll cook the bacon. Let me know when." He moved behind her, bending to kiss her neck. It sent a shiver down her skin, reminding her of younger days when such a kiss would have meant that breakfast wouldn't be made. Dane topped off her coffee cup, then his.

"You came in late. What happened?" he said.

"A family lost their daughter. She and her fiancé had their engagement party last night, then they were both killed in a car accident."

"It's in the paper," Dane said, turning the front page toward her. The mangled car in the photo looked haunting, lit up against the dark night.

"That's fast—sharks indeed," Ava said.

"Be careful driving around so late. You should call me when you're on the road."

"All right," she said, not wanting to talk further about the night before. The little girl beneath the table and that congratulatory banner struck a little too close to home for her liking. "Where did you get a paper at this hour?"

"I stole it from the Lopez yard."

"No you didn't."

He gave her a mischievous grin. "I traded Jason out. He has to mow their lawn."

"He's going to love that."

"He will because I'll mow ours for him, and the Lopez yard is smaller." Dane settled into a chair in the breakfast nook. Ava bit back a smile at Dane's salt-and-pepper hair sticking up on one side. She loved him rumpled with bed head. Dane was always put together for business with his designer suits and ties, hair perfectly cut and smoothed in place. At home, Dane was Dane again.

"Seeing you like that makes me expect Sienna and Jason to come running in wearing their footed pajamas . . . what did Sienna call them? Feet jammies."

Dane lowered the paper, watching Ava as she dipped the bread in the batter and layered it into a baking dish.

"Let's call her. We'll tell her to forget the wedding, forget college, and come be our baby girl again."

"It's not even six a.m. there. She'd kill us." Ava pictured her daughter sleeping with the covers all kicked off like she always did. They were planning Sienna's dream wedding, extravagant and luxurious, and Ava's binder of wedding plans overflowed with designs, schedules, and brochures. The months were moving too fast, like a locomotive barreling down a mountain picking up speed and gathering more and more weight.

Dane turned a page of the paper. "Not sure I'm loving this newspaper as much as I'd hoped."

"Missing technology already?"

"It's pretty nice to scroll through all my papers at once. And no ink on the fingers." He rubbed his fingers together.

Ava opened the lower oven and set the casserole dish inside. Then she tapped out a text to Sienna, hoping she didn't wake her but missing her daughter too much to keep the words in.

The only thing missing this morning is you, Ava typed and hit Send. She pictured those words traveling across the state of Texas, then New Mexico, Arizona, clipping the edge of Nevada, and up California to her daughter at Stanford University.

No one had wanted Sienna to attend Stanford—too far from home, too liberal, not Texas. It made Ava secretly proud that her daughter would venture into the unknown. But then, Ava's one year outside of Texas living with Aunt Jane had been much more than her own parents had done. Her entire life looked nothing like her parents', but Ava hoped her own daughter wouldn't feel the need to build a life wholly contradictory to the family she'd grown up in.

"I need to go in to the office today," Dane said, glancing up from the paper.

Ava's Sunday morning peace rattled like windows in an earthquake. Before she could respond, he continued.

"And . . . could you hold off using the credit cards for the next week? I may switch them over to a line of credit or consolidate a few, and I want to make sure the balances on all of them are accurate." Dane kept his face in the paper, and Ava took a moment to consider his words. In all their years of marriage, Dane had never asked her to avoid using their credit cards.

"Everything okay?" she asked, keeping her voice casual.

"Of course. It'll be worked out soon. I know wedding and Christmas shopping is on the horizon—it's just a few weeks." He chuckled slightly, but Ava knew him well enough to know he was concerned about something.

She let it go. He'd talk when he was ready.

"Have you noticed the willow tree?" Ava asked, standing at the window with her coffee cup cradled in her hands.

"Yeah, I think it's dying." Dane turned another page.

"No, you think so?" Ava muttered as she swallowed back an ache at the back of her throat. She set her cup on the counter and headed outside. The gentle autumn morning met her with the scent of leaves, freshly cut grass, and swimming pool.

Ava padded in her slippers, weaving around patio furniture at the pool and down the path to the tall willow. She touched a long weeping strand of leaves, and several fell off into her hand.

"No," she whispered. This wasn't the normal changing of the seasons. Something was definitely wrong with the tree. A sudden wave of panic flooded over her as she gazed upward into the branches and cascade of leaves. She wanted to paste the leaves back onto the branches.

It doesn't matter that much, she tried chastising herself. Compared to the heartache and tragedies she witnessed every week, like the family last night, a tree was nothing. But this willow was important to her. It had been growing in their back-yard for fifteen years, given to her by her brother as a gift when Jason was born. Clancy had dug it up from the land they'd grown up on. Her brother knew her attachment to the weep-ing willows, and Ava had cherished this tree all these years. Through the ups and downs of the past decade and a half, it was a reminder of how far she'd come, and she'd spent count-less moments of prayer sitting on the bench Dane had built beneath its branches.

Years earlier, Ava had saved the willow tree from landscap-ers who wanted to pull it out because it interfered with the Mediterranean style. Their plans had a tall fountain drawn in its place. The pool guy complained about the leaves cast in the water with every summer breeze. But Ava would never risk it being moved, and she certainly would have never removed it.

"You must make it through this. You're my *prayer tree*," Ava whispered, looking up at its weave of branches that stretched toward the blue sky, then fanned into the shape of an umbrella dripping all the way back to the ground. She'd never asked her brother but wondered if Clancy had dug the tree from the stand by the riverside. As a young child, she'd hidden within the umbrella fan with her books and dolls. Ava hadn't told her family those stories. While most of her life was an open book, there were a few secrets to keep within a tree.

The baked French toast was in the oven, she needed to check in with Hannah, and a morning with her men couldn't be wasted. Yet Ava resolved to watch the tree and to find out how to save it. It was only a tree. But she couldn't just let it die.

Three

Five willow trees had stood along the riverbank of her childhood home. Her young imagination had seen pioneers coming out west in wagon trains, settling along the bank of the Black Rock River, and carefully planting the willow trees. Maybe it had been a little girl like her who'd planted the trees, pushing the seedlings down into the soft earth and wondering if they'd someday grow.

Ava found herself daydreaming about those willows in the following weeks, surprising herself with details she'd forgotten.

Yet matched against daydreams, her schedule of real life took precedence. She stared at her electronic tablet every morning in wonder at the passing of days. Would there ever be a year she wasn't shocked at how quickly the months flew away? Jason's Friday night football games, Bible study, the funeral for the Gibson family, emergency calls to her ministry, and fall church events were just a few of the commitments filling up the boxes on her calendar. Ava kept moving "TREE" to the next day, then the next, and the next, without any action toward saving its life.

Dane kept working late, asking her to do things that he usually did. More and more she attended church and social events alone.

"It's temporary. Some issues with investors and other things, but nothing to worry about," he said, and promised to make it up to her once the company passed through their little crisis. He was distracted and seemed gravely worried, so she let her annoyance mostly slide off her back. His lack of availability wasn't new, and he'd always made up for it in the past. And she was busy too. Her Broken Hearts ministry was growing in demand as more people experienced hard times.

⚬⚭⚬

One night, Ava heard an incessant ringing, demanding that she wake. She grabbed her cell and recognized the number as Randy Hemstead's, one of the church's pastors.

"Hello?" she said, trying to sound already awake. She pulled out her notepad from her bedside table to write down the details. She suppressed a yawn and slipped away from Dane's gentle snores and onto the second-story balcony overlooking the back-yard. After she hung up the phone, she leaned on the railing, gazing down at the shimmer of blue water around the under-water pool lights. The scent of chlorine mixed with the smell of autumn leaves.

A soldier had been killed in a training mission. He left a young pregnant wife with two little boys.

Ava put on her slippers and walked down to her computer in her built-in desk between the kitchen and living room. Her phone rang again as the computer loaded. Her heart never failed to skip a beat at the thought that one day the call would be about someone she loved.

The woman was crying and croaked out her name.

"It's all right. Take your time."

After several seconds the woman apologized and explained who she was.

"You were in Bible study last spring with my neighbor June Reilly, and I visited a few times," she said between sniffles.

"Yes, Rose, I remember you." Ava recalled that June had asked them to pray for Rose's marriage.

"I'm sorry to call so late, but the church website said you were available at all hours, and I didn't know what to do."

"What's going on?"

"My husband. He's been drinking more and more. Tonight, I was really afraid of him."

"Did he hurt you?"

"No. He broke a bunch of things in the house, but I locked myself in the bathroom."

"Where is he now?"

"Passed out on the couch. I'm in my car in the driveway."

"That's good. Don't go back into the house. Do you have someplace to go? We can get you a hotel room for the night." Ava wrote down Rose's name on her tablet.

Rose's voice faded a moment, then she said, "That's my best friend calling me. I couldn't reach her earlier."

Ava paused, worried about the young woman. "Please call back if you need anything. I can meet you or get you someplace safe for the night."

"Thank you."

ᴇᴏᴏⓒᴏᴅ

After they hung up, she turned on a few lights in the kitchen and put on a kettle for some chamomile tea.

She opened a new file in the program a techie guy at church had created for the ministry. There were hundreds of files filled with stories of loss.

Ava opened an e-mail and sent a message to her team, asking for prayer and for any thoughts on how to specifically help the two families. She e-mailed her florist, a church member who gave the ministry all its flowers at cost, and ordered a huge bouquet for the soldier's family. At times Ava felt like flowers were an empty gift. Then she'd remember her Aunt Jenny's passing. The flowers had meant more to her than she could have ever imagined.

Ava closed her laptop and grabbed a notepad to make a list for tomorrow. Her pen holder was empty, and she grumbled at how everyone stole them from her desk with its convenient location in the house. She walked into the den and opened the drawer of the large oak desk. Papers covered the slot where Dane kept his pens. Then Ava noticed what the papers were. They were bills, and all of them had red ink. Late.

Ava shuffled through each one: credit cards, electric bill, phone, Internet . . . Dane was meticulous about paying bills on time to avoid late charges. The balances on their cards showed that he hadn't followed his rule of paying them off every month in quite a long while.

Ava returned the bills and closed the desk drawer. Why wasn't Dane sharing this with her? The moment she thought it, she knew the answer. He'd told her when they married that he would always take care of her. He'd never wanted her help with their finances, knowing it wasn't her strength and it was unusually stressful for her. After her tumultuous childhood when she and her brother had struggled to have food in the cupboards, Dane promised her security. He said it was another way of showing her how much he loved her, how much he hated what she'd endured, and how proud of her he was for overcoming such a harsh beginning.

But clearly they were in trouble. Maybe Dane was dealing with it as he said. Maybe he'd gotten behind in paying bills lately with all the long hours at work. Ava would ask, and she could help him. She was familiar with online bill paying—she did it for her ministry every month.

Ava returned to her kitchen desk, forgetting the pen and deciding she'd done enough for the night. She put her teacup in the dishwasher, then turned off the lights and headed back to bed. As she slid in beside Dane, she studied the outline of his strong shoulder and listened to his deep exhales. She touched the hair at the back of his neck. She pulled away as he groaned and rustled the covers before settling back into sleep.

Ava gravitated between being upset that Dane was hiding his problems from her and feeling grateful that he wanted to protect her.

When sleep wouldn't come, Ava decided to pray.

She prayed for the families she'd been meeting through the ministry, starting with the Gibson family who'd be struggling forward in the awful days after the funerals. Next she prayed for the children and wife of the soldier and their journey of life without a husband and daddy, then for Rose, whom she hoped was safe with her best friend now.

Ava's prayers moved to Sienna in California and Preston, her fiancé, then Jason in his first year of high school and Dane with his many issues at work, and for their finances and the heavy burden he was carrying in silence. The list moved forward as her eyelids got heavy.

"Everything all right?" Dane muttered in his half-asleep voice, turning toward her and draping an arm around her waist.

Ava considered the question. For those families, nothing would be the same again. And everything wasn't all right for Dane and the stack of late bills in his desk.

She kissed his cheek and settled into her pillow, knowing he was already back to sleep.

Her eyes opened at a memory.

"It always comes in threes," her grandmother loved to say, always seeming hungry for doom.

"See, what did I tell you?" she'd say whenever anything went wrong. "This is just the beginning."

Ava turned over and tried shutting out the sound of her voice. For a long time she'd lived without her grandmother's doomsday voice haunting her. Why was it back?

The problem was, her grandmother had often been right.

Four

When Ava was a little girl and thought about God, she always pictured her daddy. She'd remember him standing waist high in the slow current of the Black Rock River wearing his white dress shirt and slacks from the thick JCPenney catalog as he dipped people beneath the lazy green waters. Baptism days were Ava's favorite. All the parishioners left the stuffy church for the huge shade trees lining the river, carrying large picnic baskets, coolers, and thick quilts to stretch out over the lawn.

Daddy would raise his hands toward heaven as he talked about John the Baptist and the Jordan River. He told of the Holy Spirit descending like a dove. The way he spoke, with his moving arms and his deep passionate voice, brought the story to life. For years Ava believed she'd seen that dove descend and thought that Jesus might have been baptized by her father on one of those summer dipping days. He'd pulled people up into the new air with his eyes looking into the blue sky and shouted, "Hallelujah. Praise be to God!"

But that was a lifetime ago. It seemed like someone else's life, as if she'd watched it on a movie or read it in a storybook. Thirty years had passed since she'd seen her daddy face-to-face . . . thirty years since he'd walked the earth as a free man.

Her father nurtured Ava's faith, but later she blamed him for losing it. If God was like her daddy, how could she believe in His promises? How could she believe in His love?

The God she'd sung about with a heart so full it might explode was no longer there. For a long time, He became a dark void like the space that filled a starless night. The sky would be dark and empty, covered up by unseen clouds, and it became hard for her to believe that stars existed behind such dense darkness. Her brain knew the truth about the stars, just as she never fully stopped believing God was somewhere, but for a while, God disappeared behind the darkness.

‿❧❧‿

Ava missed her daughter's phone call during Thursday morning Bible study. She stood in the foyer of church, adjusting the autumn leaves that decorated the welcome desk, and listened to the voice mail.

"Mom, I'm coming home this weekend. Friday afternoon flight—will text you the details. Can't wait to see you guys and watch the game together. Love you!"

Ava caught how her daughter's voice sounded different—a few tones higher than normal. It surfaced the memory of a summer Sienna had called from camp the year before seventh grade.

22

"Mom, I'm sick and need to come home," she'd said. Sienna had claimed stomachaches despite how her friends begged her to stay. This was her third year of college, not summer camp, and though Dane had given her a credit card to fly home whenever she wanted, she'd never actually used it.

Ava tapped a text off to Dane with the news, and despite her concern, she couldn't wait to see her girl.

"Ready?" Kayanne came around the corner from the ladies room, picking up her Bible and study book. "By the way, you told me to remind you before lunch we need to ask a florist or garden person what's wrong with your tree. Oh, and I brought a list of what we're doing for Private Grant's family. The funeral is on Monday."

Ava looked up with the phone in her hands. "Uh . . . hmm."

"Hey, you told me to remind you. I have the text message."

"No, not that . . ." Ava thought about her plans for the next few days. She opened the calendar on her phone, hoping to rearrange her schedule so she'd get plenty of time with her daughter.

"You're canceling on lunch? Why?" Kayanne popped her hands onto her hips. Her purse slipped off her shoulder and down to her elbow.

They'd been friends since the first years of marriage, raised children together, and shared shoulders when Sienna left for college and William joined the air force. Their roles had diverged five years earlier when Kayanne's husband left her for another woman. Yet their friendship had strengthened since that time, even though their lives no longer looked like carbon copies of each other's.

Ava slipped the phone into her bag and wagged a finger at her friend. "Hold the indignation, it's usually you canceling on me."

Kayanne smiled. "You got me there."

"I need to drop off gift baskets to those families, but Sienna left a message that she's coming home tomorrow."

"Wonderful. What's the occasion?"

"No idea. It has me wondering, but of course I can't wait to see her."

"Just Sienna? Or Preston too?"

"Apparently Sienna only."

Kayanne frowned. "That's weird."

Ava loved Kayanne's bluntness, which was exactly why many of the polite churchwomen disliked her.

"She wants to see Jason play football. Her voice sounded off to me."

"Interesting. And her perfect fiancé isn't coming with her?" Kayanne squinted her blue eyes in thought.

"Don't be sarcastic. I couldn't dream up a better guy for Sienna. He grounds her where she needs grounding but supports her in everything. And I adore him."

Kayanne rolled her eyes. "He comes from a great family, he'll take care of her financially, and he's a good Christian boy."

"As if I care about the family part," Ava said, though sometimes she noticed she felt a sense of pride that her daughter was marrying into a well-connected tribe. "This would have been solved if she and William had married like we planned when they were babies. Everything would be perfect."

Kayanne sighed. "My son has less patience than I do, plus they think of each other like siblings."

"True," Ava said with a laugh.

They walked side by side out of the church. The other women had already left and the large parking lot was nearly empty.

"I'm starving and you dump me. Now you'll miss my newest dating drama. I hope you can handle the suspense."

"I do so love your dating stories."

"Yes, tragedies that they are."

"It won't always be this way, sweetie." Ava slid her arm around Kayanne's shoulders. "It might be time to bite the bullet. You ready for online dating yet?"

Kayanne snorted, then broke into a laugh.

"What's so funny?" Ava said, smiling as they walked across the parking lot.

Kayanne laughed harder. It took a moment for her to talk.

"In all the years you've known me, would you have ever imagined you'd suggest such a thing to me?"

Ava laughed with her. "I was against it, truth be told. But all those commercials with online success stories are changing my opinion."

"You're either a marketing person's dream or you know I'm getting desperate."

Ava clicked her keychain and heard the engine of her Mercedes fire to life. Kayanne was parked beside her in a sun-faded Corolla.

Kayanne set her Bible and study book on the roof of her car as she unlocked the door. "Life takes us on very strange journeys, that's for sure. *Life is weird, then you die.* That should be a bumper sticker."

"For the hopeless. I'd like something with a bit more cheer."

"You're right. How about, *God is taking us on a wild ride. Hang on.*"

"It doesn't have quite the same rhythm to it, but that's better."

"And it's true. But how do we hang on? That's always my problem."

"Mine as well."

As Ava waved and drove off, she kept hearing Kayanne's bumper sticker as if God was pressing the message home. *God is taking us on a wild ride. Hang on.*

She brushed away the thoughts. Her life was in a good place. She wasn't looking for any wild rides, divine or otherwise.

کوئی

"Dad, you aren't paying attention," Jason said as he watched a sci-fi show, one of the space spinoffs that he and Dane usually watched together. They often discussed the plot and elements of the show, but it sounded like a foreign language to Ava, with all their photon blasters, warp speeds, and light years.

Ava, Jason, and Dane lounged around the living room. Ava held her electronic tablet with her list for Sienna's weekend at home. She'd make her daughter's favorite pumpkin soup and order bread from the brick-oven bakery in town. To appease the guys, Ava would pop a beef stew in the Crock-Pot. They'd go to Jason's football game on Friday night, work on the wedding plans, attend church, and maybe have a movie night at home or see if there was something going on in town. Perhaps they could squeeze in a little retail therapy as well.

"I'm watching, buddy," Dane said in a voice that only proved his distraction. Dane leaned intently toward his laptop screen with his glasses low on his long, straight nose.

"Did you see what just happened?"

"The galactic treaty was broken again. Awful."

Jason frowned and let out a distinct groan of annoyance.

"You probably should go to sleep after this," Ava said, typing in a note to call the housekeeper in the morning.

"What time will Sis get here?" Jason asked without raising his eyes from the television.

"Her flight arrives at two thirty."

"Cool," Jason said, jumping up from the couch as his program appeared to be ending. "I'm going to bed. I want to read anyway."

"Read? As in a book? What about aliens and distant planets?" Ava said.

"My book is about aliens and distant planets," Jason said, bending down to kiss Ava on the cheek.

"Of course it is. At least it's reading."

Dane didn't move his eyes from his laptop. "Good night, buddy. We'll catch up on our shows over the weekend."

"That's what you said last week," Jason muttered with a scowl tossed Dane's way.

"You can watch it with Sienna this weekend," Ava reminded him. That seemed to cheer him up as he disappeared around the corner, his heavy footsteps tromping up the stairs.

"Our son is not happy with you," Ava typed into a chat program. She heard the sound of her message popping up on Dane's screen and smiled as he looked up in surprise.

"What do you mean?" he asked, his eyes bouncing back to his laptop.

"I keep telling you—you're here, but not here. We all notice it."

Dane nodded with his thick eyebrows scrunched over his eyes.

Jason's growing bitterness at Dane's consuming work schedule was beginning to worry her. Dane had always worked long hours, but in the last months he'd become less available to everyone. Dane continued to promise it would get better, it was the recession, that he was training someone, an essential proposal or meeting or something was going to change it, and that it was all temporary.

Ava missed her husband as well. They usually talked about everything. But Dane talked little about work now, and he wasn't there to hear what was happening in her life either. Their usually bi-monthly dates had taken a hiatus since the previous winter.

"Is everything all right? At work? With you? Our finances?" She hadn't told him she'd found the late bills. When she looked the next day, the bills were gone. Maybe he'd paid them? She'd tried casually bringing up their finances a few times, but Dane always cut her off.

"Good enough. Manageable. Nothing to worry about," he said, glancing at her, then back to his laptop screen. She stared at him, but he didn't look up.

"You aren't worried about Sienna's surprise visit?"

"She wants to see us. What's to worry about?"

Dane always brushed her concerns away as being a mom-thing. He'd once said she seemed to seek problems to be concerned about when it came to the kids.

Sometimes Ava longed for a sister or a mother—or at least for Aunt Jenny to still be alive. What would they say about her life? Ava had wondered that many times over the years. Aunt Jenny would undoubtedly be proud of her. But Ava's mother had died when she was a child, and her memories were like images smudged with rain.

An e-mail popped into the in-box, distracting her from her thoughts. A note from Corrine Bledshoe caught her eye with the subject line: "With Concern"

Dear Ava,

I have wanted to talk to you about Broken Hearts. This is a difficult subject for me to broach, so I hope it comes across accurately via e-mail. Your schedule has been too demanding for a face-to-face, so e-mail seems right to begin this conversation. I hope I am not mistaken.

Ava rolled her eyes. She could guess where this was going and she opened her mouth to comment, but the intensity in Dane's stiff shoulders and his tight lips kept her silent. She returned to reading the e-mail:

I was reviewing our work in the past year. Last month, we helped organize a fund-raiser for Professor Timothy Torini. Professor Torini is well known for his very liberal opinions and outspoken pro-choice views.

Just a month earlier, we sent meals to that family with the son who was an antiwar protester and got paralyzed in a demonstration in DC.

Mixed in between those, we've been offering supportive services to the families of our lost soldiers and that one who came home after losing both his legs.

There was also that woman who had been married five times, though I can't remember what we did for her.

Do you see how our support of all of these varied people might offer a confused view of what we believe and what our church is about? What kind of message are we sending to the community? Should we support any kind of sin as if we accept it?

I'm wondering what Pastor Randy would think of this? I know we need to reach beyond the borders of our church, but should our funds be used to promote sinful, anti-Christian behavior?

I know that you were instrumental in starting Broken Hearts, but I think this might be a good time to reevaluate the mission statement and direction. I want God's blessings on all we do. Do you as well?

Ava hit Reply before finishing the e-mail.

We aren't sending a message to the community other than if any-one is in a desperate state, we will be there to help you. Jesus didn't condemn, so why should we? The gospel is about grace. And you are just a mean, spiteful woman! And by the way, Broken Hearts is not supported through church funds, so don't give veiled threats—Pastor Randy supports everything we do anyway . . .

She closed the program without hitting Save or Send. This was Angry Draft. Tomorrow she'd be better prepared to write a more diplomatic e-mail.

Annoyance pulsed through Ava as she rose from the couch, picking up the remote to switch from television to a music sta-tion playing acoustic guitar. In the kitchen she turned on the teapot and pulled down three packets of tea. Sleepytime for Jason and herself, and a black for Dane.

She opened the French doors and stepped out to take in the scent of an autumn night. Her mind wandered until she realized she'd walked down the path to the willow tree. Its silhouette cut against the night sky, and the leaves and branches fluttered softly as a wisp of a breeze moved through the yard.

In the low light it was harder to see signs of further degen-eration. For a moment, the tree appeared as whole and healthy as ever.

But the last time she'd viewed it, the tree was certainly going downhill. It wasn't just losing autumn leaves—they'd become brittle and dry.

Ava sensed that she needed to stay here, to rest beneath the branches and wait for God to guide her. A whisper to her heart said, "Wait a moment."

Her life was filled with blessings. They'd had a long season with everything going well, yet something nagged at her. Her childhood had taught her to expect the worst. Every good season was shadowed with the fear of what bad would surely come. It was like swimming in a perfect sea with the fear of sharks lurking beneath every kick and stroke of her arms.

A wisp of wind pushed harder through the leaves, perhaps God's display of His presence. *I am here.*

Ava's restlessness got the best of her. She paused on the walk back toward the house, stopping by the pool, newly protected for the winter with a thick plastic cover. Their yard guy would be there in the morning, but Ava liked the mess of leaves that decorated the pathway and deck chairs.

She gazed through the window with the sense of an outsider's view of her family. A light switched off from the window above her. Jason was going to sleep, and her husband was still working on his computer. He'd moved from his spot on the couch, yet he hadn't wondered where she'd gone or why Jason was annoyed at him again.

Dane's distraction was taking a toll like the small bites of a piranha that soon ate entire creatures whole. After all these years, she could still so easily go from prayerful and peacefilled to anxious, as if the fears and stress crowded around the corners of life, seeking any opening to steal themselves inside.

The autumn breeze curled around her, softening her mood

as she looked up at the stars. God was with her, tugging at her to draw closer. It was time for her to listen even more. Wasn't that the advice she'd give at Bible study?

Back inside, the kettle whistled from the stove, sending out a plume of steam into the air. The microwave door was fogged, and most of the water had evaporated. Jason was sleeping anyway. She poured Dane a cup and herself a half cup. She popped the tea bags into the water, which made her think of Aunt Jenny, who would've insisted she use loose-leaf tea.

"The willow tree isn't getting better," Ava said as she set Dane's cup of tea onto the table beside him. He didn't raise his head from the computer and made only a slight grunt in response. She didn't expect Dane to jump up and rush out to save the tree, but his complete lack of concern nipped at her. He and little Sienna had helped her plant it those many years ago. He knew it was special to her—why else had he built the bench there one Mother's Day? Dane didn't thank her for the tea, but took a sip and set it back down as if she weren't there at all.

"Am I talking to myself?" Ava said, staring at her husband.

Dane glanced up, then returned to studying his computer. "Tree isn't looking good," he repeated in a monotone voice.

"I hope it doesn't die after all these years," Ava said flatly.

Dane groaned and stood abruptly. "I need to go back in."

Ava looked up at the large clock on the wall. "It's almost ten."

"I'm aware of that." Dane closed his laptop and stuffed it into his bag.

"But—"

"Call Leo about the tree. That's what we pay him for," Dane said as he grabbed his keys and kissed her good-bye.

"We pay him to clean up the yard."

"See if he can fix a tree as well."

"What's his number?" Ava said testily. Why wouldn't Dane offer to call him? They lived under the unspoken agreement that she handled the inside of the house and he did the outside.

"I'll text it to you," he said over his shoulder.

"I want to talk about some things. What time will you be home?"

Ava tried to think what she'd advise someone else in her shoes. She'd tell the woman to pray for her husband, try to be supportive, but to also be clear in verbalizing that she needed from him. She'd seen too many couples take severe turns in opposite directions and end in divorce within a year or two of being happy and solid.

"I'll be late. Can't talk tonight. How about this weekend?"

"Sienna will be here this weekend." Ava followed him to the garage.

"That's right, well, we can still talk when she's here."

"What is going on at work?" she asked pointedly.

It tapped at her thoughts, the fear of every woman when her husband started working late. She'd seen it a thousand times, and she knew her life wasn't immune to such crisis.

Dane stopped, turning around. His tense expression softened as he looked at her face. He reached for her hand, but she kept it stiff and unresponsive.

"Hey, I'm sorry. Really I am. The board is meeting for a special session in the morning. Some investors are flying into Dallas on Thursday, and we're having a crisis with the portfolio getting finished."

"So this is about the merger? Is everything all right?"

Dane shrugged. "With this economy, nothing is all right."

"So . . . what does that mean? In laywoman's terms."

"Let's talk tomorrow night after the game. We'll sit on the balcony and have a glass of wine. I'm sure Sienna will be visiting old friends anyway. Oh, can you grab her from the airport? I sent her a text that I can't pick her up. We're having that meeting with the board all afternoon."

This wasn't like Dane. He always picked Sienna up from the airport. Dad and daughter had a special relationship, as if they'd been woven together using the same ingredients.

"Sure, I can. What's the meeting about?"

"A few tricky things. Don't worry." He came around and kissed her neck. His lips were cold, making her flinch.

Ava turned out the house lights and locked the doors.

Don't worry.

Five

"THIS IS AVA KENT," SHE SAID, ANSWERING THE PHONE BEFORE she was fully awake. Her hand reached for her notebook and pen in the drawer as she bumped her head on the edge of the bedside table.

Sitting up, she rubbed her head and glanced at the space beside her. Dane's side of the bed was empty with the pillow untouched.

"Is this Aunt Ava?"

"Uh-huh," she muttered, then her eyes flew open. "Um, who are you calling?"

"Aunt Ava?"

"This is . . . Ava," she said, trying to figure out who'd call her *aunt*. Her mind was still muddled with sleep.

"This is Bethany."

"Bethany?" Ava knew a few Bethanys, but this voice didn't match those faces. "Is there something I can help you with?"

"Do you remember me?"

"Uh, I'm really sorry, I was sound asleep. Who is this again?"

"Bethany. Jessie's daughter."

Ava's back straightened. Her cousin was Jessie, and yes, her daughter was Bethany.

"Of course. How are you? Is everything all right?"

"Yeah, we're fine. Sorry for calling so late."

Ava glanced at the clock. No one called at this hour unless it was a tragedy. She braced herself for the news.

"Do you remember me and my sister, Debbie?"

"I do, it's just been such a long time. The last time I saw you, you were running around with a doll in your hands." Ava rubbed her eyes.

"It was an old doll, and after that, you sent me and Deb both a baby that sucks on a bottle and had eyes that open and close. It was the first doll that we didn't have to share. Remember?"

"I do sort of remember. I'd forgotten about that. How old are you now?"

"Sixteen," she said softly, and there was a long pause.

"Bethany, did something happen?" Ava asked, sensing the girl wanted to share something.

"What do you mean?"

Ava cleared her throat. "So nothing bad happened?" *You're just calling a long-lost relative after midnight and no one is dead or dying?*

"No, um, not really. Everyone is fine, I mean."

Ava was sure the girl wasn't telling her something. She

opened the bedroom door and walked to the staircase, leaning over to see if Dane was downstairs somewhere. All of the lights except for the one over the kitchen sink were still turned off.

"I just hadn't talked to you in a real long time. You still living in Dallas?"

"We do."

"Mama says you live in a mansion."

Ava wanted to laugh at that. Compared to many of their friends, their house was quite humble. As she leaned against the upper banister, the low light caught on the crystal chandelier hanging from the tall ceiling in the foyer. She thought how she'd have viewed this house from the perspective of herself as a young woman like Bethany.

"It's not really a mansion, but we've very grateful to be here. Do you get to Dallas often?" Ava hesitated to offer a full invitation. If she opened this door, there was no guessing what relatives might follow.

"I went there a few years back when Deb's boyfriend went into the army. We drove on up to the airport and back home. I wanted to go to the mall but Mama wouldn't let us. She said I'd get discontent with wanting more than I need."

Ava glanced at the clock. It was nearly one in the morning.

"Well, maybe you'll have to come visit sometime," Ava said, cringing at the thought. For a number of years her family had periodically popped into their lives, always wanting something. Dane did more than she thought he should—it fed the monster. It was one thing to help family, but they wanted large sums to invest in their business ideas, which included her cousin's invention of a solar-powered distillery, a pyramid scheme that would make them rich without having to work, a partnership in a dilapidated bowling alley (Ava and Dane would buy it and her Cousin Frankie would run it), and a loan for something no one would explain, yet Ava knew was most likely drug related.

Ava had stopped it. She cut the ties despite the angry calls and letters saying they would disown her. She'd hoped they had.

Now after years of silence, this girl was calling and Ava opened the door.

"I might take you up on that," the girl said in a cheery voice.

"Well, I have to get up early tomorrow," Ava said as nicely as possible, amazed again by the lack of manners. Her daddy hadn't allowed phone calls after nine o'clock when she was growing up.

"You got a job to go to?" Bethany asked.

"I do a lot of volunteer work, and Sienna's coming home from California for the weekend."

"She's in college, huh? I was so jealous of her growing up. And I always wanted to be just like you, marry a rich guy and give my kids really nice stuff."

Ava bit her lip. "That's not exactly what happened . . ."

"I know, didn't mean nothing by it. Anyway, maybe I'll call you again sometime? If . . . that's okay . . ."

"Is everything really all right, Bethany?" Ava had the sudden awareness that there must be something wrong, that was why the girl was reaching out to her. Here she'd jumped to the conclusion that this was another family member wanting something. But hadn't she once been a girl trapped in that same family? Perhaps Bethany was looking for a life preserver like the one Aunt Jenny had been for her.

The girl didn't answer, and Ava heard some rustling in the background.

"Bethany? Are you there? You can tell me if there's a problem."

She heard muffled whispers before Bethany returned to the phone.

"I'm fine . . . well, I'm good enough, if you know what I mean. But nice you asked it. Nobody asks me that."

"If you need somebody to talk to you, go ahead and call me . . . anytime." Ava squeezed her forehead as she said it.

"Thank you, Auntie Ava. I 'preciate it. Maybe I'll come to Dallas and visit. Maybe someday I'll go to college too. Just don't tell Great-Aunt Lorena, she already thinks I have the devil in me."

Ava shook her head. So Aunt Lorena followed in Grannie's footsteps. "Don't listen to that, okay? You don't have the devil in you."

The girl giggled. "Okay. Thanks again. Talk to you later."

After hanging up the phone, Ava saw an unread text on her phone from Dane.

Sorry, sweets. Working at the office through the night. Hope this doesn't wake you. I'll come crash in the morning. Love.

Ava sighed. She'd have little sleep now. Something was going on in their lives, as if the prelude to an unknown. Ava had never done well with unknowns.

Six

AVA DROVE INTO A PARKING AREA AT THE DALLAS-FORT WORTH
International Airport. She'd arrived early but carried a novel
on the passenger seat to read while she waited. She'd been on
the same novel for months now, finding little time to concen-
trate on her favorite author's new release.

Sienna needs you.

Ava paused at the thought. Was that God speaking to her
heart, or was she letting her imagination get the best of her?

What was there to worry about?

It wasn't the first time such words had bubbled into her
thoughts when thinking of Sienna or even when she wasn't
thinking about her at all. There was nothing she could pin-
point, other than the whispers.

Sometimes Ava couldn't wait for the wedding to be behind
them. The idea of her daughter safely placed with such a great
guy soothed her heart. Sienna and Preston were moving back
to Dallas, and Ava had imagined sharing recipes, meeting her

daughter at their favorite boutiques, going to lunch, and picking out colors for the nursery before long. Ava had already volunteered to babysit if Sienna wanted to continue working.

Dane loved Preston as well, always slapping him on the back with a wide grin. They were both grateful to have Sienna with someone grounded and responsible in comparison to Sienna's first crush—a hippie Christian singer who wore jeans tighter than their daughter's and who rarely wore shoes.

Preston came from a stable family, had grown up in a church much like their own, would finish grad school before their wedding, and had already interned at an international finance company. Life didn't usually wrap things up so nicely. It was a blessing indeed.

As she turned off the engine, her phone flashed Kayanne's face above the number.

"Let me guess, you're already at the airport because you can't help being early everywhere you go?" Kayanne said after Ava answered.

"You know me too well," Ava said, knowing she wouldn't be reading her novel now.

"Hang on, I need to take this call. It's my delinquent date."

"Where are you?"

"The grassy knoll," Kayanne said matter-of-factly.

"The what—where?"

"You know, the grassy knoll where JFK was shot. Tell you all about it soon, but gotta go for now. I'll be back before you can say conspiracy theory."

The line went dead, and Ava stared at the phone and shook

her head. Kayanne's dating adventures never failed to amuse and worry her.

Ava opened up the wedding files and her to-do list on the tablet. She and Sienna would work on wedding plans over the weekend. They needed to decide on a guest list—particularly Ava's side of the family. After her cousin Bethany's late-night phone call, did that mean she'd need to invite them all? Ava pinched her forehead at the thought.

She still wondered about her daughter's voice—the tone of it. The little-girl-lost tone she'd caught, despite how Sienna later sounded when they'd talked. Her daughter assured her that everything was fine. Preston had a guys' fishing trip, and she'd decided on a whim to come home.

Ava pulled up the guest list for the wedding. Preston's family filled several page-long columns. Sienna's family was less numerous unless they invited the whole dysfunctional clan, but Sienna hadn't seen them since she was a child. Ava recalled their last visit had been a family reunion where Bethany and Deb had seen Sienna's doll. The girls were so taken by it that Ava had sent them each their own.

The wedding already exceeded their initial budget, but six months earlier Dane had given his daughter carte blanche to have the wedding of her dreams. Dane was more indulgent of Sienna than Ava would have liked, but their daughter hadn't turned into a spoiled monster as she'd feared. Sienna was a lovely young woman now, and she tried keeping the wedding within reason—whatever that meant.

Ava stared at the list with only her brother, Clancy, moved

into the "invite" row. She had three aunts still alive, numerous cousins, and unknown numbers of their children. They were like a troupe from *The Beverly Hillbillies*, but not half as nice. Sienna had given her the option to invite all or none of them. Her children didn't know their mother's family other than a few visits from their Uncle Clancy.

Perhaps Preston's family had seen the invitation list—or lack of one on Sienna's side—and that was the problem. What if they made her daughter feel as if she didn't measure up to their family?

Ava had been made to feel that way. Dane's mother, Norma, had wanted him to marry her best friend's daughter. Dane's family was oil people. Who was Ava? She was the daughter of a poor family who'd come from Oklahoma and tried to pass themselves off as Texans—South Texans of all things. Dane had the heritage of true Texas blood. His ancestors fought in the Spanish-American War, died in the Alamo, and secretly leaned toward Texas as an independent country. Ava's relatives wore gray in the War between the States, although why this mattered, Ava didn't know. Dane had rolled his eyes about it.

Even worse, Ava had left God's country to live in California—California of all places! If Norma knew her granddaughter was doing the same, she might come back to life and put things right.

At Ava's engagement party, Norma had downed a few too many sangrias and whispered loudly, "I guess we should thank our stars that she's on her first marriage, at least as far as we know."

Dane took Ava's side, which put his mother in tears. Insults were flung, glasses broken, and the scandal helped Norma accept an elopement instead of a wedding, much to Ava's relief.

This wedding was resurrecting the memories. Ava hadn't realized what a wonderful few decades of peace it had been without much interference from the mess of blood relatives on either side of the family.

Her phone buzzed on the passenger seat.

"I can't talk long, we're going to dinner soon," Kayanne said out of breath.

"Are you seriously on the grassy knoll?"

"Yes, and this guy is now fully convinced that there was more than one shooter in President Kennedy's assassination. He's up in the Texas Depository right now."

"Isn't that a museum?"

"It is, and he's at the window checking it all out. He just called and said that not even a professional could have shot JFK from there."

Ava glanced at her watch to make sure she wasn't late meeting Sienna. "I'm still unclear as to why you are on the knoll."

"This is the site of the suspected second shooter—or one of them."

"Yes, I know."

"John asked me to stand on the grassy knoll so he can see my location from the window where Lee Harvey Oswald made his shots."

"How old is he? Where is he from? Who is this guy?"

"He's from Topeka and is kind of a JFK history buff."

"O-kay."

"I didn't know that part of his personality until right before he flew out."

"He flew out to meet you? And you were going to tell me this . . . when?"

"He came out on business. We met on Christian Daters."

Ava smacked her forehead with her hand. "What? You joined?"

"I didn't want to tell you. It's only been a few days."

"And he wanted to meet you after a few days."

"Since he was out here anyway, he asked if I wanted to meet. Don't worry, it's all very safe even if he is a bit odd."

"I'm more than a little freaked out by this."

"I'll text you my locations. And we have the fail-safe word too."

Ava's electronic tablet popped up an alert.

"I need to grab Sienna—my flight app says she's about to land. Remember I'm out at the airport if you send the fail-safe word."

"Good to know—and I don't know what to tell you."

"About what?"

"Asking Sienna if there's anything to be worried about." Ava had forgotten she'd sent Kayanne a text about her niggling concern over her daughter.

"I'm afraid I'm making this about me. And my past."

"Could be. You need to figure that out before you say anything."

Ava leaned her chin onto her hand and thought this over,

examining her hands that were showing more veins beneath her skin. The years were inching their way into her body, and yet Ava didn't feel any different from the young girl she'd been, climbing the branches of a willow tree and playing in the tall grassy fields of South Texas.

"Prayer," Kayanne said with the sound of wind crackling the line.

"Yes," Ava said with a smile. *Of course, that was exactly right.*

"I often repeat the advice you give me. But I just received a text and my date would like me to move four steps to the left. I gotta step."

"Be careful!" Ava said, but Kayanne was already gone.

Seven

"Oh my girl," Ava said, pulling her daughter into a tight hug as she came through the doors into baggage claim. Sienna had lost weight, but Ava didn't want to comment on it—at least not yet. Her makeup was hiding dark circles, a surefire sign of stress and exhaustion.

"Hi, Mom." Sienna hugged her, squeezing tighter than she had in a long while. This wasn't her independent, confident daughter. Now that Ava could see for herself, her heart raced with concern.

"Let's get you home," she said, weaving her arm around Sienna's waist. Her daughter slumped into silence as they waited for her luggage.

"Did your flight go all right?"

"Yep."

"Are you feeling okay?"

"A little tired. But I'm excited to be here."

Ava didn't see any excitement in her daughter.

"Maybe you can take a nap before the game."

"In my old room." She smiled then. "That sounds really good about now."

"It seems like I haven't seen you in forever." It had been since their wedding shopping weekend in New York in August. Sienna couldn't find a dress. Every store they visited looked at them hungrily at first—they could spot people with expensive taste the second they walked in the door. But within fifteen minutes, the salespeople also identified a difficult client. Sienna had no vision for what her dress should look like. She offered no direction whatsoever.

"I'll know it when I see it," she'd stated much to everyone's chagrin. That shopping trip, as well as the one in Dallas, all the online research, and way too many hours watching wedding shows on TLC had yet to provide Sienna with any sense of "knowing it." They were planning another trip to LA after the holidays, though Ava was toying with a surprise trip to London and Paris as a Christmas gift to her daughter. Dane had loved the idea, though Ava wondered if it crossed the line of extravagance and indulgence and other such "ance" words that she herself had never known as a child.

Sienna had been a little girl with big wedding dreams. She'd created an elaborate wedding plan when she was thirteen and going to marry Orlando Bloom in a castle in Scotland.

The wedding was eight months away, and the wedding planner kept reminding them that they were now a month behind the schedule she'd given them. Sienna hadn't tackled the list of questions Ava e-mailed her, but Ava knew her daughter was busy with her classes.

"Do you want to talk about it?" Ava asked as they reached the car. The interior was hot with Indian summer popping them back into eighty-degree temperatures. Ava opened the trunk and helped Sienna slide her lone overnight bag inside. When had her daughter gone anywhere without a suitcase and carry bag?

"What do you mean?" She sat in the passenger seat and bit on the edge of her nails as Ava hopped behind the wheel and turned the key.

"Do you"—she turned to Sienna—"want to talk?"

"Talk about what?" Sienna stared out the front window as if enthralled by the parking garage. She turned to look at Ava with an innocent expression, then bit again at her nails.

"What is this surprise visit really about?"

"I miss my family." Sienna shrugged.

"It took you three years of college to finally miss us, huh?"

Sienna laughed. "I've missed you before now. But it just seems like more lately. I even miss Texas."

Ava's mouth dropped in exaggerated surprise. "This from the girl who couldn't wait to get out of her hick state?"

"I'm getting nostalgic in my old age."

"Don't get too old, that means I'm much older."

"Where's Daddy?" Sienna said, in a voice that conveyed a trace of disappointment.

"He said he sent you a text."

"He did, but I hoped he'd still surprise me."

Ava rubbed her daughter's arm. "I'm sorry, sweetie. He's at work. Emergency board meeting or something. That's all he does lately."

"He's pretty worried about the company."

Ava glanced at her daughter as she drove. "I know, but he makes it sound like everything is all right."

Sienna looked at her. "He doesn't want to worry you."

They all said that. Ava didn't think she was an especially worrisome person. She prayed instead of worrying. Well, mostly.

Ava paid for their parking, thanking the attendant before driving away.

"What's for dinner?" Sienna said, settling into her seat and looking more relaxed.

"You'll like it, but from the looks of you, I need to make a few more courses."

Sienna groaned. "I was waiting for that one."

"Just wait until you're a mother." Ava wondered if that came a little too close to the feared subject—marriage, future babies, Preston.

"I've lost some weight, it's true."

"Why?"

"I don't have my mother's cooking in California."

"Why else?"

Sienna was texting now, further distracted as she frowned at the phone.

"What about you, Mom? What are you going to do with all your freedom in another few years?"

"That's a change of subject."

"A good one," Sienna said with a sly grin. "But seriously, you're not far from an empty nest."

Ava had already planned her five- and ten-year goals at the beginning of the year. She could nearly recite them from memory.

"As a matter of fact, once Jason is in college, I'm going to devote more time to the ministry I've been doing since you left. I'd like to learn how to garden a little more. I want to go on a short-term mission trip, as long as it has water and showers. And eventually I look forward to being a grandmother."

"Sounds pretty neat and tidy." Ava frowned as Sienna continued. "You've told me my entire life that whenever something is too neat and tidy that . . ."

"God has a way of shaking it up," they said in unison.

Sienna laughed, but Ava felt a flash of nausea sweep through her stomach. She believed this truth, had seen it again and again. But she'd worked hard to reach this place in life and having it shaken up did not appeal to her.

"I've been known to be wrong," Ava said with a shrug.

⋆⊚⋆

Jason raced down the stairs when they arrived.

"It's about time!" he said, sweeping his sister into a bear hug that lifted her off the ground. "Did you lose weight or am I growing?"

"Both, but really, who are you and what happened to my scrawny kid brother?" Sienna stepped back and looked Jason up and down. He towered over her by a foot now.

"You can marvel at my awesomeness later. I can't stick around, but I thought you were going to miss my entire season. Crazy Californian, you've forgotten what it means to be a football fan."

"Oh hush," Sienna said, socking him in the arm. "I gotta make a call—be right back."

"Mom, I can't find my socks." A look of panic spread over Jason's face.

"On the dryer," Ava said, setting her bag and keys in the cubby above her desk.

"My game socks."

"On the dryer."

He started to rush down the hall, but came to a sudden stop. "Did you wash them?"

"They need washing," Ava said nonchalantly.

He stared at her as if she'd committed an unpardonable sin. "Mom, please. Do not tell me that you washed my lucky game socks."

"Is it a new tactic to defeat the opposing team by the stench of your feet? Because that seems unsportsmanlike to me."

"Some guys don't change their underwear. Be grateful. But you didn't wash them. Right? Come on, Mom."

Ava smiled. "Of course I didn't wash them."

"Whew. That really freaked me out."

"It's killing me not to, and be careful. You might knock off a few of your teammates with that smell."

"Maybe I should lose a shoe on the field and blow away the entire defensive line?"

"Those socks could do it."

Jason raced down the hall and returned a moment later sliding across the floor in his socks. "What movie has Tom Cruise doing this in his underwear?"

"Easy one," Sienna said with a mock yawn, returning from the backyard with the phone in her hand. "*Risky Business*."

Ava frowned at his dingy, stained socks. "Get your shoes on or take those off, you're rubbing toe jam all over my clean floors."

Jason made a long skid right up toward her, grabbing her arms as Ava let out a scream. He laughed and kissed her cheek.

"Bratty kid," she said, tossing a dishtowel at him and missing by a mile.

"See you at the game!" he yelled as he grabbed up his large sports bag in the hall shelf and slung it over his shoulder. "Glad my sis finally made it!"

"Did you get something to eat?" Ava said, then saw the plate in the sink.

"Four eggs and a bagel. I'm ready for the game. See you guys there!" he yelled as the front door closed.

⌘

"How did you know Daddy was the right one for you?"

Sienna sat cross-legged in a living room chair. With her daughter home, Ava felt a sense of rightness where she hadn't realized anything was wrong. She wished she could turn time back to nights of story reading, footed pajamas, and the excitement of Christmas morning. In the passing of years, there was

54

no holding on to such moments, and the fact that they were forever gone had not found peace within her.

Ava picked up a folded blanket from the large basket between the couches and draped it across Sienna's lap despite the warmth of the afternoon.

"You used to ask about your dad and me all the time when you were little. Don't you remember the story of how we met?"

Sienna nodded, but the usual sparkle in her eyes seemed dulled with more weariness and a lack of wonder.

"You were at a beach bonfire when you heard a guy talking with a Texas accent. He was visiting California for the first time, but after you met, he dumped his friends to hang out with you. You avoided him as much as you could. Daddy says when he saw you across the fire, he just knew. It was love at first sight for him."

"He was from a wealthy family, and I wasn't. I wasn't planning to ever return to Texas."

"Because of your bad childhood."

Ava nodded. It sounded strange hearing her daughter say that. Her children didn't fully know what *bad childhood* meant.

"But there was something special there, like he was my home—my real home." Ava smiled and sighed deeply.

"Is that how you knew?"

Ava could see that her daughter needed the truth, not the rosy, fairy-tale version.

"I had doubts all along the way. I don't know if that's normal though."

"What were the doubts about?"

"I guess with my . . . background, I had a lot of distrust

from when I was young. I sometimes revert back to looking for the bad in people instead of the good."

"Really? Why?"

"Maybe to protect myself, until I find out what I'm dealing with."

Sienna nodded in thought. "You're always so nice to people. I didn't know that about you."

Ava kicked off her slippers and sat on the opposite chair. "What are your doubts?"

"Just normal stuff, usual pre-wedding jitters. Pledging myself to someone for life is a big deal." Sienna chuckled, but there was fear in her eyes.

Ava bit the edge of her lip. "Is he treating you well?"

"Preston? Of course. He treats me too good, I think," Sienna said with a small laugh. "It's nothing like that."

"Then what it is?" Ava's heart started beating faster, but she tried to remain calm in her daughter's presence. Her mind was already running a track of worrisome thoughts: was she pregnant, had she met someone else, were they having second thoughts?

"I just need to pray more," Sienna said and sighed deeply, the usual sign that she was about to open up. Then her pink phone buzzed on the arm of the chair.

"It's Preston, finally," Sienna said as if apologizing.

"It's all right. Talk to him."

"I sort of need to. But thanks, Mom. By the way, I was out back, and the weeping willow doesn't look too good."

Ava felt her heart shudder as if she'd forgotten something

essential. The tree's demise felt oddly important. Was it just her old superstitions trying to flare their ugly heads, or was God trying to get her attention?

When Sienna returned there were no signs that anything was different. Her daughter had never been an open book, unlike Jason, who still told her everything, even when it got him into trouble.

Ava hoped there would be a way to talk about her concerns. Time before the wedding was quickly running out.

Eight

THE PARKING LOT WAS OVER HALF FULL AS THEY PULLED IN EARLY, just like every Friday night. Even with Dane's schedule, he hadn't missed a game, either at home or away. On Friday evening, half the community showed up to watch the rumble on the green with numerous businesses shutting down for the night or bringing their goodies into the stadium grounds in booths. The rich scent of barbecue filled the air as several groups gathered around tailgates where mini-grills smoked with sizzling steaks and burgers.

Dane ran a few steps ahead and turned suddenly with his cell phone pointed at them.

"I need a picture of my beautiful gals."

Sienna slid her arm around Ava's waist as they posed for the photo. Ava wore her favorite jeans, high black boots, and a deep purple sweater she'd found at Saks that matched Jason's school colors. Her purple-and-white striped scarf added to her school spirit, but this was as far as she was willing to go, unlike some mothers who painted their faces purple and white and rang cowbells during the game.

Ava checked out the picture. She liked her new haircut above her shoulders, while Sienna was growing her hair out for the wedding. Their brown hair, light eyes, small chins, and heart-shaped faces were enough for anyone to see they were related.

"This looks like a picture to frame," Sienna said, leaning in to view the photo.

They walked toward the field and Dane pointed out the teams already warming up. The band tuned their instruments and a whistle blew from either a coach or the bandleader.

Ava walked with her arm through Dane's, though he nearly tripped as he tapped into his phone and checked his e-mail. Sienna stopped frequently as they wove through people with hugs and exclamations of excitement at seeing her again.

Friday night football was a community reunion. Since Ava had started her ministry, she'd been with a number of these families during the loss of a loved one or other tragedy. Dane was a social animal and had connected with much of the community at various sporting events since Jason was five.

Ava noticed more people than normal looking their way and whispering over Sienna's visit. Ava felt that mother-pride in her daughter. Sienna hadn't married right out of high school, she attended a prestigious school, and she'd left Texas to do it. But more than that, today they were together.

They searched for number twenty-two on the sidelines where the team huddled together getting last instructions from Coach Ray. Jason was sitting on the bench, which was unusual for the starting lineup.

"Do people always stare at you guys?" Sienna asked, leaning toward Ava.

"Never. They must be murmuring over how amazing our daughter looks."

"I'm sure that's it," Sienna said, rolling her eyes. "But this is so strange seeing all the familiar faces. I can't believe I'm here," she murmured as she waved to someone as they walked up the stairs of the home team bleachers, searching for a seat.

"What do you mean?"

"It's just so weird. You think high school is never going to end. Now my little brother is here, and I'm an alumni coming back to watch the games. The football players seemed so cool and grown up. I can't quite get my head around the idea that Jason and his annoying buddies are out there, and I'm one of the old alumni we used to make fun of, wearing their high school jackets and T-shirts."

"You made fun of my high school jacket?" Dane said with a shocked expression.

"Maybe a little." Sienna winked at her dad.

Dane glanced out onto the field. "I'm sure Jason's buddies would love to see you again. They all had crushes on Jason's big sister."

"They read my diary. I'll never see them as anything other than little punks."

Near the top of the bleachers, they found a row unoccupied and settled in with their bleacher seats and blanket. Ava buttoned the large buttons on her jacket as the evening breeze carried a chill that crept around her neck. Dane had barely sat down before he hopped back up.

"I'm off to get some food high in trans fat and cholesterol."

"What's that—my daddy learned his first foreign language?" Sienna said.

"Doc said family history can't be ignored, even though my physical said I could still be playing college ball. What do my girls want?"

"What's the hurry?" Ava glanced at her watch. They still had twenty minutes before the game began.

"You never know what kind of line there's going to be down there. I don't want to miss kick off."

"Nachos. The works." So Sienna was eating, Ava observed with relief.

"Pretzel with salt and mustard. And two Diet Cokes—right?" Ava glanced at her daughter.

"Of course."

Dane kissed each of them on top of the head before heading off, but Ava frowned as he slid his phone from his pocket. More business—would it ever end? At least, she hoped it was business.

"Are you still in love with Dad?" Sienna studied her face.

Ava squinted her eye as she studied her daughter in return. This was more than wedding jitters.

"Why?" Ava asked.

She shrugged. "I don't know. Just wondering."

"Earlier you asked me how I knew your father was the one."

"Is there a law about asking my mom questions?" Sienna said with a smile.

"There just might be."

"Tell me," she said. "These are important marriage secrets that should be handed down woman to woman like in the tribes of old."

Ava thought about the question. "It's different from how it was at the beginning, but I'm most certainly still in love with him. It's more than just . . . exciting and heart racing."

"Do you miss that?"

Ava smiled. "Sure, in a way. And there are moments when it comes back. But the steadiness is even better. Settling in and knowing your best friend is always with you, that you have one another for life . . . that's a pretty incredible thing. And though the beginning of a relationship can have a lot of passion, there's a lot of fear too."

"Yes, that's true."

"What are you worrying about?" Ava asked.

Sienna shook her head wildly and said with drama, "Absolutely nothing! I'm going to enjoy the moment. Isn't that what I'm supposed to do, Mama?"

Ava laughed and let all seriousness go. "You better believe it."

Soon the announcer started in, giving the players' names and numbers and announcing a raffle.

Dane returned with his arms laden with food and a teetering drink carrier.

"I haven't had these in far too long," Sienna said, taking a tortilla chip covered in nacho sauce and chopped jalapeños.

"This is the first time this season I've eaten a pretzel," Ava said as they tapped a piece of mustard-slathered pretzel to nacho chip in a food toast. Ava had put the household on a health kick for the past year after Dane's blood pressure was high and Doc threatened medication. He was still a big meat-and-potato man at heart, but he'd adapted to more chicken, salads, and a few vegetarian dishes.

"I shouldn't be having this with the wedding coming." Sienna cradled the large nachos on her lap, piled with chili, jalapeños, olives, and salsa. "What's the nacho cheese made of anyway?"

"I don't think it's cheese, but right now, you don't want to know. Just enjoy."

"Something interesting happened," Dane said after settling back into his seat and pulling his attention away from his phone.

"What?"

"Hey, Dane, how's it going?" Ava looked up at Peter Riley, another team parent. Dane shook the man's hand and greeted him.

"It's great you guys are here. Way to show your support." The way he said it sounded odd.

Dane gave a quizzical expression. "Why wouldn't we be here?"

"Exactly. That's the attitude!" Pete said and tipped his hat to Ava. He headed up the stairs toward where his wife was warming up her cowbell at every name that was announced.

"That was weird," Dane said. "We're here every Friday night. Rico Rodriquez said something similar when I was down getting food. Jason didn't get hurt, did he?"

"I'm sure we'd know. Maybe it's because you missed that scrimmage a few weeks ago?"

Dane's jaw clenched. "Yeah, that's right. I missed a practice game so I'm an awful parent."

Ava put her arm on Dane's arm. "Don't let him get to you. Rico hasn't worked in a year, so maybe that's his way of feeling better about himself."

Dane simmered, seeming to consider the thought. They chatted and ate their food as the game finally got underway.

Jason sat on the sidelines. He'd been first string the entire season. Dane mentioned that perhaps the coach was trying something new. Dane always supported the coaches whether they played Jason or not, unlike many of the parents who seemed to think they were assistants to the coaches.

At half-time the team was behind. Jason was one of their best players, yet he remained benched. Before the team disappeared into the locker room, Ava saw Jason turn to study the bleachers as if searching for them. He held his helmet under his arm, and the expression on his face read sheer frustration. Ava wanted to rush down and find out exactly what was going on. Suddenly she understood those pushy parents much better.

The next two quarters continued the Wolves' downward spiral as the Hawks scored two more touchdowns and a field goal.

The final buzzer rang with the crowd grumbling, one man yelling toward the referee, and a cowbell tossed onto the field.

"We could've used your kid tonight," a man shouted as he walked down the middle stairway.

"I know it," Dane said, shaking his head.

"I can't believe they didn't play him," Sienna said, disappointed.

The crowd dispersed while they hung back in the bleachers until it was pocketed with groups of parents waiting for their sons on the team.

Ava caught a few parents' remarks that made it sound like it was Jason's fault or their family's that the coach didn't play him.

"Hey, Mr. Duke," Sienna said, waving at an older man standing on the sidelines with his hands shoved deep into his football jacket.

"Sienna, well, well!" Mr. Duke called back, walking toward the bleachers. He'd been one of Sienna's favorite teachers—history, Ava recalled—and assisted on the football team. "What are you up to?"

"Came out for a visit and to watch my brother play, but what happened out there? My brother could've been an asset tonight."

Mr. Duke lifted his ball cap up and down on his head. "That's not the coaches' fault. We needed him. He's let the whole team down."

"He . . . what are you talking about?"

Ava noticed two of the other mothers in the bleachers suddenly lean in to whisper something to one another. She looked at Dane, then at Mr. Duke, who now looked as confused as they did.

Mr. Duke walked the distance separating them at the railing. He glanced around, but the coaches and players had all disappeared into the locker room.

"Coach Ray didn't reach you?" He said this to Dane, then glanced at Ava with a concerned expression on his face.

"I have about fifteen messages on my phone right now," Dane said, pulling out his phone and scrolling through it. "I was in meetings all day and evening."

"Oh," Mr. Duke muttered. "Think you better talk to him or Jason—or both, for that matter."

Dane glanced at Ava as if she might know what was happening.

"What's going on?" Ava asked more to Dane than to Mr. Duke.

"Oh." Dane turned the phone toward her.

"What is it?"

"A text from our son. It says that he's suspended from the game."

"Why?" Sienna and Ava asked at the same time. They all looked at Mr. Duke, and Ava felt a sudden anger that Dane hadn't seen the text earlier because he was wrapped up in his work again.

"I'm not sure I'm the one to discuss this."

"Just tell us, please," Sienna pleaded.

Mr. Duke rubbed the gray stubble on his chin. "This afternoon Jason was chosen for a random drug test. Sorry to say, he failed it."

Nine

THE DAY OF HER FATHER'S ARREST, AVA SMOKED HER FIRST CIGA-
rette to save her brother from a beating.

She didn't want to smoke. And her brother didn't want to
be saved, especially by his big sister. Clancy was in a fight every
other day it seemed. But when she came around the corner of
Jem's Frosty to the view of her brother surrounded by Doug
Bell and his cronies, Ava knew Clancy had bitten off more than
he could chew.

Doug Bell had a crush on her and it was years in the making. In elementary school he called her names, chased her on
the playground, and slipped a Snoopy Valentine into her bag
that professed his love, except he didn't sign it. Ava figured out
her secret admirer when she saw him staring at her. In high
school, his teasing continued, and rumor had it he'd beat up
anyone who planned to ask her to prom.

Did Doug think she'd be endeared to him with his harass-
ment of her brother? Doug wasn't the smartest kid in school,

though he knew enough to put to use his skills in physical manipulation and all-around terror.

When Doug spotted Ava, his demeanor changed. He took a step back, unclenching his fists, and his grin turned like a light switch from menacing to sheepish.

"Hey, Ava," he said, taking a step back. Clancy was poised, ready to pounce.

"Hi, Doug. Clancy, I was looking for you. Could you help me with something at home?"

"What do you need help with?" Doug asked.

"The desk in my room has a broken leg on it." Ava was making this up as she went.

"I'll do it," Doug said with an excitement that made her shiver.

"No guys allowed in my room, but thank you, Doug." She walked toward him, trying to act all feminine and sweet.

"Want a smoke?" he asked, pulling out a mangled pack of Camels from his back pocket.

Ava hesitated, glanced at her brother in his ready-for-battle glare, and then closed the distance and reached for a cigarette.

"I don't smoke," she said, which seemed to make Doug even happier.

"I'll show you how," he said, lighting her cigarette.

They arrived home with Ava smelling like smoke and Clancy still fuming but without another busted nose or black eye. To their surprise, Grannie came out of the house and met them on the front porch.

Before they could say hello, she said, "Your daddy is in jail. You're gonna have to live with me for a while."

Guilt washed over her as if smoking had sent God's judgment. If their grandmother caught wind of it, she'd think just that, and Ava would get a licking despite being in high school.

"Why?" Clancy asked, and Ava realized she'd been more distracted by Grannie's arrival, the horror of having to stay with her again, and the fear of being caught smoking. Grannie's words sunk in. Her father—arrested?

"The devil is making his move. They have him up on charges of manslaughter and embezzlement."

"Manslaughter and embezzlement?" Ava asked, looking at Clancy.

"They say he's been stealing from the church 'cause he's breaking something in the bylaws. It's all hogwash. The manslaughter, well, he got tempted by the drink and got behind the wheel . . ."

The memory came to mind as the family drove home from the football game. Jason wasn't going to be arrested like Daddy. There was no Grannie to be terrified of now. No one was being bullied. But something about this stirred the memory.

Dane drove with his hands gripping the steering wheel. Jason sat slumped in the backseat beside his sister, not uttering a word.

Replaying that night, Ava wanted to rewind the entire game and hide under a hat, or better yet, just remain at home. It felt as if the entire crowd of parents, community acquaintances, and old friends had all known about Jason before them. Of course, not everyone knew, but news did travel like a wildfire in Dallas circles. Yet her family had spent the game as if nothing was going on, because they didn't know. What fools they must have appeared to everyone.

Ava's initial concern was about how this looked to the people in their church and among their friends—instead of the fact that her son might be doing drugs. The truth was, she was more embarrassed than angry, more humiliated than worried. And this disgusted her.

The worry was there. He'd failed a drug test. Her son, the athlete, the God-lover, the baby of the family . . . he'd failed a drug test? Maybe it was a mistake. She'd heard poppy seeds in muffins could make a false positive. There might be other foods as well. Or perhaps he'd been slipped something. What kind of drug had it been? She wished someone could tell her that.

"When did you find out?" Dane asked with a stern voice.

"Right before the game," Jason murmured. Ava couldn't believe the news had traveled through the parents that fast.

"When we get home, go straight to bed and we'll talk about it tomorrow. You are obviously grounded from everything," Dane said in a severe tone as if trying to keep the volcano of fury from exploding.

Ava wanted to address it tonight, not tomorrow. But she decided to wait until they were alone before talking further to Dane about next steps and appropriate punishment.

As they pulled up to the house, Jason practically leaped from the car and raced for the front door. Sienna followed more hesitantly, pausing to see if her parents were coming, then went inside when neither moved from their front seats.

"I can't deal with this tonight," Dane said after the car door shut. He didn't turn off the key.

"You can't deal with this tonight? What does that mean?"

"I'm sorry, but I have to go to the office again. I told you I had to."

Ava realized her hands were shaking. "I would remember if you told me you were going to the office in the middle of the night again. Didn't you say we were drinking wine on the balcony tonight?"

"That was yesterday. I'm sure I mentioned it this afternoon."

"It doesn't matter, though you didn't tell me. We need to be united about this."

"I can't tonight."

"And so what am I supposed to do?"

"Let him go to bed or talk to him if you want. I almost didn't go to the game with everything that's going on. You don't realize what I'm dealing with, Ava." He enunciated her name in a way that sent her blood pressure skyrocketing.

"I don't realize because you don't tell me. You just disappear at all hours." He didn't turn from where he stared out the front window. "Just go then."

Ava hopped out of the car and shut the door hard as if to shout her anger. But Dane didn't shut off the engine. He didn't get out of the car and follow her. He didn't even roll down the window.

Instead, her husband pulled out of the driveway before

she reached the front door. Ava stood in the cold of the night watching the red of his taillights disappear around the corner and down the street.

Jason was in bed with the covers pulled over his head and his football cleats sticking out from the bottom of the blankets. She wanted to tell him to change his clothes. Instead, she leaned down and unlaced his shoes one at a time and then covered up his stinky socks with the blanket. The rancid smell dissolved her anger and put her on the sudden verge of crying for him. This boy was what mattered, she chided herself. Her son was in pain, humiliated, and was going through something that she'd been completely unaware of. He didn't move from beneath the covers.

"I love you," she whispered, bending down to kiss his thick hair. At the door she added, "We'll talk tomorrow. Get some sleep."

"K. Love you," he whispered back.

Sienna waited in the kitchen with the kettle already bubbling on the stove.

"Where's Daddy?" she asked with a frown.

"Office," Ava croaked out, trying to rein in her tempest of emotions.

"What?" Her eyes narrowed and she bit the edge of her lip just as Ava always did. It brought a smile, even as Ava tried to reconcile her thoughts. Jason and drugs? Sienna at home for no reason? Dane and work? When had her husband not addressed an issue with the kids, ever? Something was undoubtedly going on, and she needed to quit hiding her head. Obviously her family wasn't as healthy and flawless as she believed.

"Mom, it's going to be okay." Sienna hopped up onto the end of the counter.

"I'm sure it will," she muttered half-heartedly. "I just can't believe everyone at the game knew before we did."

"Why do you care?" Sienna asked defiantly.

Why did she care? Ava had never considered herself to be vain. Her childhood was enough to slam humility into her any time she thought of herself or their family with anything other than gratitude. Sometimes in the middle of a social event, she had the sudden awareness of the child she'd been. Tangled hair, hardened feet from running around outside without shoes, dirt on her sunburned cheeks, a stained homemade dress handed down from a woman in church with older daughters. They'd clean up for church, Daddy insisted on it, but on all other days, she and Clancy lived the life of ragamuffin orphans.

Once when she spoke to a group of women at a country club, she had a momentary flash of panic with all of them arriving in luxury cars and sitting at their linen-covered tables wearing designer suits. There were women from old money, oil families, and Texas society. Would they see her true self? Would they turn away as if they saw her standing with matted hair and skinned-up knees? Yet they always surprised her by being full of broken people. Perhaps these women had grown up wearing expensive brands, but inside they were so much like her.

Ava rarely spoke about her childhood, and even then it was mostly hints and snippet stories to get a point across. Few people knew what it had been like, and those who did didn't have the full impact of what had occurred.

So why did she care if her family had looked like fools? Was it the attention? Was it the props she'd built that created an illusion of perfection? She'd wanted to be real, transparent, and open to the people around her . . . except for the full image of her extended family. That was a past she hadn't processed herself. It was like bread dough that rose and needed pounding down. Someday she might let it rise fully, she might take it in her hands and knead it into a dough that could be baked, sliced, buttered, and shared with others, nourishing them by the story she'd endured. But Ava wasn't ready for that.

"It's normal for kids to experiment a little," Sienna said, interrupting her thoughts.

"That's all it is, you think? Wait . . . you did stuff like this?"

Sienna's eyebrow rose as she bit back a grin. "A little, but nothing to worry about."

"What?" Ava pinched the bridge of her nose and leaned against the counter. "We don't know how bad this is. He could be kicked off the team. College scouts are coming next week. Sure, he's only a freshman, but they groom them early."

"Oh," Sienna muttered as the full weight of the possible consequences rolled over her.

"How could I have missed it?" Ava said to herself. Was the ministry distracting her from knowing that their own son was falling apart before their blinded eyes?

Jason was the one who could never keep a secret from them. He told on himself about things they would have never found out, like the time he stole a pack of gum at the grocery store or when he'd started a small fire at church. So why did her kids need to keep secrets now?

"What if he has a real problem?" Ava said, following Sienna toward the living room with a cup of tea in her hand.

"No way, Mom. I'm sure you experimented a little, or did a few rebellious things as a kid."

Ava stared at her daughter. She'd never told Sienna about her high school or college years.

"I wasn't a Christian then. And there're so many chances for problems, big problems like drug addiction, accidents . . ." She had dozens of real-life cases she could present from her experiences with Broken Hearts.

Sienna pursed her lips to hide a smile. "Mom, I know. I'd rather this didn't happen either, and I wish I could have listened to everything adults told me so that I didn't make mistakes. But isn't life about messing up and hopefully learning and growing from it?"

Ava smiled while staring at the ceiling. "Listen to you, trying to calm me down. But I'm a mother, I want my kids safe. Mistakes mean the possibility of something that can't be easily fixed—or fixed at all."

"I'm just a big sister, but I can appreciate those fears. And

I've also seen how you trust God with our lives and with your own. It's been the best example, and I'm seeing the value of that more and more." She bit her lip and Ava waited to hear the rest. "I need to do that more. And Jason probably does too. You've put that into our lives, Mom. You should trust that."

Ava wanted to argue with her daughter and explain how it never felt like enough. Too many good families had lost their children to the world; she couldn't just sit back and trust. Instead, she kept it inside. Her daughter would understand when she became a parent some day.

"I promise to try," she said, smiling at her daughter.

"Great, then let's make some kettle corn and stay up late without the guys around."

"You have a deal."

❧

The weekend should have been baked French toast casseroles and time spent with their daughter and son.

Dane called from the airport. He'd taken an unscheduled trip to New York. He hadn't come home at all, but said he'd be home late Sunday. He promised Sienna that he'd fly out to California soon to make it up to her.

Ava's indignation twisted with a sense of helplessness. She couldn't force him to come home. She could try tears, shouting, insisting, stating his wrong, or she could not be home when he arrived—but those tactics had never helped in their early years of marriage, and they surely wouldn't help now.

Mostly, Ava simply couldn't believe this was Dane.

Ava and Sienna sat at a little table in the corner of their favorite café, cradling cups of coffee in their hands. Jason was on restriction until further notice, but he didn't want to talk to anyone yet. Ava and Sienna had left him at the house and ventured out for breakfast.

"I'm sorry about your daddy," Ava said, wondering if Sienna's lack of disappointment was an act.

"It's all right. He's trying to protect us. Something is really wrong. We should support him."

"That's more mature than I'm feeling right now," Ava said, wishing she could argue and state her grievances. How long did she have to endure his career emergencies? Ava sensed Sienna wasn't about to back her up on this one.

"The student becomes the master," Sienna said.

"We haven't discussed the wedding."

Sienna bit her lip. So many of her daughter's traits were similar to Dane's that it always delighted her to see a few traits of herself in their girl.

"Can this be a wedding-free weekend?"

"Really? Most brides-to-be can talk of nothing else."

Sienna shrugged. "I was having wedding overload. Next week I'll get back on track. Or for sure over Christmas break . . . once I'm done with finals."

Ava studied her daughter's face, sensing again there was something more. "You're talking to our drill sergeant of a wedding planner then."

"I'll e-mail her when I get home."

"Preston is a really good guy . . . ," Ava said.

Sienna sipped her coffee and glanced around for the waitress. "I know," she said in a clipped tone. The waitress arrived carrying two large plates. She set down Ava's eggs Benedict and Sienna's frittata. It was time for Ava to tuck away her concerns and enjoy breakfast with her daughter.

The tension dissolved as they discussed plans for Thanksgiving and Christmas—Sienna wanted to be home for the tree-cutting and cookie-baking days. After breakfast they shopped for a while, then they watched a movie in the evening. Jason remained in his room, though Ava tried to coax him out. He wouldn't even talk to Sienna.

Sunday morning, Sienna announced that she needed to take an earlier flight back to California.

And the weekend was done. Her daughter was on a flight back to California, Dane was in New York, Jason would hardly leave his room. Their family was more fractured than Ava could ever remember.

Ten

MONDAY MORNING, AVA DROVE TO THE HIGH SCHOOL TO MEET with the principal and Coach Ray. A Crock-Pot of stew sat in a box in the passenger seat for the funeral of Private Grant being held in a few hours. She told herself that no matter what happened at the meeting, she had a lot to be grateful for. Their family was going through a trial, but it was nothing compared to what Private Grant's family was facing. Still, this was a first—she'd never met with school officials about disciplinary action for either of her children.

Ava pulled up next to Dane in the school parking lot. She locked her car and slipped into the passenger seat of his luxury SUV. She didn't look at him and barely grunted a greeting. She knew little of his trip to New York that had stretched beyond his promised Sunday afternoon arrival. He'd come to the school straight from the airport.

"I think we should pray," Dane said before she could utter a word. Ava turned toward her husband, wondering if she'd heard him right. She was the one who brought up prayer. With her irritation high over his many disappearing acts, Ava hadn't thought to pray before this meeting.

"You're worried he'll be off the team?" she asked, irritated.

Dane leaned back in his seat. "I've been thinking about a lot of things lately. I know it appears I'm consumed with work. But having the company in trouble, it's made me think about what's really important."

"And what is that?" Ava wanted to take this in, but her anger and suspicion weren't easily abated.

"Our family. Us." He studied her face in a way he hadn't done in such a long time that she shifted in the seat, wondering what he saw. Did he notice the lines around her eyes, the tiredness in her face? Dane had grown better-looking with age as some men did. He could turn the heads of women half her age, and surely did, while Ava struggled with an extra fifteen pounds and didn't work out as much as he did.

Ava turned away with her head against the headrest, savoring the scent of Dane's cologne and the warmth inside his vehicle.

"I guess we should get inside," she murmured.

"Or we could make out in the backseat and pretend we're in college again," he said with a slight smile.

"What?" she said, surprised by his words.

He took her chin with his fingers and guided her face toward his. His kiss was long and tender, awakening a surprising amount of feeling throughout her body.

"Where did that come from?" She scrutinized his face. "Are you having an affair?"

"What?" Dane leaned back surprised.

"Tell me the truth. Are you?" Ava studied his face, searching for the lie. Dane's lips curled into the edge of a smile as if barely holding back a tumult of laughter.

"Why would you ask me such a thing?"

"So you are." A cold shot of adrenaline raced through her.

"No, I'm not. Why would you say that?"

Ava wasn't sure she believed him. "Then are you looking at pornography online? Or something like that?"

"Ava. What is this?"

"When a man is having an affair or doing something wrong, anything wrong, he starts acting differently at home. First, his schedule changes. Then often he starts complimenting his wife, buying her gifts or flowers. It's the guilt. A classic sign of a man's betrayal is suddenly becoming a good husband."

"I'm glad I haven't bought you flowers." Dane laughed, only making her angrier.

"It's not funny."

"Listen, I'm not having an affair."

Ava heard a bell ring across the school grounds.

"We're going to be late for the principal," Ava said and opened the car door to a spillway of cold air. Something was wrong. Something had changed. A man didn't make such fluctuations overnight without something happening.

Before she could rise from the car, he leaned across, his body pressing against hers as he reached for the door and closed it shut.

"What are you doing?"

"We're going to pray. And then I'm going to kiss you again."

"Then do it," she said in annoyance, and something else—respect, fear, excitement.

Dane took her hand and prayed for Jason, for them as parents, for their family, and finally for their future.

"Everything is shaky right now. Whatever path you have for us, help us to know it and have the strength to take it."

Could prayers be amended? Ava wondered. "Whatever path" sounded too open-ended with the growing unrest in their family.

❧

Dane held the door open, then followed Ava inside the administration building, humming a death march. Ava didn't find it humorous but tried smiling anyway.

"We have an appointment," Ava said, but the receptionist rose from her chair as she recognized them. The older woman's grim expression further unsettled Ava's stomach.

"Go on in. Principal Landon and Coach Ray will be there shortly."

Through the glass window Ava saw Jason already sitting in a chair off to the side and slumped low in the seat. She had an instant vision of him as a five-year-old in kindergarten. She'd been called in because he'd freed the classroom lizard.

"He hated that cold cage and wanted to play outside on the playground," he'd told her, not understanding why he was in trouble.

"Hi, honey," Ava said as they walked into the office. Jason raised his head as they sat beside him.

"Hi, Mom," he said in a low monotone.

Dane greeted their son, but Jason didn't respond. Before either one of them could remind Jason to respect his father, the door reopened as the coach and principal arrived.

"Hey, buddy," Dane said, shaking Coach Ray's hand. The coach didn't respond with his usual quick humor and hard slap on the back.

The greetings became more subdued as they pulled up seats, with Principal Landon moving around his desk and opening a file.

"Sit up, son," Dane said in a firm tone. Jason sighed loudly and slid up a few inches in the chair.

"We know why we're meeting, but do you have any questions?" Principal Landon asked.

"What kind of drugs?" Dane asked, more to Jason.

"The test doesn't specify. But from talking with Jason . . . Do you want to tell them?"

Jason shook his head. His eyes didn't leave his shoes.

Ava wanted to burst into tears. She couldn't believe this was happening.

"It seems there has been an instance of marijuana and a somewhat regular use of prescription drugs," Coach Ray said.

"What?" Ava and Dane said in unison, with Dane much louder.

"You've been taking prescription drugs?" Dane said, his face red with anger. "And smoking pot? When did this start? Are you an idiot?"

"Dane!" Ava said, putting her hand on Dane's arm. Jason winced at Dane's anger, but made no other response.

"I know this is tough to hear," Coach Ray said. "My middle son went through something like this, and yeah, I pretty much lost it. But let me finish."

Dane leaned back in his seat, his body rigid with the pent-up fury.

"He's been taking scripts—as the kids call it—because apparently he hurt his knee at football camp."

"But he did physical therapy and is fine now," Ava said, glancing between Jason and his coach.

"Not as fine as we thought," Coach Ray said.

"So what's going to happen?" Dane asked, cutting to the point as he often did.

"He's out for the rest of the season."

"Out?" Ava asked. "You mean off the team. Completely?"

"Yes. You should know that this is a huge blow to the entire team. We need Jason. He's let us all down. As well as himself."

"And he's suspended from school for the next week," Principal Landon stated.

"We have a zero-tolerance drug policy. One more instance of this, and he's expelled."

"Why, Jason?" Ava heard herself say.

"Mom—" Jason began, and she could see the tears filling the corners of his eyes. He looked at his coach. "Do I have to be here?"

"You can sit outside, if your parents don't mind."

"Fine. Whatever," Dane said.

Jason rose from his chair and tossed his backpack over his shoulder, quickly leaving the room.

"Honestly, I know Jason is a good kid," Coach Ray said.

"His teachers all say so," Principal Landon echoed.

"Obviously something is wrong," Ava said, though her voice sounded far from herself.

"He could have a dependency problem. I think he was medicating to keep playing. The pot, well, I don't know why he was messing around with that. He knows we do the random testing, all the guys know it."

Dane leaned forward with his elbows on his knees, staring at the ground while the coach spoke.

"After the money we've donated to the sport program, you can't do us a favor?"

"Dane, we can't ask things like that," Ava said.

"Of course, that was wrong of me to ask. I'm sorry."

Coach ran his hand through his thinning hair. "I'd like to do something, I really would. But the news is already out. Once the team knows and the community starts to hear, we have to follow the rules or we open ourselves up for a lawsuit."

"No, it wouldn't be right anyway. Rules are rules," Dane said.

Jason waited on a bench outside the door. As they walked out, he returned for a moment into the office. Ava thought she heard him apologize to the two men, but she couldn't be sure. The three of them walked to the parking lot together. Jason's suspension began immediately.

"You're grounded from all extra activities at home as well," Dane said. Ava could see his expression soften as he studied their son. "This is very disappointing. But you've let yourself down most of all. You may have ruined your college career with this move. But in the end . . . it's gonna be all right, buddy," Dane said, wrapping an arm over his shoulder.

Jason shook off his arm and walked ahead of them.

⁓☙☜⁓

Her son didn't speak as Ava drove them away from the school. Dane had rushed off to work with more empty promises that he'd tackle their home problems soon.

When she dropped off the stew for the funeral of Private Grant, she could no longer gather up gratitude. Jason didn't want to leave the car. Ava thought it might be good for him to see the grieving family, but she didn't want to subject the family to her moody son.

Ava found Barbara, another member of the ministry team, organizing food in the kitchen. She gave Barbara the stew and then returned to Jason in the car. As Ava drove away, she thought of the gratitude of the families they helped.

Ava's involvement in women's ministries had led her to start a program to help people during times of crisis. She had three other women who worked with her consistently, and a list of volunteers for when a greater need arose. They didn't do earth-shattering work. They didn't build wells in Haiti, save victims of natural disasters, or rescue children in sex-trafficking stings, but she hoped what they did mattered to individuals in need. People called when they were going through anything that could be described as heartbreaking: divorce, abuse, abandonment, death, or loss of any kind.

Once when a car hit a little girl's dog, they sent the girl a stuffed animal dog and a gift card to Chuck E. Cheese. A contact of Dane's had the governor of Texas sign a card to the girl, and he included a story about how he lost his childhood dog in a similar way. He wrote that he hoped their dogs were in heaven together.

Ava enjoyed helping children the most. They dealt with pain on such different terms. It broke her heart to see their tears, to hear their questions, and yet they had such innocent belief. Ava knew that this precious hope would wane in the years to come. Ava hoped to leave them with comfort, with hope that might soothe. She understood childhood pain.

Ava let her friend Kayanne do more of the dealings with the adults. Kayanne wasn't moved by their anger, by flowers being tossed in her face with harsh words like, "Is that all God is going to do for me, have someone bring flowers? Why won't God give me my son back?"

The ministry reached beyond the church membership to most anyone touched by tragedy in the Dallas-Fort Worth region. Ava was busier in this role than she wanted to be.

As she rode with Jason slumped in silence beside her, she realized that helping others had taken a lot of her time in the past few years. Her son was going through something serious, and she had been completely oblivious.

She could help other families, but she didn't know how to help her own.

When Ava called Sienna, her daughter was stunned by the revelation, no longer offering assurance that this wasn't serious.

The next night, Ava found Dane in the kitchen when she returned home from a late planning meeting where she'd removed herself from helping with the Christmas program.

"Have you talked to Jason?" she asked.

"He won't talk. I think it's his form of rebelling or something. But it's only going to prolong his restriction."

"Restriction's all well and good, but how are we going to deal with the drug problem? We don't even know if he's addicted, if he needs rehab, or what. And does he need more physical therapy for his knee?"

Dane carried a bowl of ice cream with sprinkles on top and sat down at his computer on the dining room table. Sienna and Dane always put sprinkles on their ice cream, it was one of their "things" and brought on the missing of her daughter again.

"I know. I'll get him to talk. He might just need a couple days."

"I'm worried about this family."

Dane nodded, and she saw the weariness in his features. Ava realized that except for the other day in the car, he hadn't looked at her the way he used to in a long time. He walked around as if with blinders on his eyes. He didn't say she looked beautiful or seem to notice anything outside of his narrow vision.

"Would you tell me if you were seeing someone else?" she asked.

Dane's head shot up with a surprised expression that turned comical.

"Why do you find that so humorous?" she asked, annoyed at his response.

"Because if you could see inside my head and follow me around all day, you'd see that someone other than you is the last thing on my mind."

He set down his bowl of ice cream and rose from his chair. He took her hands, pulled Ava toward the couch until she was sitting on his lap. She rarely did that anymore.

"Then what is happening?" she said, fighting the urge to wrap her arms around his neck.

He took off his reading glasses and rubbed his eyes. People asked him if he was a pilot or a former football player. Ava studied their family photograph to see if she was outdistancing him in age, but she couldn't judge.

"I haven't wanted to worry you."

"Me worry? I could have prayed. Have you been praying?"

Dane set his spoon down. "I actually have. Not as much as you would. But yes."

"Wow, it is bad," she muttered as a joke, but there was truth there. Dane attended church with them, and he gave money religiously, but he was the first to admit that God wasn't front and center in his life.

"Yes, it is. But we'll figure it out. I know God isn't going to let my company fail. I've been praying too hard about it. He won't let this family fall apart either."

Ava nodded. She didn't remind Dane of what she kept

thinking lately. That God didn't always do what we thought was best for us. In fact, He rarely did.

This appeared more like the wild ride, the unknown, the untidy that kept creeping into her thoughts like dark clouds gathering on the horizon. Ava had run from the image, yet that had never stopped a storm. There was no time for preparation—the tempest gathered at their doorstep.

Eleven

THOUGH AVA'S MOTHER DIED DURING AVA'S KINDERGARTEN YEAR, her daddy's sermon topics stemmed from her mother's betrayal for many years to come. Seemingly out of the blue, he'd preach messages around the unfaithful or villainous women of the Bible. At times he'd mention Leanne by name, lamenting about how his own wife had gone the way of Delilah and Jezebel. His eyes would fill with tears as he expressed how he prayed for her soul.

She'd divorced him, left them for a man who told her all about the world and promised to show it to her. She and her new boyfriend were killed in a car accident on a highway outside of Chicago. It was God's hand of judgment, the church members murmured, as if to console Daddy.

That Daddy was flawed and full of mistakes only served to make his congregation love him more. Over half the women swooned over him, married or not, from teenagers to the elderly. Ava never questioned if he slept with any of them, at least not then. She didn't think of such things as a child. No one accused him of it except a few disgruntled husbands.

Even after he was convicted, most people in his congregation stood by him, believing the devil had come in to destroy a wonderful man. His stiff sentence given during a time when Texas was being stricter about law enforcement was another sign of Satan's devious plan.

He was sentenced to life, though everyone said it would be appealed or he'd one day get paroled.

Ava breathed in the October air as she sat on the bench in what she called her private Garden of Gethsemane, located behind the modern three-story church building built for Sunday school and youth events. Ava and Dane had attended this church for fifteen years, first coming because of the great children's program and warm welcome of the congregation. Over time the closeness had been lost with the growth of the church from the hundreds into the thousands, but Ava knew that every church underwent stages of growth, decay, renewal, change, reassessment, even crisis.

Today she'd taken an hour between a leadership meeting and a private meeting with Tammy Blake, a woman she mentored in planning her first charity ball for kids with health issues. The little garden was an oasis between conversations, worries, planning, and schedules. Here she could reflect and breathe, eat her lunch with the sound of birds singing. She could pray without thinking about what she was actually saying. Her "poured out" prayers happened in solitude like this. Today, her thoughts overruled her prayers as she thought about Daddy and his sermons about Mama. Ava hadn't thought of that in years, and she wondered why so many childhood thoughts kept returning lately.

Kayanne's ringtone startled her. Ava picked up her phone and sighed. Carrying it to her Gethsemane had been a mistake. She'd already been tempted to text Jason and see how he was doing at home, though he was restricted from his phone. Sienna had sent a text that she needed to talk to Ava soon. And now Kayanne . . . all in a matter of ten minutes.

"Hey, can I call you back in—"

"No, listen, I found him." Kayanne's voice was out of breath.

"You found him? Who? Oh, as in . . . *him*?"

"No, *him him*."

Ava rolled her eyes and dropped her fork back into her salad. She closed the plastic top. "You found *him him* as opposed to just *him*?"

"Remember how *him* turned out?"

"Do I ever? If you would listen to your best friend when she tells you that *him* is not a twenty-eight-year-old guy who does professional Celtic dancing all around the world—"

"I know, but for a few weeks, we seemed so connected. This is different, I hope."

"Okay, who is he? Where did you meet him?"

"He's my new match on As You Wish."

"Hmm."

"Did I tell you I joined As You Wish dot com?"

"No, I think you were on Dallas Singles, Marriage-in-Your-Future, and some other one."

"Wait. I'm sorry."

"Sorry?"

"I was in my divorce group and we were talking about friendships and how easy it becomes as a single person to become pretty self-involved. And I realized that in our friendship, sometimes all I talk about is my single life. It's just so stressful being single after all these years."

"I know it is, or I can imagine."

"But you have things happening as well. Like what's going on with Jason."

"He won't talk to us. He's taking his punishment without argument, he was suspended from school, and he has all sorts of additional things he has to do for the football coach, like cleaning all the equipment."

"But he won't talk to you? Not Dane either?"

Ava dropped her salad container back into the bag. She cleaned everything up as a cold breeze inched beneath the edges of her clothes. She worried about leaving her son at home alone—what if he had a hidden stash of drugs in the house? Dane had searched his room and Jason had promised there weren't any drugs there, but what if he ran away? But Ava knew she needed to keep her routine, and Jason could either come with her or remain in the house alone.

"He's not talking to anyone, so there's not much to say there. Now let's get back to *him him*."

"No, more about you. Dane? Sienna? You?"

Ava laughed as she walked back toward the main church, a tall, red-brick building with stained-glass windows. Ava appreciated Kayanne's attempts to be a better friend. Since Kayanne had become single, her search for a soul mate often became all consuming. Their friendship had shifted considerably, which meant Ava was most often listening or giving advice and Kayanne sometimes neglected Ava's struggles as less important.

"I'm leaving the church after I meet Tammy. We're going over her budget to look for a few areas to cut."

She carried Kayanne inside the glass doors and toward the office kept available for ministry volunteers like her.

"You deserve a medal, and okay, I don't want to be a bad friend, but I can't wait to tell you about our first date."

"Tell me."

Kayanne launched into the details as Ava sat down at her computer, opening the file on event planning she used when she coordinated charity events. Ava listened, making comments and asking questions as usual.

"What?" Ava muttered as she perused her e-mail.

"Are you listening to me?"

"Yes. He sounds like a pretty nice guy. But I don't think he's *him* or *him him*."

"Don't say that yet. You're going to jinx it."

"Then I take it back. But are you ready for me to share my concerns?"

"No, no I am not. Let me have a few days of unchecked euphoria. Reality can be a bitter pill and I'm enjoying the moment."

A knock sounded on the office door.

"Hey, I need to go. Tammy's here." She opened the door to the woman's exuberant squeal.

"We're down to just days until Dallas is blown away with my Children's Charity Ball!" Tammy said, swishing into the office.

Kayanne said good-bye as Ava set aside her own cares for a while to help Tammy. It was time to focus on other people and Ava enjoyed the reprieve.

Twelve

THE NEXT MORNING, AVA WAS SITTING IN HER FAVORITE CHAIR with her Bible and journal when she heard the leaf blower rev up in the backyard. With a glance at the clock, she slipped on her shoes and pulled on a sweater before heading outside. Leo was emptying the leaf blower bag in the compost bucket. He jumped when he turned and saw her only a few feet away.

"Mrs. Kent. How are ya today?"

Ava shook his outstretched hand in greeting. He never appeared comfortable around her, and in the many years that he'd been working on their yard, they'd had little interaction. Dane organized that part of their lives. She gave Leo a container of homemade Christmas cookies with his bonus during the holidays or sometimes she took out a pitcher of ice-cold sweet tea or lavender lemonade on a hot Texas day, but that was the extent of their relationship.

"I'm doing well, thank you," she said, trying to sound cheerful. "How are your wife and son?"

"Good, ma'am, very good. Can I help you with something today?"

Ava stuck her hands deep into her sweater pockets as the cold of the day worked its way to her skin.

"Yes, there is. Do you know what's going on with my tree—the willow over there? Are you trying to kill it?"

Leo's head whipped up. "No, ma'am, of course not. I wouldn't do that."

"I was kidding, Leo. I know you wouldn't do that." She bit the edge of her lip. This wasn't going well.

"I'd say so." He nodded his head with a look of being insulted.

"Really, it was a joke. I apologize, all right?"

Leo frowned as he stared at his shoes. "Okay. I did see the tree is dying. We need to pull it on out."

Ava turned to the tree, then back to Leo.

"No."

He raised an eyebrow and rubbed his chin. "What's that? We can pop a new tree in there. You can even buy them already growed up if you don't like waiting for shade. I could bring over a catalog for you and the mister to see what you like."

"No, I don't want to pull it out."

"And why not?"

"Does it matter why not?"

He stumbled over his words. "No . . . I . . . you're right. It ain't my business if you're committed to it. I'm just saying. I'm no master gardener, ma'am. I know how to fix things, trim, prune, cut the grass, and blow the leaves. But something's right wrong with that tree. In my experience, that could be the start of something for all your trees. Have you heard about the mountain pine beetle in Colorado? It's eaten through entire forests."

"And you think this tree has that beetle though it's not a pine and we're nowhere near Colorado."

Leo shrugged. "Don't know. I'm just saying. If it does have that or some bacteria or worm or something, it might start knocking out everything around here. Why would it die out of nowheres? I been caring for this yard for, what, eleven years? That tree's been growing and doing just fine through winters and summers. Something ain't right."

"But that's so extreme."

"Why do you like it so much?"

Ava considered the man for a moment. "I had a grove of them back along the river where I grew up. They remind me of the few good times I had when I was a kid."

Leo's frown deepened as he studied her. "Where you from?"

"A little town out in the middle of nowhere Texas," she said with a smile that felt somewhat forced. She remembered the wide river lined with weeping willows just like this one. Were they still there? What was the lifespan for trees like this? Maybe it had come to its end, as all things eventually did.

"I know towns like that. Always thought you were from Dallas, a city girl."

Ava smiled. "I hide it well, then?"

He nodded with a slight smile. She thought he seemed more at ease with her suddenly. "I'd say so."

"It never leaves me, though. Guess that's why I'm so attached to something like a silly tree." Ava felt a stab of guilt over calling it "silly." Her eyes wandered down the pathway to where its bare branches reached up toward the sky and bent down back toward the ground.

Leo scratched the dirt with his shoe, then cleared his throat.

"I don't even like this tree. Too messy for one thing and roots shallow, running close to the ground and messing up the lawn. Never liked these willows."

"The roots aren't deep?"

"No, look how they run through the lawn." Leo bent down and pointed at roots threaded through the ground.

Ava couldn't help wonder about the significance of that.

"I like it much better than that scraggly looking eucalyptus. They sure do grow a lot, but ugly with a capital U. But like I say, I'm good at yard cleaning and fixing things, but no good at plants. Seems like I should be, but I'm better with the remains and keeping them looking nice. You need me to find somebody?"

"No, I'll see what I can find. Thank you." Ava took a few steps away, already plotting her next move. Perhaps there were some master gardeners at the college or someone they could hire to save it. It couldn't be too late, though something nagged within her that perhaps it was. Perhaps she'd neglected it too long.

"I'm sorry about your tree, ma'am."

Ava saw genuine regret in his eyes, and she appreciated the sentiment. But she wasn't about to give in.

"Thank you, Leo. I think there's still hope for it."

"Hope is good, but I say you should prepare for bad news."

"I live too much of my life preparing for bad news," she said with humor in her voice, though this truth was a painful reality. "Can't one thing be hoped for without the fear of disappointment?"

Leo took off his hat and wrung it in his hands, then he slapped it against his dirty blue jeans. "In my experience, there ain't much that comes back from the dead."

Thirteen

AVA LEFT THE BACKYARD WITH ONE DETERMINED THOUGHT IN her mind. She had to get down to the business of saving the weeping willow.

"Jason, get your shoes on," Ava called as she walked toward her bedroom, pausing at Jason's room. He was on the floor of his bedroom, building a house of cards.

"Why?" he asked with a frown. Grounded from friends, technology, television, and video games left few options. Ava had seen him doing his school work in between wandering aimlessly outside, sleeping a lot, reading a little, cleaning his old snowboard, and pulling boxes of toys out from the closet.

"I want you to come on an errand with me. We're going to save the willow tree."

"Do I have to?" The cards crumbled silently onto the carpet. Jason dropped the stack onto the floor and rose with the energy of an old man.

"You need to get out. I'll get you a milkshake at Sonic."

"Okay," he said, still scowling.

Ava drove toward the nursery with photos of the tree taken on her phone at all angles, a bag of its leaves in the backseat, and Jason sitting wordlessly beside her. Maybe this excursion would resurrect both tree and son.

Jason slumped into the passenger seat with his eyes out the window. Ava explained where they were going with as much enthusiasm as if they were off on a great adventure. Jason mumbled in response, and Ava gave up on small talk after a few miles. She turned on a new audio book she'd ordered, a mystery she hoped Jason might enjoy as well. He sighed loudly and leaned his head against the window.

A gate barred the entrance to the nursery with a Closed sign spray-painted onto a piece of plywood. Plastic pots and gravel piles implied the place had gone out of business, not just shut down for the season.

Jason glanced at her.

"We'll try another place," she said, putting the car into reverse.

At a larger nursery, she pulled into the lot and parked beside neatly stacked bags of soil and mulch.

She hopped out, making it clear Jason should join her, and carried her bag of leaves into the nursery. Ava breathed in the rich scent of earth and flowering plants.

"I love that smell," she said cheerily to her uninterested teenage son.

An elderly man tipped his cowboy hat at her as she made a turn down an aisle of decorative grasses. A misting machine shushed overhead as they moved through an area of ferns and mosses.

In another life, Ava would have put her energy here, into soil and growing things, having them multiply, bear fruit, go to seed, and grow again the next season. It sounded peaceful being a gardener, spending days with plants and watching them grow beneath a careful hand.

"Can I help you with anything?" a deep voice asked as Ava reached a section of potted trees.

"Yes, I hope you can," Ava said to the young man walking toward them wearing a polo with the nursery's name written over a pocket. He pulled off work gloves and reached for the handful of twigs and leaves Ava removed from the bag.

"Please tell me my tree can be saved. It's been looking funny for a while, and now it's in a pretty bad state."

The man broke the branch and touched the end. He studied the leaves.

"I have pictures as well." She pulled out her phone and opened the first of a dozen pictures of the tree, the trunk, the branches, and leaves taken from different angles as she explained every detail.

"This is the tree you're trying to save?"

"Yes," Ava said with conviction.

The nursery worker scrunched his eyes and smacked his mouth. "I'm sorry, but from what I see, there's not much hope for it."

"Not much? But that means there is some."

"The only hope I can give is to wait till spring and see if it comes back. Or cut the whole thing down about two feet up the trunk. Some trees sprout back up from the old trunk."

"But . . . why is it dying?" Ava wanted to tell the guy that he was much too young to know the tree was dead for sure.

He shrugged. "Could be all kinds of reasons. Too much water, bacteria, fungus, insects, age, competing plants in the yard. Have you had any construction work done in the last year?"

"My husband had a new shed built in the backyard."

"That might be it, if the roots were compromised. Or sometimes they just get old and die."

"It was planted from just a sprout of a tree when my son was born." She motioned to Jason.

The man scratched his head. "Sometimes we don't know. A plant dies. Same as how some people just go out of the blue."

The man looked at Jason. "Shouldn't you be in school? You helping out yer ma?" he asked heartily.

"Not helping that much," Jason muttered.

"Play football?"

That seemed the question most people asked Jason. Ava wondered if it was just a Texas thing.

Jason and Ava glanced at one another as Jason said, "No."

"Kid your size, you should be playing ball."

Ava walked across the parking lot to find Jason leaning against the car waiting for her.

"I found another guy for a second opinion. But he said the

same thing." Her determination to save the tree struggled to recover. Her eyes swept the rows of bushes and trees, many dormant for the winter, looking similar to the willow. Perhaps the first guy was right and the tree would surprise her come spring.

Jason responded with an unconcerned grunt.

"Do we have to listen to this, or can we just turn it off?" Jason said when she turned on the engine and her audio book came to life.

Ava flipped the power button off and set the bag of leaves behind Jason's seat.

She remembered her grandmother saying she'd never grow anything. The little houseplant she'd been given as a prize at school died within the first month she'd had it. Grannie would also regurgitate the story of how Ava forgot her Barbie doll outside in the fort she'd constructed with Clancy. The dog chewed off one leg. Grannie whipped her good for that one, Ava clutching the one-legged Barbie. She'd cried even longer when Grannie confiscated the Barbie after the spanking and gave it back to the dog.

"Maybe that'll teach you. I just hope you never have children. They probably won't survive you being their mama, just like you can't grow anything."

Neither Ava nor Jason spoke the rest of the drive home. Ava went through Sonic and bought Jason a chocolate milkshake, but she'd lost her appetite for one. As soon as she pulled up to the house waiting for the garage door to rise, Jason opened his car door.

"You know, I would've appreciated you being a part of this

today. That tree is special to me, and you made it harder than it already was. You're acting like I did something wrong and you're punishing me. I haven't done anything, Jason. So knock it off."

"I'm not . . . punishing *you*," he muttered.

"Are you ever going to acknowledge that what you did was wrong?"

"What—today or the other thing?" he muttered.

"I guess both."

"Of course," he said, his voice cracking. "I just want to go up to my room. Can I?"

"We need to talk about this."

"Can we later? I just want to go to my room." He clenched his jaw, but to Ava, he appeared boyishly meek and small.

Ava wished she could crack his closed expression or force him to open up.

"I guess," she muttered, and off he went.

Fourteen

AVA LEANED IN TOWARD HER VANITY MIRROR, TOUCHING HER finger along the slight lines below her eye. They appeared more pronounced lately, accentuated by the faint bluish shade that always gave away restless sleep.

She stared at the face in the mirror. Ava had always thought her cheekbones were too pronounced for the roundness of her face, and her grandmother said she looked like a doe with her large eyes and narrow face.

It surprised her when men started treating her differently in her early teens. Daddy and her grandmother wouldn't let her wear makeup or jeans; it was dresses only. Daddy went to prison and she decided to do what she wanted. Then she spent every tip she earned waitressing after school at the diner on jeans, makeup, and trips to the small beauty shop in town. Grandmother said she was a vain tramp and that men only liked her because she dressed like a harlot.

In California Aunt Jenny told her she was beautiful with or without makeup. She showed her how to use blush to accentuate her cheekbones and eye shadow to bring out her eyes. Ava lived in San Francisco for five years, going to college, working at Nordstrom, and discovering a world beyond Texas. Aunt Jenny said she transformed into a lady during those years. Grannie wrote her letters about her backsliding ways. Clancy had joined the military, Daddy was sitting in prison, and Mama was in the grave. They were a family that would never exist again.

Even now after so many years of luxury, Ava could see her face transform into a wild child with matted hair or the teenager putting on too much blue eye shadow.

Ava pulled her hair into a short ponytail and slipped into her designer sweats and jacket. There was a slight chip in one of her nails, and she had just enough time to get it fixed before picking up Dane's tux from the cleaners.

She touched the silver Vera Wang dress that Kayanne insisted she buy for tonight's charity event, exclaiming that if she had curves like Ava, her search for a man would be over. The dress did hug her hips, which twenty years earlier might have been nice to display except that curves weren't popular then. Now that they were, Ava felt too old to be wearing a form-fitting gown. She'd pulled a less flashy black dress as a backup and hung it up beside the silver—she'd decide tonight which to wear.

Ava rushed down the stairs, enjoying the fresh scent. Martina had been in today. Ava loved Martina days, when the house was even cleaner than usual, dinner was popped into the oven, and the laundry was actually put in everyone's drawers instead of folded on the laundry room table.

Ava grabbed her keys, chiding herself for spending too

much time thinking and not getting going. What did reflection accomplish anyway?

The sound of the garage door stopped her. She walked toward the garage, but the door opened before she reached it.

Dane jumped when he saw her.

"What are you doing here? This is a surprise," she said. He'd left for the office early, promising to be home in time for the ball.

"Yes, it is a surprise." Dane's voice sounded weary.

"What's going on?" She kissed his cheek, noticing how his deep lines and dark circles were much more pronounced than her own.

He took in the bag on her shoulder and keys in hand. "You're on your way out. When will you be home?"

"Few hours. Just errands—nails and dry cleaners."

"We'll talk when you get back."

"You remember it's the Charity Ball."

He chuckled and muttered, "Of course it is."

"What does that mean?"

"I'm sorry. Nothing. We'll talk after the Charity Ball then."

Warning flags waved in her head.

"Is it about us?" she asked, following Dane as he walked down the hall and turned into the den.

"It's about us," Dane said solemnly, dropping his messenger bag on the desk. He looked up then, seeing her face, and his expression changed. "No, not about us, as in our relationship. Nothing like that. I need to make some calls, but don't worry. It'll be all right."

Don't worry. Everything is going to be all right. How often she'd heard her father say that, all through his trial, and even into the first years of his conviction. And Dane often assured her with such words—he'd been saying them for years—but in his case, everything *had* turned out all right.

"Is it the company?"

Dane nodded. "Always the company. There will be some allegations against it. They aren't true, but in this day and age, you have to prove your innocence. We're being investigated. The company is on the verge of crumbling, and out of nowhere, we're being investigated for securities fraud."

"I'm sorry."

"It's going to affect us. We need to talk about it."

"So . . . what does this mean?" Ava realized this wasn't being processed in her brain at all. It felt like she was talking about someone else.

"It will take a few days or weeks to know for sure." Dane cleared his throat and sighed. He sat down in his favorite leather recliner in the corner of the room, closing his eyes. Dane didn't rest when things went wrong, he fought back. This sight sent flutters of fear through her.

"I don't want you to be late for your nail appointment," Dane said with his eyes closed, then he opened them. "But don't use the American Express card when you pay."

"Okay," she said, standing in the doorway wondering if she should really leave.

"I just need a little sleep."

"Of course," she said, gathering a blanket that was draped over the leather couch on the opposite wall.

She closed the door behind her, but Ava set down her purse and sent a text to her manicurist, canceling her appointment. She fixed herself a cup of coffee and sat at the kitchen table.

Words assaulted her from a voice much like her grandmother's. *You've been acting all high and mighty. Now you face the very hard fall.* In the first years after the old woman's death, Ava was haunted by them. Grannie saw the devil in nearly any misfortune since he was always trying to destroy them. She'd often exclaim that the world was getting so bad, Jesus was going to return soon.

As she fixed an early lunch for Dane, she told herself that everything was going to be fine. She prayed it as well. God had taken care of her through much worse than a financial glitch.

Dane emerged from the den, rubbing his eyes.

"I forgot to ask if you talked to Sienna this morning?"

"No, why?" she asked as she sliced homemade bread for his sandwich.

"Did you know she and Preston were having so many problems?"

"What do you mean?"

Their daughter often called her father when debating a big decision, then Ava would be the second call. She didn't mind, even loved the idea of her daughter having a strong male force in her life. What would that have been like to have a father to talk to, especially as a young woman?

Dane studied her face. "So you don't know? Sienna called off the wedding."

Fifteen

YOUR TIMING IS IMPECCABLE, AVA NEARLY MUTTERED AS DANE drove them into downtown Dallas for the Children's Charity Ball. The high-rise buildings shimmered with light and glass brighter than she remembered.

They'd driven in silence with Ava trying to find a viable excuse to not attend the event. Her hands clenched together to keep them from shaking and to keep herself from bursting into tears before they arrived. Her phone sat on her lap in anticipation of Sienna's return call. Ava's calls went unanswered, but Sienna had sent a text saying she was talking with Preston and would call them when she could. Ava prayed their talk would turn this around. What was her daughter thinking?

"How bad is all of this? I really want to know the truth," Ava said, turning toward Dane. The dashboard lights illuminated Dane's strong chin and neckline. She hadn't realized how attractive he looked tonight.

"Sienna hasn't been sure about this marriage for a long time. I liked the guy a lot, but I'm not marrying him."

"I was asking about your company."

Dane pulled in front of the Hyatt Regency. "The company. That's better discussed later."

The valet trotted up to the car, waiting for them to emerge.

"I think I want to know now."

He took her hand, studying her face a moment. "It's pretty bad."

She stared into his dark eyes, wondering what he was thinking. Dane released her hand and rose from the car. He gave the keys to the valet and walked around the car, then opened her door and reached again for her hand. Ava felt the strength in his fingers as he gently led her out.

"Let's enjoy tonight and talk later at home."

Ava squeezed his hand, making him stop as the antique light posts along the entrance blurred momentarily. "Tell me now."

He spoke, and Ava only heard bits and pieces. "Investigation. Freezing assets. Investors pulling out, allegations of . . ."

His words turned to gum in her head. Ava had never understood the financial world. Dane explained it off and on, but he could see her eyes glaze over. He said something about failed mergers and insider trading, but she couldn't get off of the thought, *What are we going to do?*

As more arrivals came up behind them, Ava became aware that they were standing outside in what must have appeared a very intense conversation. "All your investments are gone?"

"Personal investments have been for a while now, but the company investments—I'm hoping we'll salvage the company and the market will come back, or . . ."

"Or what?" she asked as Dane led her toward the entrance of the hotel.

"Or the company goes under and I look for a job, though probably not in Dallas."

Ava stopped again. "We'd move from Dallas?"

"That or I'd commute. The east and west coasts have always been better for my line of work, you know that."

They stepped inside the luxurious entrance. The sound of people talking and laughing in the crowded ballrooms reminded Ava of crows squawking from a telephone wire.

Let me just paste on my smile and pretend our life isn't imploding around me.

"We can't bid on anything," Dane said with such a deeply apologetic look that her heart ached for him.

"Oh, of course. I expected that." Ava reached out her hand and touched his face, trying to reassure him. She had been making this about herself, not considering how painful and humiliating it must be for her husband.

Dane had three rules in life: be a man of integrity, provide well for his family, and build close ties with his wife and children. Ava had told him that something about God should be first on that list, but he said God was a given, not a mission statement. Now that he'd been praying for the company, Ava wondered if his faith was shaken by the outcome.

Before familiar faces surrounded them, Ava tugged on his

hand and led him away from the hall where the main ballroom was located.

Ava said with more strength than she felt, "I know we will get through this. Just please don't tell anyone tonight."

Dane nodded and Ava caught a quick flash of worry in the clench of his jaw. "It'll be known by Monday. The papers got it."

Ava took a deep breath and bit the edge of her lip. "The papers? Really?"

"It's news, especially in Dallas."

"Well then, tonight we should dance a bit. Let's enjoy it, okay?" she said, wondering if she could actually dance to this tune. Dallas society wasn't an easy contender. The women of the city could bind together in a crisis, or they could tear someone apart when scandal was revealed. Ava straightened the sleeve of her black dress. Perhaps God was teaching her not to care what anyone thought . . . or it might be much more than that.

"And to think I planned to bid on that ten-carat diamond bracelet," Ava said with a laugh.

"We can. But it might be embarrassing when our credit card isn't accepted."

Ava swallowed hard even as she snickered at his joke. The reality was setting in, breaking out beads of sweat down her back.

"Can't we go home and pretend that we're sick?"

He gave her a sad expression. "We can do whatever you need to do. I've been trying to protect you from this, and what happens, I drop the bomb on you during one of the most inappropriate times. I know these events are already stressful enough for you."

Ava appreciated the sentiment, but it didn't ease her tangled emotions. "We're already here, and I did force you into telling me."

"We can leave," Dane said, looking deeply into her eyes.

"I can hold my head up high. After all, I have the most handsome husband in all of Dallas," she said with gusto.

They stepped back into the hallway and toward the ballroom. A photographer snapped pictures as if the attendees were movie stars. Dane walked with his hand pressed against Ava's back, which provided a surprising amount of strength.

Ava took shallow breaths as she tried to remember what this night was about. Tammy Blake had worked on this event for a year with Ava meeting with her monthly to offer advice and ideas. After her young son's death from a rare genetic disease, Tammy had turned her energies toward helping other families whose children were suffering. The ball was her first gala event.

"I'm impressed," Dane said, drawing her closer as they entered the ballroom. The elegant décor was layered with reminders of childhood. The tables sparkled with china dinnerware and centerpieces, and each setting had a card with a child's picture and the story of their dreams as well as a short description of his or her illness.

"I'm so proud of her," Ava said, spotting Tammy leaned in toward a hotel staffer with an intense expression on her face.

At the far end of the ballroom was the dance floor and stage with instruments propped up on stands awaiting the musicians to bring them to life.

As Ava and Dane took in the ball, they greeted familiar faces, and Ava tried to cling to his hand and stay joined together. But they were soon separated as Dane was pulled away by a group of men he'd met at a golf tournament, and Ava turned to a tap on her arm, then the careful hug of a longtime friend.

"You look amazing as usual," Jean said, looking up and down at Ava's black dress. Ava thanked her and complimented her gown, which sparkled with sequins much too daring for Ava's taste. She enjoyed how Jean was bold in that way. In her early sixties, the woman stood out with her flashy everything: car, purse, clothing, giant belt buckles with tight jeans. Her hair was always twice the size of her head, even when pulled into a bun.

Once, when they'd roomed together at a women's conference, Jean had tried brightening Ava up with bold red lipstick and sparkling jewelry. Ava felt like a Christmas tree and had to tone it back, despite Jean's disappointment. But Jean could pull it off. Her entire demeanor flashed with style and personality that people said was the epitome of a rich Texas trophy wife.

"How's our girl Sienna and that wedding planning?"

Ava glanced toward Dane as if seeking a life preserver.

"She came for a visit last weekend. She's doing well."

"And she'll get back to Dallas once they're married, correct?"

Ava wanted to avoid lying, but she hadn't spoken to her daughter about the breakup yet, and she certainly wasn't letting the news loose in this room until she knew the details.

"Oh perfect, I'd hoped we would see one another here," Corrine George said to Ava, bustling up to them in her floor-length gown that rustled as she walked. "Hello, Jean," Corrine said coolly.

Ava realized she'd never responded to Corrine's e-mail about the direction of Broken Hearts.

Jean looked at Corrine with distaste, ignoring her greeting. "I'll talk to you a little later, Ava. I believe we're sitting at the same table."

"I declare, Ava," Corrine said as Jean walked away, "you seem to surround yourself with people who surely won't be like iron sharpening iron."

"What are you talking about?" Ava said, staring at the woman. Corrine would be almost pretty if she didn't have a near constant scowl on her face.

"That woman cheated on her first husband with the man she's married to now."

"They've been married for twenty-something years, and it's none of my business, Corrine."

"It is your business who you have in your life."

Ava sighed, searching for Dane and a way out of this conversation. Sometimes it surprised Ava that she was involved with church and other Christians to the extent that she was. After a childhood of religious constraint and domination, she sometimes reexamined her reasons behind her involvement and the core of her faith. Why should she believe? Why should she subject herself to the multilayered complexities found in any church?

Her faith came down to trusting and seeking God, and the belief in Him she'd found outside of what her childhood had told her about God. She wanted to know the real God, not the one forced down her throat in childhood. What surprised Ava most was that her love for other Christians had returned. As a child she'd loved the people in her daddy's congregation. And flawed as they were, Ava often was warmed by the love that overtook her as she heard the stories and tried comforting the tears of people who wanted to truly know who God was.

But the people who acted like Pharisees, who reminded her of her grandmother, those were the hardest for her. Corrine was a thorn in her side, but Ava tried to be patient. There was some kind of pain or fear that was the engine running Corrine's attitude. If Christ loved this woman as much as He loved all the rest of them, shouldn't Ava try harder as well?

"Did you receive my e-mail?" Corrine asked with a smile.

"I did. We'll have to talk about it soon—I had my daughter visiting recently and this week has been quite busy."

"I was sorry to hear about your son," she said, and Ava's stomach clenched.

"My son?" she asked, frowning.

Corrine leaned close to her. "The incident at his school."

Ava nodded and smiled. "Yes. Teenagers are certainly a challenge at times."

"I say this because I care, truly."

Ava waited for the "but" that was coming next.

"But as your sister in Christ, I have to tell you that this incident with your son might have something to do with what I was writing about in that e-mail. It might be related to the people you associate with. I always examine my own life and heart when these things start happening."

Ava didn't speak for a moment. She'd grown up being told that everything bad that happened was because of your own secret sin. When she'd broken her arm climbing a tree, it was her fault for disobeying her aunt. When she and Clancy had to stay at Grannie's house where she sometimes locked them outside for days, it was Clancy's or Ava's fault, something they'd done wrong that sent their father off evangelizing at other churches to make amends for their sins. Ava remembered sitting in her bed as a child, afraid to get out because she would begin sinning, and who knew what harm would come to her or her family because of it.

"I appreciate your concern." Ava glanced around, spotting another friend waving her over.

"I'll keep praying and expect to hear from you about the e-mail soon," Corrine said with frank disapproval.

Later, while standing in a group of women, Sonya Peters—a woman Ava suspected had a crush on Dane by the way she tried flirting with him at every social event—set her hand on Ava's arm and said, "Ava, honey. I want you to know we've been really thinking of your family. We heard about Jason. And I know a great rehab center that my brother went through."

Ava stared at the woman. "Thank you, but I don't think he needs rehab."

Sonya raised her eyebrows. "Please don't get defensive. I really mean this with the best of intentions. You can't ignore these things. And when someone is in trouble beneath our own roofs, we can't be blind to the severity."

"I appreciate your concern. Now if you'll excuse me." Ava stepped away and heard another woman whisper, "I think her husband's company is in trouble as well."

Ava found Dane holding a glass of wine and staring off while standing in a group of people discussing politics. She took his arm and led him away.

"I'm feeling ill now. Can we go home, or will that make a scene?"

"Scene or no scene, let's get out of here."

They walked toward the door as inconspicuously as possible, when a voice came over the sound system, silencing the room. Ava watched as the coordinator of the event, Tammy Blake, stepped onto the stage holding a microphone.

"Run for it," Dane whispered, tugging at her hand. They took careful steps through the crowd, stopping here and there to avoid notice.

"We are just thrilled to have you all here tonight. We have a wonderful night planned for y'all. Before we get started, I've got to thank my mentor in all of this, Ava Kent. This could not have occurred without all your guidance. Will you please come up here with me?"

"We almost made it," Dane said, kissing her cheek as the room full of faces turned toward her.

Ava smiled and waved, hoping Tammy would let her remain where she was, but people motioned her forward.

"I'm guessing that Ava or her handsome fella are going to be bidding on that ten-carat diamond tennis bracelet. We'll let her have a first go at it, but please bid against her. Be generous now. It's for the children."

After the crowd gave her a round of applause and Tammy gushed further about her help, Ava walked off the stage. She was directed toward the tables of the silent auction, but motioned toward the ladies' room. "Just a minute, I'll be right back," she said to a few people who tried to stop her along the way.

Dane met her near the bathrooms, and together they raced for the exit. Ava turned and saw Corrine coming from the bathroom. Their eyes met and Ava had a sudden shiver wash over her, but she refused to go back to the belief that God was punishing her or her family. Instead, perhaps He was opening new doors that would change their lives forever.

Sixteen

AVA OPENED HER EYES TO JASON STANDING BESIDE THE BED studying her with a strange look on his face.

"Are you sick?" he asked. He was fully dressed with his backpack on his shoulder.

"No, I'm fine. What time is it?" she muttered as she saw the time on her alarm clock. She sat up fast and felt a sharp rapping on the side of her head.

"Headache," she said, squeezing her eyes shut.

"You don't have to get up. Dad's taking me to school. I was just coming to say good-bye, but want some medicine?"

She blinked her eyes. "Your dad is taking you?"

"Yeah. And he made me waffles."

"He did? With bacon inside?"

Jason only liked bacon waffles or else he wanted pancakes instead—a quirk she indulged despite the fact it was the same batter for both.

Her son smiled, something she hadn't seen in over a week. "We were out of bacon so he used your salad bacon bits. Not quite as good, but worked for me. He made one for you but without the bits."

"That was nice." Ava leaned back on one elbow. Dane had made only a few breakfasts in all their years together—she could count them on one hand.

"I made the coffee. It's kind of strong."

"Strong sounds exactly right for this morning," Ava said. Jason agreed and lingered in the room as if wanting to tell her something. "Are you all right? You're finally speaking."

"Yeah," he said sheepishly.

He sat on the edge of the bed with a look of shame. His backpack slumped onto the bed next to her legs. The instinct to take him into her arms nearly overwhelmed her.

"I'm sorry, Mom. Really sorry."

Ava didn't respond, fighting the compulsion to say that it was all right, for him not to worry, that all was forgiven. She didn't want it to continue, whatever was going on with her son.

"Can you tell me why?" she asked, sitting fully up in bed.

"What do you mean?"

"*Why* is a pretty straightforward word."

Jason leaned his head onto his hands. "Well, okay, you know I only did that stuff once."

"Which? The pot?"

Jason nodded. "I guess, in that moment, I was tired of being the church boy, as they call me, or the Christian. It gets old. It was stupid, though."

"You know, I do understand," Ava said, setting her hand on his arm. Jason looked as if he didn't believe her.

"Did I ever tell you I was suspended from school once?" Ava said, sitting up in bed and brushing back her hair.

"No you weren't," he said, scrutinizing her face.

"For fighting."

His eyes bugged out and he laughed. "You're making that up."

"I'm not."

"You, fighting? What for? I can't believe this."

"It's true. I was more defending myself, though. I kissed this girl's boyfriend at a dance."

"Mom!"

"Well, I didn't know he was her boyfriend, but she didn't give me time to explain."

"And they suspended you for that?"

"Well, it might have had something to do with the fact that I'd been drinking at the school dance as well. Otherwise I would've never had the guts to take the dare that made me kiss the cutest guy I could find at the dance."

Jason's face couldn't have appeared more stunned if he'd seen a ghost. "Does Dad know this?"

Ava thought for a moment. "You know, I don't think I've told anyone that story before."

"Why not?"

"I don't really like revisiting the things that happened when I was a kid."

"I thought your dad was a pastor."

"He was. But this was after . . . after he wasn't a pastor anymore. And I was tired of being the pastor's kid, the goody two-shoes."

"It was after your dad went to prison?"

"Yes. Your Uncle Clancy and I were living with our grandmother in a house full of people, which brought the rumor that we lived on a commune or in a cult. And looking back, that probably wasn't too far from the truth. It was very hard. But that doesn't excuse it. Everyone is responsible for his or her own choices. I did my share of rebelling, but it only hurt me further. It didn't really harm anyone else and no one started looking up to me because of it."

Jason nodded as if understanding fully.

"I'm sorry that your tree died too."

Ava bit back a smile at the way he said it, though the reminder made her inwardly groan. It wasn't dead, she still hoped.

"Now, the prescription drugs."

"They made me able to play ball without my knee hurting."

"Why didn't you tell us about that? I already made an appointment to see Doctor Andy, but we should have done that months ago if your knee wasn't healing."

"I think it's fine. I haven't taken anything since that night : . . and it doesn't hurt."

He admitted he'd grown dependent on the pills. People at school easily provided what he needed. Ava didn't fully believe her son was fine. None of this was normal or all right for a fifteen-year-old. She wondered if his long silence and moodiness, such a contrast to his normal self, had been part of him coming off of his dependency. Ava swallowed down the emotions working their way through her.

"Did you apologize to your dad?"

Jason nodded. She suspected the incident had something to do with the strain in Jason and Dane's relationship as well. They'd all been affected by Dane's absence.

"We're going to get more help, all right? I believe what you're saying, but we need to have your knee checked and talk to the doc about the prescription."

"You mean, to find out if I have a drug problem?"

"Yes."

Jason sighed, blowing out his cheeks. "I guess I deserve that. But I promise you, Mom, I'm not a druggie. So many other kids are worse than me. And maybe God let me get caught 'cause I was feeling so guilty, or so that I'd never do it again."

"You're still grounded, and you'll have periodic drug tests at school, you know. You don't deserve bad things, honey. But there are consequences. This time you got some pretty harsh ones. You lost out on being on the team, and this certainly harmed your shot at college ball."

Jason frowned at the punishment, then he said slowly, "Dad wants him and me to go on that father-son camping trip."

"You mean the one at church?" She'd mentioned the trip to Dane months ago, but he hadn't appeared receptive.

"Yeah, guess he already talked to Pastor Matt to see if we could still go since it's such short notice, but with football ending . . ."

"It's in a few weeks, right? And you want to go?"

Jason nodded as if contemplating that. "Guess so. What else am I going to do since I'm grounded for all eternity?"

Ava laughed and ruffled up his hair.

Dane called up from downstairs. "Jason, we gotta scoot, buddy! Aves, text me if you want me to pick you up anything. I'll be back in a bit."

"Bye, Mom." Jason leaned down and popped a kiss onto her cheek. She'd barely croaked out a good-bye and he was gone, his feet pounding down the stairway. When he was a boy, Ava compared his running to that of an elephant stomping through the house. She stuck her feet out from under the covers when she heard the sound grow louder again.

Jason popped his head into her room. "Dad said he'll give you two kisses when he gets home. But I wanted to be sure you're okay. I can skip school and take care of my ailing mother." He grinned mischievously.

"Would love that, but you can't miss any more school after your suspension."

Jason groaned. "Okay. Well, love you, Mom!"

"Love you too," she called as he raced back down the stairs.

❦

Ava longed to remain in bed all day, especially after she checked her e-mail on her phone. She immediately closed the program. By the subject lines in the e-mails, news of Dane's company being under investigation had hit the news and gossip lines. She found a number of texts as well, including several from Kayanne.

Kayanne's most recent text read, *I'll be there in thirty minutes if I don't hear from you.*

With the Jason incident not even two weeks earlier and now this scandal with the company, Ava sensed their family's honor might never recover. She kept her phone on vibrate as she headed toward the shower. Before the water turned hot, she heard the rumble and checked the number before answering. The area code alerted her to the location. She touched the screen to ignore the call, but the phone slipped off the counter and onto the marble floor.

Grabbing it up, she was checking it to see if it still worked when she heard a girl's voice.

"Hello? Aunt Ava? Are you there?"

"Hi, Bethany," Ava said, putting the phone to her ear.

"What are you doing?"

Ava bit her lip. This was getting a little too casual.

"I was about to hop in the shower."

"Are you going somewhere?"

Ava thought this girl was the oddest person she'd ever met.

"A friend is coming over and my husband is home from work today." She wondered if the news would find its way to her hometown.

"That's nice. Do you have a lot of friends?"

"I have a lot of people I know, but only a few close friends." Ava looked into her closet full of clothing, but saw nothing to wear today other than the pajamas she had on.

"You go to church a lot, right?"

"Um, yes," Ava said, wondering what that meant to the girl. "It's not the same kind of church that I grew up in back home."

"That's probably a good thing. I quit going there. They said I was going to hell for everything I did."

Ava didn't know how to respond. The girl was in obvious need of someone in her life. She thought of how Aunt Jenny's influence had changed hers and shaped a distinctly different future. Perhaps Ava was supposed to be that for this girl. Wasn't that how it worked in paying it forward? Ava had hoped her work with anyone except her extended bloodline would make up for anything she'd been given. But perhaps God didn't allow trades like that.

"Is that why you go to a different church now?" Bethany asked.

"Sort of. I heard a lot of things like that when I was younger too," she said carefully. Ava pictured family members calling her up and telling her off for leading Bethany astray. But more than caring what they said, Ava wished for everyone to discover how Jesus offered grace and redemption, not judgment and damnation. God wasn't some scary deity lurking in the corners, anxious for someone to sin so He could pour wrath upon them. That discovery had turned Ava's life completely around from what she'd lived with her entire life.

"They make it seem like they're the only people going to be saved in the whole world. That's just not true, right?"

"No, it's not true, Bethany. God's grace is for everyone who wants it."

A muffled commotion sounded in the background.

"Just a minute," Bethany said. The back noise grew silent. "I had to turn down the TV."

The clock read well past the time of Kayanne's threat. She'd be there soon, and Ava expected Dane would need her today as well.

"Bethany, I can't talk long right now. Would you like me to call you back?"

"No, that's okay. I'll call you later. Do you like flowers?"

What is up with this girl? Ava wondered, and then immediately felt guilty for her impatience. She set down her toothbrush and tried to give the conversation her full attention.

"I do like flowers."

"What's your favorite kind?" Bethany asked.

"My new favorite is dahlias."

"Dahlias? I don't know what those are."

"What are your favorite kind of flowers?" Ava took a thick towel from the cupboard and carried it to the bathtub. Today had turned into a bath morning.

"I love all kinds, but if I had to pick, I guess orchids. I read a book once about orchids and I didn't know what those were, so I looked them up online. They're really pretty. I'll look up dahlias next time I'm at the library—that's where I get online."

"Orchids are very beautiful too. You like to read?" Ava hoped her voice didn't betray too much surprise. Orchids and books certainly didn't fit with most of her family's interests.

"If it's a good one. Mostly I read trashy romance novels, but I'm trying to read more better books."

"Maybe I can send you some of my favorites."

"Really? That would be great. Oh, I gotta go. My boyfriend just got here and he doesn't like me talking on the phone."

"Wait? What?" Ava stopped short.

"I'll look up dahlias soon. Bye." And Bethany was gone.

Ava stared at the phone, wondering if something was mentally wrong with this poor girl. She jumped as the phone buzzed again.

"You haven't called me. I'm getting really worried." Kayanne sounded like she'd been running.

"I thought you were coming over."

"You hate when people just show up at your house, so that was a threat to get you to call me."

"Oh, I was expecting you any moment."

"Then why do I hear the bath water running?"

"I got behind. I keep getting phone calls from my cousin."

Kayanne took a deep breath. "*Your* cousin? But you don't talk to your side of the family."

"I know. She's younger than Sienna, and suddenly she started calling me."

"What does she want?"

"I don't know."

"What does Dane say about that?"

"I haven't told him yet. He's been gone so much."

"Listen," Kayanne said dramatically. "You are in a crisis situation from what the newspaper says. So you need to get on the same page with him. You can't be the next marriage fatality. I'll lose all faith in love. Do it for me if for no one else."

"You are too much. We won't be another marriage fatality," Ava said, pouring her favorite bath salts into the steaming water that filled the bottom of the tub.

"You aren't being you, so I'm very concerned. I heard you snuck out early from the Children's Charity Ball."

"Yes, and Sienna broke off her engagement with Preston."

"What?! When? Why? Never mind, I'm coming over."

"I probably need to return to my therapist," Ava said, sitting the edge of the tub and watching the swirl of salts in the water.

"You're a Texan, remember? We stuff down our issues and find fulfillment in anything that has cream and butter. Take your bath and I'll be there soon, with donuts."

Seventeen

AVA'S PHONE KEPT HER FROM ENJOYING THE HOT BATH. SHE ignored the calls, but checked the numbers to be sure it wasn't Dane or Sienna. Finally she rose from the bath water and tip-toed to the walk-in shower to start her normal morning routine before Kayanne arrived.

As she gathered her Bible and journal for her morning meditation, another call interrupted her thoughts.

"It's about time. I've been worried sick about you."

"I know, I'm really sorry." Sienna's voice sounded regretful, but Ava also noticed a definite change from the last time they'd talked. Her daughter sounded happy again. But Ava knew Sienna was making a terrible mistake.

"What's going on? What happened? Are you all right?"

"I'm fine, Mom, really. I think I've known for a really long time, but I didn't want to see it. It's hard, but it's kind of a relief."

"So this is why you couldn't find a wedding dress?" Ava said as she sat on the stool at her vanity counter.

Sienna laughed. "Probably."

"How's Preston? And his family."

"Preston's taking it hard. His family hates me."

"No, they don't. But before you take this any further, I want you to slow down. You're under a lot of pressure. You know we wanted you to wait to marry until after you finished school. Maybe stress is making you confused."

"I don't think so. And, Mom, I can't marry someone just because you and Dad love him."

"Of course not," Ava shot back as she wrapped her robe tighter around her.

"Anyway, I need to talk to you about something else," Sienna said.

"What is it?" Ava said softly, still unable to let go of the end of this perfect future for her daughter.

"Two things. First, I'm on academic probation."

"What? Why?" Ava's head spun.

"I've been burned out with school for a while."

Without intention, Ava walked down the hall into Sienna's room full of cool shades of red and black. There was no clutter, no posters on the walls, no frills or fluff. That was Sienna— organized and ambitious. Her daughter had certainly never used such words as *academic probation* or *burned out*.

"What's really going on?" Ava had a moment of imagining the worst.

"My life has been all about Preston, school, and the future for years. I'm tired of it."

"Do you want to take a semester off and come home?" Even as Ava said it, she thought about the repercussions. Sienna had a plan all figured out. She wanted to be in law school by the next year with a degree in international law before she was twenty-five. For years Ava and Dane had teased Sienna about their need to invest in a Dutch airline for all the flights they'd need to make to and from the International Tribunal in The Hague. When she'd met Preston, Ava savored the idea of her daughter practicing law in Dallas while she helped out with any grand-babies who came along.

"No, Mom. But—"

"But what?" Then it hit her. Sienna already had a plan. Of course her daughter wouldn't toss everything away. Instead, she'd revised her plan, and Ava sat at her daughter's desk, waiting to take in what it was this time.

"Well, it might sound a little crazy . . . Oh, hang on a sec, I need to answer this call." With that, Ava was on hold.

Ava opened the top drawer of Sienna's desk and fiddled through a pad of Post-it Notes. The buildup to whatever Sienna was about to tell her was eating a hole in her stomach. Ava liked her ducks in a row and secretly thought people who did spontaneous things, lived by the seat of their pants and all that, were somewhat foolish. They were missing out on being the best they could be. Why not instead hone your life into the best possible version of yourself? Sienna ascribed to the same sort of logic, yet suddenly she was breaking up with a longterm boyfriend and wanting time off from school.

"I'm back," Sienna said.

Ava inhaled and steeled herself for what would come next. "Tell me."

"I want to live in Nepal for a year."

Ava burst into laughter. "Okay, Sienna."

Nepal was as ridiculous as Sienna saying she was running away to join the circus. Even with her innate desire for justice in the world, Sienna required a certain level of luxury: five-star accommodations, pedicures, and just the right labels in clothing.

"Mom."

"What it is?"

"I'm serious. There's this guy—"

"Oh no . . ." Now this was making a little more sense, and Ava knew her daughter wasn't ready for a new guy in her life.

"No, it's not like that. There's nothing going on."

"Okay."

"He's this professor at the university. He teaches Greek. I started going to this group, and they want to really tackle a lot of the social justice topics."

"So is this like an internship?"

"No, Mom. It's just me and some people going to Nepal."

Again Ava waited for her daughter to reveal that she was teasing her, but then Sienna kept going on about the plan this group had created.

"It wouldn't be just Nepal. That's where we'd start. I'd like to explore all over Southeast Asia—Indonesia, the Philippines, Malaysia . . ."

Sienna talked on in her rapid, excited tone that was usually reserved for something profound like an article in the *Atlantic Monthly*, a documentary about children in Africa, or a deep theological study. Sienna loved to learn, but that had never sent her to scary places before.

"Those are really dangerous places. Your dad will never agree to this."

"I already talked to Dad. He was worried, but he thinks it's exactly what God wants for my life."

"When was that?" Ava felt a sudden sense of betrayal between the two of them. How could they leave her out of this?

"A few days ago."

"A few days ago?"

"Mom, this is totally out of my comfort zone, and it's not like anything I've ever done. It sounds crazy to me, so I know it's terrifying for you. But it's also exactly what you've always wanted for me. You wanted me to go on mission trips in high school and understand people from different cultures than ours."

Sienna had always been good at turning a subject around. It was one reason Dane teased Sienna about becoming a lawyer when she was a little girl. If they talked much longer, Sienna might convince Ava that it was her idea for her brown-haired, blue-eyed, All-American girl to drop out of school and gypsy around Southeast Asia.

"Why right now?" Ava asked, stopping Sienna mid-sentence. The question was directed as much to God as to her daughter. Ava knew God's timing was intentional and coincidences weren't that at all. So why was He allowing all of this at the exact same time?

"I don't know exactly," Sienna said, her voice becoming sincere. "I'm seeing things differently than before. I wanted to go into law to stick up for the underdog and punish people for harming others."

"Ever since you were almost expelled for pushing Kelsey Blakely down after she put gum in Trina Glasgow's hair?"

Sienna laughed. "Yeah, I always needed to defend those who didn't defend themselves."

"It's a beautiful attribute."

"But I realize that while I was defending people, I felt superior to them. That's what I want to change. I want to be among people who aren't from my world, to learn from them, and not just come at them with my Americanized ideals. Then I'll be truly effective in my career."

Ava fell back onto her daughter's bed, staring at the ceiling Sienna had looked up at all of those years as she grew from a girl to a young woman. How could she argue with Sienna or with God over her daughter's epiphany and longing for more? Yet Ava couldn't imagine a year of her daughter loose out in the world, especially in some of the most dangerous places.

"You're doing this because of the breakup. Instead of a rebound guy, you've got a rebound trip."

"No, this is one reason I knew Preston wasn't right for me."

"Because he didn't support you running off to third-world countries?"

"They're called developing nations now, not third-world countries. And some of the countries are quite advanced."

"I guess I have a lot to learn too."

"Mom?"

"What, sweetie?" Ava closed her eyes, wishing for her own year away. Why couldn't the world just freeze for a while so that she could rest, regain her strength, and catch up with it all?

"Just pray about it, okay? I'm going to get my grades up this semester. This wouldn't start till summer."

"This summer?" Ava wanted to grab hold of all of her loved ones and rein them all in. She'd counseled many women stressed-out with their children in the home. They had no idea how much harder it was when you didn't have them safely beneath your own roof.

Ava sat with the phone in her hands after Sienna had hung up. She watched a blue jay outside swoop down from the trees and onto the edge of their neighbor's birdbath sitting in the front lawn. The autumn leaves were nearly gone now and the winter drab was coming soon.

"Why can't anything good remain?" she whispered.

Eighteen

KAYANNE AND HER DONUTS DID LITTLE TO SOOTHE AVA. HER best friend struggled to hide her excitement over Sienna's decision to see the world. Since her divorce Kayanne had gone on several mission trips to Haiti and Costa Rica. Her financial crash had forcibly changed her perspective as well.

"I know it's scary, but . . ."

Ava wasn't ready to process the benefits of an adventure. She also knew her daughter would expect them to fund the grand journey.

"She'll figure it out," Kayanne assured her. "She's going to learn the truth about your finances anyway—and she can handle it. It's not like your childhood and being told there might not be food to eat."

Ava was stung by the truth in Kayanne's words. She tried protecting her children from the fear she'd known as a child, hearing her grandmother harp about the lack of money as if the world were on fire and soon they'd all burn up.

When Kayanne left, Ava tossed the donuts and ran two miles on her treadmill until her legs stung with pain. She'd slacked off on her running in the past year and had gained some weight, but suddenly she needed to do something or else climb the walls waiting for Dane to return.

Dane arrived in late afternoon and appeared so weary that Ava stuffed back her anger over his approval of Sienna dropping out of college for a trip to Asia. He wore jeans and a pullover sweatshirt instead of his usual business attire.

"Where were you?" Ava asked as he sat in the dining room. He set his elbows on the table and rubbed his eyes.

"I met Jimmy for lunch since the office is closed."

Jimmy was their personal lawyer and a friend since right after college. Ava hadn't realized that the entire company was closed.

"What does he say?"

"Confirms everything I suspected."

"Tell me. Stop trying to protect me," Ava said in frustration.

Dane nodded softly as if giving up. "Our accounts are currently frozen while the investigation is going on. I basically have no job and can't move on to something else until this is cleared up."

"So we have no money and you have no job." Ava sat at the table across from him.

"Not much money. I have an emergency fund in the safe, but it won't get us through many months . . ."

Ava listened with her hands flat against the wood. She saw her fingerprints smudge on the polished surface. They'd sat in these same positions when they'd planned the funerals of Dane's parents when they'd died six months apart from each other. These weren't their usual seats when eating dinner, but perhaps this was their necessary placement when facing a crisis.

Dane's head hung forward as he kneaded his temple with long fingers. Ava asked random questions as they came to mind. He answered with little emotion, painting a bleak picture.

"So what were all those late nights and the trip to New York about?" Ava asked, gazing toward the window where a deep sunset painted the western sky.

"It was about saving the company. Obviously a failure now. We were wading through the recession, but this investigation will fold us. That's exactly what our competitors planned. It's a smart but devious move. But big picture, it doesn't matter. I prayed and prayed about this."

"You believed God would pull you through."

"I did believe that. And I put too much energy in trying to save it. I'm tired."

"What happens now?"

He rubbed his forehead. "I don't know. I'm hoping God has a better plan than the ones I've tried."

"He does. I just wonder what it is." Ava's heart raced with the uncertainty.

"Do you want to pray together?" Dane asked.

Ava swallowed hard as she moved to the chair beside her husband and took his hands. Times like these broke couples apart or joined them together. She wanted to escape, but where would she go? Still, the compulsion welled up strong within her, despite what her mind and heart were telling her. Her husband was praying for them, and she'd longed for such intimacy for a long time. So why now did she want to yank away her hands and rush out the door?

That night, Ava gave an abbreviated explanation to Jason, and Ava heard Dane talking with Sienna over the phone. Ava wished she could keep her children safe from what this might mean to their lives, to Sienna going to law school or Asia, to Jason who'd asked for a snowboarding trip to Utah over Christmas break. And Christmas was coming. Would they have a Christmas without gifts? And what about their house? How long could they live there before being booted out? Ava felt somewhat guilty over the relief that they didn't have to tell their daughter they couldn't afford her wedding.

As Ava's questions crowded in on top of one another, her husband's prayer offered little solace.

In the next few days, Ava tried adjusting to the instability. Dane hadn't given her an actual budget to work with. She didn't know if she should look for a job or what. Dane was inundated with talking to colleagues and corporate lawyers, answering questions from investigators, shifting through documents—and he was sleeping. A lot.

Dane never slept in. He rose at five during the week and five thirty or six on weekends. Dane never understood people who wasted the day in bed or shuffling around their lives instead of grasping it with two fists.

Now her husband slept with his mouth open and one arm up by his face. She picked up his shirt and pants off the floor, pulling a balled-up sock from under the bed. Dane's nighttime routine included his clothes going straight to the hamper. They joked about his obsessive-compulsive behavior, and in their early years of marriage it had been an issue with Ava's own neatness suddenly not good enough.

In college, Ava's roommates had teased her about her organized shelves, the organizing baskets under her bed that was always made unless she was in it. But compared to Dane's rigid habits, Ava felt like a slacker. They'd eased into a workable routine. Now, twenty-six years later, Ava didn't know what to do with this sleepy man with a scruffy chin rapidly turning toward beard material.

With Dane home and Ava avoiding most social events, she found more time for a last attempt at saving the willow tree.

Ava read online tree forums, posted and responded to advice, then searched the local university for a plant specialist. She sent pictures in, met with the arborist and his intern, and stopped in at several nurseries. The conclusion from the experts and second and third opinions were conclusive. The tree was dead.

Leo held the chain saw, looking more glum than usual. He stared at the saw and peered at her sideways, not meeting her eyes straight on.

He cleared his throat. "I ain't never been as sad to cut a tree as this one, and I don't even like the thing."

Ava smiled while biting her lip, but her throat felt thick with emotion. Why was this affecting her so?

"Maybe we should wait till after the holidays or till springtime. If the leaves don't bud, then we will know for sure."

Ava wanted to continue hoping. But some things couldn't be saved. Maybe some things shouldn't be saved, she mused.

"Let's get it over with."

He studied her a moment longer as if to be assured of her certainty. Then Leo pulled the handle, and the saw roared to life. Ava stepped back, covering her ears.

She thought of the five willow trees along the Black Rock River. The bench beneath this tree would soon be surrounded by all sky as her beloved willow was turned to wood chips or burned in Leo's fireplace.

Leo bent forward, bringing the roaring teeth toward the smooth bark.

"Wait!" she yelled, making Leo jump back.

"What?" he yelled with a terrified expression.

"Don't do it!"

Leo shut down the saw and the noise died away. He cursed beneath his breath and with a frustrated wave of his arm headed for his truck parked outside the back gate.

Ava stared at the pathetic branches of what had been her full, luscious tree. It was gone. It was over.

But she just couldn't cut it down.

Nineteen

AVA ARRIVED EARLY TO THURSDAY MORNING BIBLE STUDY. SHE walked through the garden, praying as she went, and then sat in the empty room well before the start time. Finally women arrived, greeting her and getting coffee and talking together. There was an air of uncertainty in some of the women—Ava knew those were the ones who'd heard about Dane's company, or Sienna's breakup, or Jason failing his drug test. They might wonder what she was doing leading a Bible study at all. Ava realized that everyone in her family was coping with a very personal challenge while also living with the effects of everyone else's. Except for her—she didn't have a personal issue to deal with on her own like they did.

She turned the pages of her Bible and for a moment let the rest of the conversations in the room disappear around her.

As a child Ava had loved her daddy's Bible. Sometimes she'd crawl onto his lap during a Bible study meeting or when he was studying it in the morning with the Word sitting on the table in front of them. She'd lean against Daddy's chest to hear the rumble of his voice as he talked about Jesus walking along the Sea of Galilee or of Moses climbing that great Mount Sinai or of Ruth following her mother-in-law to a foreign land, saying that Naomi's people would be her people and Naomi's God would be her God.

Ever so gently, she'd rub the thin pages between her fingers and listen to the sound of them turning. Daddy turned the pages quickly with a swooshing sound, but he never once tore that thin paper.

Ava would lean very close to the slim edge of gold that, when put together with all the pages as the Bible closed, made one solid gold layer. She'd touch the words in red and imagine Jesus' voice speaking them. At first Jesus sounded like Daddy. Later He took on His own voice, a more humble and rich tone that didn't get frustrated or pound the pulpit in anger or burst with emotions both up and down.

"Who would like to open in prayer today?" Kayanne asked from across the table. Ava usually opened this way, and she realized that the women sat silently, waiting for her to begin.

"We are praying for you and your family, Ava," Jillian Latoya said with a sincerity that Ava appreciated. A few of the women wore confused expressions, others showed empathy, and one had the pruned up look of impertinence.

"Thank you. And for those of you who don't know, my family is experiencing a few challenges. Our daughter, Sienna, has decided to break off her engagement. Our son has made a few mistakes—high school, you know. And my husband's company is . . . well, it's not in the best place at the moment."

A few surprised gasps were heard and mumbles of, "That's so hard." "Oh no. Poor Ava." "Oh we understand."

Ava gazed at the faces of women she'd come to love through all their issues, flaws, and struggles. The weekly gathering had bonded them, not always in friendships that extended outside the doors, but in a deep, soulful way. For wouldn't they be sisters forever?

"Sometimes I try to be your fearless leader, and I forget that you don't need me to be perfect or without struggles. We just need to be real with one another. I really do need your prayers and support." Ava gazed around the room at the faces.

"I see God working in our family through it all. This morning John 16:33 popped into my mind. 'I have told you all this so that you may have peace in me. Here on earth you will have many trials and sorrows. But take heart, because I have overcome the world.' Jesus was talking to His disciples, but don't we all know that there are many troubles in this life.

"Before this week, I didn't think I could get tired of my husband being around," Ava said with a laugh. "Let me just say, he's driving me a little nutty."

Corrine cleared her throat from the other end of the long table as she always did before speaking in a group. "You shouldn't criticize your husband just because he lost his job. It's not about the money. You have to love him for richer or for poorer."

All eyes jumped back toward Ava with surprised expressions. Kayanne leaned forward ready to defend Ava when she interjected.

"I didn't mean it like that," Ava said with her annoyance unchecked. "For twenty-six years, Dane has been at work during the day, and since Jason started kindergarten, I've had the house to myself during the day. Suddenly we're tripping all over each other."

"I know exactly what you mean," Leslie Hammond said, plopping her purse on the table and digging out her cell phone. "Look at how many texts I've been getting from my husband and kids since I got here. Ten messages in, what, five minutes? Jimmy has been out of work for seven months now, and I don't know how much longer I can take of it. He actually told me that maybe I should get a job. What in the world would I do? I got a liberal arts degree and haven't worked . . . well, ever."

"Oh, Les, that's awful," Jillian said with a look of horror. Ava saw Kayanne purse her lips to keep back a laugh. Leslie and Jillian had been raised wealthy and expected to die the same way.

"Some of us in the room would be grateful for a husband," Corrine added with a sympathetic glance toward Kayanne.

"It's not all fun and games over on the marriage side," Shawna Normandy stated as she tapped her nails against the wooden table. "I'm ready to strangle my husband, and if he ends up strangled to death, none of you can tell the police that I just said that."

Ava chuckled, but with an edge of tension. Shawna was an avid hunter with enough firearms in her house to take out half the forest. Surely she was kidding about her husband.

"Men are much worse out in the big, bad world though," Kayanne said with a sigh.

"You think so? Do you have to clean up the progressive messes of a man who leaves smelly toenails all over the bathroom floor and eats cheese with his ice cream?"

"You've got me there," Kayanne said with a laugh. "Though cheese ice cream is actually a flavor in some countries."

"But not here, and this isn't cheese-flavored ice cream, it's cheese in his ice cream." Shawna shook her head in disgust.

"Let's rein ourselves back in. I want to say that I appreciate this group. I don't say that enough," Ava said. She held up the Bible study guide. "Chapter twelve this week."

An hour later, the women dispersed and left the room with Kayanne remaining.

"What were you scribbling away about during Bible study? Your shopping list?"

"I was making notes about the study," Ava said with a smile, then held up her notebook as proof. She turned the page and revealed a list of to-dos. "But, okay, I also have this."

Ava usually tapped everything into her little techie devices, but during Bible study she only used pen and paper.

"Why exactly do you continue to lead this Bible study? It's not like you get anything out of it."

"I get a lot out of it, and I hope others do as well. Wasn't that obvious by my rambling confession today? Why do you keep coming?" They walked from the room and down the hallway toward the entrance of the church.

"Because I certainly need it. I'm a divorcee, I'm neurotic, I spend a disgusting amount of time plotting the ill-will of two other human beings, one of whom I promised to love and cherish until death we did part . . ."

"You're still plotting their ill-will?" Ava hoped Kayanne would somehow forgive her ex-husband for his affair, but Ava had no advice on that front. It had only been three years after twenty-seven years of marriage. Ava wasn't sure how she'd forgive Dane if it happened to her, let alone the fact that Ava's ex-husband and his mistress had married and moved to an island in the Caribbean while Kayanne was left with their small business that eventually went belly-up.

Kayanne glanced around, and leaned closer to Ava. ". . . and I'm so tired of being single that I may run away with that older usher I always thought looked like a magician with his slicked-back, overly dyed hair and Liberace suits."

"He doesn't wear Liberace suits—they aren't that bad. But isn't he in his late seventies?" Ava said in an exaggerated whisper.

"My point exactly. See my desperation. Know my need for God."

Ava wrapped her arm around Kayanne's shoulder.

"I'm sorry, and I haven't been a very good friend. Let's pray about it."

"Yeah, yeah."

Ava bit the edge of her lip to keep from laughing.

"Really, let's pray about it right now."

"See, this is why you don't need Bible study," Kayanne said with a sigh.

"Believe me. I need it."

Someone cleared her throat, and Ava and Kayanne noticed Corrine waiting by the double doors that led to the parking lot.

"Do you have a minute, Ava?"

"Of course," she said, meeting Kayanne's eyes.

"I'll call you later," Kayanne said, waving good-bye.

Corrine waited with her arms crossed over her Bible and study guide.

"Did you want to discuss the e-mail that you sent me a few weeks ago?" Ava continued walking toward the parking lot with Corrine coming beside her.

"Not at this moment. I just want to first ask, have you and Dane been praying?"

Ava frowned at the woman's brazenness. "Yes."

Corrine stopped, forcing Ava to remain in the cold morning shadows outside the church. She shivered, thinking of her jacket in the car.

"I just feel in my heart that something is wrong, that there is some unspoken sin that needs repentance."

"Where is this coming from?"

"I think the Spirit is leading me. God does reveal these things though others. Sins always come to light."

Ava had always been a woman who wanted the truth, no matter how painful. If Dane was doing something behind her back, she wanted to know.

"How long have you been feeling this way?"

"For a while," Corrine said. "Maybe since last summer."

Ava tried to remember what significance last summer might have.

"What specifically are you talking about?"

"I have no idea," Corrine said with alarm. "But I'm talking about you."

"Me?"

"Yes."

"You think I have some dark secret sin?" She racked her brain to be sure she hadn't deceived herself.

"I didn't say that I think you do. But I've been trying to tell you, all these things you mentioned in Bible study and what I've been hearing, they're happening for a reason. And I fear that reason is you."

⌒☉☉⌒

By the end of the week, Ava's cupboards begged her to fill them, with Jason seconding that request. "I can deal with stupid rumors about Dad's work and about me and my supposed drug issues," he told her, "but I can't survive without food."

She ventured out to a grocery store across town to avoid seeing anyone she knew. In the checkout line Ava stared at the numbers growing on the cash register. She counted the cash in her wallet, looking at the row of useless credit cards tucked neatly in their compartments. When was the last time she'd worried about those numbers? Their first year of marriage, but more from habit than necessity. Before that, there were the lean college years, and her childhood that was more famine than feast.

But for over twenty-five years, Ava hadn't feared the checkout line. Sometimes she remembered the anxiety, the counting and recounting of what was in the basket before moving to the checkout, the horror of being short several dollars and having to put things back.

The cashier moved each item over the scanner with Ava's heart rate rising. She counted the cash in her wallet a fourth time and barely responded to the cheery small talk. Then the total, and Ava exhaled in relief. She had twenty dollars to spare.

When Ava pulled up the cobblestone driveway to their two-story house that suddenly appeared taller to her, as if it were too much for them to keep, Dane was outside the garage waxing Old Dutch—the 1966 VW Vanagon.

Old Dutch had joined the four-car garage after Dane's father passed away.

Every six months, Dane pulled the old bus out of the garage. He and the kids washed it and checked all the fluids. Then they piled in for a drive or sometimes drove it to church. It was a reminder to all of them that what they had was a gift, and that they'd worked hard to get it.

"This was my dad's first brand-new car," Dane reminded the kids, though they'd heard it a hundred times. Their children had grown up with luxury cars. Dane bought Sienna a Volvo for her eighteenth birthday, believing he wasn't spoiling her because he'd made her drive one of their cars for the two years prior. That was the life Dane had grown up in, and Ava just couldn't explain the vast difference between hers and all of theirs. Could they ever grasp what it was like to ride a bus to school through high school, to buy clothes at secondhand stores, not because it was vintage, but because it was necessary, or to scrape off mold from a loaf of bread and eat it or eat nothing?

The door to her section of the garage rose and she drove inside. Dane put a hand up as a lame wave, then continued waxing Old Dutch without helping with the load of bags she carried in her arms. She didn't think he even noticed.

She called him in to lunch. Instead of eating, Dane fussed over his food with a scowl on this face.

"What's wrong?" Ava buried her annoyance. Dane had never needed her sympathy or coddling. His moodiness was getting old. She realized the irony that she listened to people share their concerns and stresses all the time. She'd listened to women talking about their husbands going through a depression—the topic had grown in the past few years. Men who'd lost their jobs, who couldn't find work, who had to work out of town. Why didn't it irritate her to hear their stories, yet Dane's moodiness was touching on her every nerve? And Kayanne wondered why she continued to do Bible study—she might need it more than anyone.

Ava realized, too, that her life wasn't tied to those women. She didn't have to live with them or gauge their moods and have it affect her life. Advice and understanding were much easier to offer when it didn't involve her and her family.

Dane didn't answer. He went to the French doors and stood gazing out at the pool.

"I didn't do anything wrong, so I'm going to ignore the fact that you're being rude right now."

He closed the sliding door. "How generous of you. You're always generous, aren't you? Generous to everyone else."

Ava glanced at the clock. This was the last thing she needed. "Why do we have all of this?"

Ava set down her purse. "Why do we have all of what?"

"This stuff. This house, the cars, the clothes, the toys."

"Because you earned it, and we enjoyed buying it. It's less than you had growing up."

"It seems my work should amount to more than this. Not just stuff that people hardly use. Important things."

So this was what a midlife crisis looked like, Ava thought. Instead of buying a sports car, he wanted to get rid of everything and live like a hippie?

"You're unhappy. What do you want to do?"

"I wanted to walk on the Antarctic, cycle across America, boat down the Amazon, go ice caving . . ." His voice drifted off, as if imagining each one.

"You should have, and still can. I wouldn't have stopped you."

"Yes, you would have stopped me."

"When have I ever stopped you from doing anything?"

"You always have some irrational fear or reason why it won't work out."

Ava couldn't believe he was blaming her. "I offer some realistic thoughts—that's all. And you've been so consumed with work for the past fifteen years, your kids would've never seen you if you'd become Mr. Adventure. Then you'd be sitting here with all of these excursions and great photos to prove it, but two children who didn't know you. Would that satisfy you?"

"See, you always knock down my ideas unless they're about work."

"I don't." Ava felt floored by his biting words. She picked up Dane's plate and caught the scent of pastrami from the mangled remains of his sandwich. She set it on the counter, regretting that she'd splurged on the expensive pastrami instead of plain lunch meat.

"You said you'd never marry a guy who wasn't stable."

"When did I say that?"

"Outside Grady's Pub during that really bad hail storm."

Ava vaguely remembered them standing under the eaves of their favorite Irish pub in San Francisco. Her memory was of a romantic hour huddled together sharing their hopes and dreams. She'd thought Dane felt that way as well.

"I was crazy about you. So when the guys asked me to do that Alaska expedition, I didn't go."

It was as if everything she'd thought was wrong. The image she had of their courtship, marriage, and two decades together wasn't the same as his. She thought it was like a photograph they could all view and see the same image. But their lives weren't a photograph.

"You act like I've ruined your life, when my entire life has completely revolved around you, your work, your activities, your everything."

He shook his head. "What are you talking about? My life revolves around you and the kids. Everything I've done has been to give you the best of everything. I was the guy who could have lived in a tent in the wild country, exploring the world or taking wildlife videos. But I went the corporate route for my family."

Ava wanted to shout, "Liar!" She thought about how much pride Dane took in his work, in golf and community activities. Now, suddenly, he was acting as if all that was for her? Maybe his favorite channels were Discovery Channel and National Geographic, but she hadn't guessed that he watched them with a sense of loss about his life.

"I guess this has all been a huge mistake," Ava said, seething. Dane walked out without saying more.

⟨⊙⊙⟩

Saturday morning, Ava rose early to cook for the funeral of a young boy who'd died of leukemia. The parents had no extended family, so the women of the Broken Hearts were providing the food, and donations were helping with expenses. Ava usually spent her own money on meals, but this time she used ministry funds to buy the ingredients.

She baked a homemade macaroni-and-cheese dish, a corn casserole, and a lemon torte. The sun filtered through angry rain clouds outside. The trees appeared barren in the backyard this time of year with only a few leafy stragglers dangling on to autumn. Her willow was among them, but Ava didn't see the harm of a dead tree among the dormant ones. They appeared the same, at least for now.

Dane slept while she showered and got ready. He and Jason had stayed up late watching old Westerns. Ava had watched them from the doorway before going to bed. She told herself it was good that this financial disaster had given Dane more time with Jason, but another part of her couldn't swallow the bitterness of that thought.

She was packing up the casserole dishes in her food travel bag when she heard footsteps down the stairs.

"You're going somewhere this morning? I was hoping we could talk." Dane rubbed his eyes as he walked to the cupboard for a coffee cup.

"It's after nine," she said with a bite in her tone.

"It felt good to sleep."

"I'm sure it does." *Some of us still have a life*, she wanted to spout.

Dane wrapped his arms around her waist, and Ava thought of how her dress might wrinkle.

"Why don't I carry out your casseroles? I'll do anything you want to put you into a happy mood."

"I'm late, that's all."

"You, late? I don't believe you."

Ava ground the back of her teeth when she saw the clock, and she felt a sudden rush of anger sting through her veins. For months now Dane had rushed out the door no matter what was happening to deal with his work, but now he popped awake and wanted to talk to her? He had no respect for her schedule or what she was doing. For that matter, she suddenly thought over how supportive he was of her ministry. He acted proud, but in the way he acted over something cute the kids had done, like making a macaroni necklace. Did he realize how grateful the families were that they helped? Did he care that what she did with the ministry really mattered?

"What do you want to talk about?" She picked up the casserole dish with two hands.

Dane took the dish from her and carried it to her car as she gathered up her purse. He returned for the other dishes.

"We can talk later," he said after the car was packed.

"What are you doing today?" she asked, her anger softening despite how she tried to cling to it.

He shrugged.

"You could go for a ride or golf?" Ava wished for some remnant of her over-achieving husband to return.

"I don't feel like either. I might organize the garage or see what Pastor Randy is up to today."

"Those are good, yeah, maybe do both," Ava said, feeling like she was talking to Jason instead of Mr. Driven himself.

He'd cooked dinner.

Ava stared at the sight of Dane at the stove with ingredients covering the counter. The stove sizzled with strip steak in a wine sauce and water boiled for pasta.

"What is this?"

"A surprise for my wife."

"Where's Jason?

"I gave him a free pass, but to youth group only."

"Why? Are we okay?" Ava asked in a softer tone.

"I hope so. First of all, I'm sorry. I didn't mean what I said yesterday. I really wouldn't be happy living in the wilds of Alaska—you and the kids mean everything to me. Come here," he said, pulling her into his arms.

Ava resisted momentarily, striving to cling to her anger. But it slid away faster than she could hold it in.

"What do you think of Jason and me going on that church trip?"

Ava leaned back and studied his face.

"Jason told me you had mentioned it, but I assumed you weren't going."

"I've been missing something."

"What?" Ava leaned in. Was he discontent with their life? Was he wanting more?

Dane's eyebrows seemed pained at the thought. "I don't know. I've been so busy building a company that I don't even own now. But something's not right."

Ava didn't know how to give Dane room to sort this out. She worked within the parameters of Dane's and the kids' lives.

She should be thankful. Maybe her husband would start seeking more of God. So why wouldn't this worry settle?

"You do work that is important. You change lives. I want to do something like that. I'm really proud of you."

Ava bit the edge of her lip and tucked a dark strand of hair behind her ear. "Thank you for saying that."

"I don't give you enough credit, but there's something else too. I want us to be closer."

"You don't think we're close?"

"Do you think you hold something back from me?"

"What are you talking about?" Ava said with a chuckle.

"There are things about you that I still don't know. I get surprised by them, and I don't realize what they mean. Like how important that willow tree was to you. I knew you liked it, but it's more than that, isn't it?"

Ava nodded with her head against his chest. She could feel his heartbeat and the echo of his words in his chest.

"So why don't you let me and the kids into the reasons and into your childhood. You're a shoulder to so many people, helping to pick up the pieces all the time. You're extremely loving and generous."

Ava moved away from Dane now. She sat on a bar stool as he hurried to stir the pasta. "Get to the heart of this, without all the compliments. What are you trying to say?"

"I want you to give us all of your heart."

Ava had the growing sense that her entire life had been a lie. Or perhaps not a total lie, just a movie playing out behind a fuzzy screen and Ava was wearing 3-D glasses even though the movie wasn't in 3-D.

God, is this true? Have I reserved myself from my family? Avoided risking my heart by loving them too deeply or sharing with them?

Dane ran a finger along his eyebrows.

"I'm not explaining this perfectly. But it's as if you keep a very thin covering between us."

"Between who?"

"You and me. You and the kids. You and everyone else, for that matter."

"I've devoted my entire life to all of you. How could you say this? You make me sound so cold and empty."

Dane reached for her arm, but Ava pulled away.

"That's not how I meant it. I want to see you fully let go of that wall you've built up."

Ava stood up, knocking her purse off the edge of the counter.

"I can't believe you're telling me this. First you tell me I've kept you from doing what you really wanted with your life. And now, after all these years, you don't feel loved by me. You feel like I'm distant from you and the kids."

"That's not all the way true. This is the life I wanted, and I shouldn't have said that. It's been hard lately, stopping suddenly and taking inventory of where we've come. And you love us greatly. But you have parts of yourself that you seem afraid to let us see. You've never told the kids much about your family or childhood. You've told me only pieces. You won't let us be part of what you've gone through."

Something in his words rang true to her, though Ava fought to deny it to herself.

Dane kissed her on her forehead. "Listen, I love you. I'm not going anywhere—well, except for a youth camping trip, but other than that, I'm not going anywhere. This is our chance to build something even better than what we've had. We've had money. We've had trips and possessions and have provided for many others. We've been able to support people who needed help. Now it's time to see what God has for us. Sometimes losing everything is the perfect way to start something better."

Ava pulled away and hurried up the stairs to their room. She didn't want to lose everything. She didn't want to have a new start or to build something different. What was wrong with the life they'd had? And how could she ever open doorways inside of her that had closed long ago?

Twenty

THURSDAY MORNING, DANE AND JASON WAVED OUT THEIR CAR windows as they drove down the driveway. Ava watched them leave, waving in return, then turned back toward the house. With several days alone, she wondered where she'd start— either deep cleaning the house or working on the yard. With their finances in crisis, Leo and Martina were luxuries that had to go. Dane had given them each two month's extra pay when telling them that he didn't know how long till he could hire them back.

Every time she saw Dane pull out cash from the safe in the den, her heart raced. At some point it was going to be gone. They had utilities to pay, fuel, food, and the holidays looming ahead. It was just over a month till Thanksgiving, and Ava was usually clicking away at online Christmas shopping by now. She liked to have her presents purchased and wrapped when they brought home the tree Thanksgiving weekend.

Now Dane was gone with the promise that he'd do something about their finances—maybe put the house on the market—as soon as he returned from the father-son trip.

Ava walked through the quiet rooms of the house, from the downstairs to the upstairs.

The rooms and walkways felt hollow without the family moving through them. Jason would be leaving in a few years for college, and the house was large for only two people. It didn't feel overly spacious with the many kids so often staying over. But with Jason's departure, they'd be leaving as well. Dane and Ava had talked about downsizing when the kids had left, or moving to something on a golf course for Dane's pleasure or with a view of water for Ava's.

Now they might not have a choice. The house might not be theirs to decide upon.

She pictured them moving out and the neighbors asking where they were going. The auction papers taped to the front door. Ava had seen other realtor signs stuck into the dry lawns with "foreclosure" stamped across the top. She'd felt empathy for those families. She'd handed out advice to several women about how to hold their heads up high, and if they'd tried all they could, then they hadn't done anything wrong. God would repay what the locusts had eaten. She hadn't used quite that cliché of a comeback, but now that she was the one facing the chopping block, she realized just how deep the humiliation ran.

And this wouldn't be her house. Someone else would have favorite places like the sunken tub, the window seat in Sienna's room, the organized shelves in the pantry, the patio barbecue and fire pit, and the bench beside a dead willow tree. Another woman would cook in the kitchen, other children would swim in the pool, and a different man would place his tools on the workbench.

Dane said he was doing everything he could for them to remain in the house. But in that quiet place, Ava knew God was telling her to let it go. That her home wasn't here, that her family wasn't made up of a place, and that she needed to release everything into His hands.

The Lord gives and the Lord takes away. Blessed is the name of the Lord.

It was easier said than done. Ava wanted to hang on to everything they possessed. She didn't want to let it go. She didn't want to go back. Losing everything couldn't help feel like failure. And possessions provided a security she hadn't known as a child. She didn't know how to live like that again.

Ava ignored her phone calls that day. She might be depressed, but she needed the quiet, only texting Kayanne and Sienna to tell them she was enjoying the time alone and asking them not to worry.

The cold on her bare feet brought Ava fully from her sleep. As she realized where she stood, Ava took in the leaves of the willow tree and how they drooped.

I'm here again.

She was in her pajamas beneath a cold harvest moon. And

she'd been dreaming, or remembering, Ava couldn't be sure which. She hadn't sleepwalked since childhood, and even now she wasn't sure if she'd meant to walk out here or not.

Soft light glowed along the backyard pathways and around the covered pool from the small solar path lights. The moon, too, reflected down, casting a hazy light.

She shivered and knew she should go back inside. Dane and Jason were gone, and being outside in the middle of the night was not a good idea. Yet her feet wouldn't move, cold as they were. She hadn't been sleepwalking, but she'd come out here in a kind of a trance as if the moon or the tree had called to her, lulled her out to a past she'd closed the book on and set up on a very high shelf. But the book wanted to be revisited, and this dream played itself out.

A girl had run through the grass beneath the moonlight. She ran with tears stinging her eyes, but the farther she ran down the dirt road away from the house, the more free she felt.

The soles of her feet were hard and calloused from a life playing outdoors without shoes. She'd be in school soon where shoes were required, and her cousins said no one was going to like a wild girl like her. Ava would surprise them, she'd planned, but for now, she could be free for just a little while longer.

She ran to the willow trees that lined the Black Rock River. She could see the shape of them silhouetted against the moon-filled sky.

A car flew down the road, lights bouncing. Ava lowered herself down against the trunk of the tree, not even bothering to duck behind it. The strands of willow limbs and leaves cascaded like a beaded curtain around her. They wouldn't see her here.

Aunt Lorena screeched out her name, head half out the window as her man of the week drove the car. Ava wanted her mommy, but Aunt Lorena said she wasn't ever coming back.

Daddy didn't come to the funeral, though people came out to the house with their edible offerings and black clothing that reminded Ava of the black crows who gathered at the fence and stared with small, knowing eyes. He didn't officiate over the bodies of his ex-wife or her lover. Instead he barred himself inside his room during the first days after news of the car accident.

While Ava sat beneath a table covered in food, she overheard Aunt Lorena say, "That ungrateful whore got her just desserts."

And so she'd run to the willows. She hid when Aunt Lorena tried to find her. She heard her aunt's panicked voice say, "We have to find the little witch before Danny finds out. I promised I'd keep an eye on the kids."

Ava spent the night of her mother's funeral beneath the willows. She thought of her mother's perfume and the silk of her slip that she wore while doing her hair and putting on makeup. The night didn't stretch out long enough for Ava to get rid of the missing.

Clancy led them to her in the early morning light. Grannie and her aunts and uncles stared at her, ready to give her a beating, but Daddy carried her cradled against his chest as they held back like pit bulls on a chain. He set her down onto her bed and covered her dirty feet and scratched-up legs with the patchwork quilt.

After that day, Daddy split his time between the farm and an immaculate apartment in town. With Ava's mother dead, her daddy couldn't raise two kids on his own, so he shared them with his mother-in-law in a kind of ignorance that Ava would forever resent. Could he not see the raised marks that regularly covered their legs and back from the switch that hung next to Grannie's favorite chair?

A lady washed and pressed Daddy's clothes and the fancy set he kept for them. On weekends, they changed into the town clothes when they first arrived.

Being with Daddy meant church, usually all weekend. There were tent revivals and visiting evangelists. There were potlucks and socials. There were youth nights and kids' clubs and baptisms down by the river.

Daddy wore his pin that said "Rev. Daniel Henderson". He checked their faces, smoothed their hair, and at church, he cried while sharing how happy he was to have his children on the pew that week. He'd put his hand in the air and the church members would too, shouting and praising Jesus. Ava would look at the gleam of pride in Clancy's eye and wonder if her face showed a similar shine as well.

The crickets filled the night with a loud chorus of song. The frogs joined in, though they could never get the rhythm despite how they tried. The river lapped the soft shoreline, and sometimes the fireflies dotted the tops of the tall grasses and Ava put out her hand for one to land.

Ava's eyes focused on her backyard in Dallas that was decades beyond the memories. The immaculate landscaping.

A pool house and pool like nothing she'd seen as a child. Once she and her brother, Clancy, had pressed their faces against a wooden fence where a knot had broken out. They could see the pool of the wealthiest family in town. The kids laughed and dove off the diving board, and it might as well have been Disneyland to the two of them—just one more place they'd never go.

Ava lived a life unlike any she'd dreamed of as that little girl. That little girl didn't know such a world existed.

She sometimes feared it was all made of paper, and any storm or fire or fist of God might smash it all to nothing. Perhaps He was doing just that after giving her too long a blessing, too long a time of feasting. *No, no, no,* she whispered, fighting the pull of the past.

Ava squeezed her arms tightly against her chest. A lone car traveled the suburban neighborhood. Tires against pavement, not gravel and dirt like the roads of her youth.

Every time she came to the tree, Ava couldn't escape her childhood. It was the safe place she'd run to in her past, and she didn't need it anymore.

Ava walked to the tool shed and opened the door. The automatic light switched on, and Ava spotted the ax hooked to a shelf.

She carried it back down the path and paused for a moment longer, gazing up at the drooping branches.

She swung hard and hit the trunk. The ax stuck into the wood, and Ava had to fight to pull it out. She swung again, and again.

Taking a breath, Ava could see the marks in the trunk like

deep nicks in the wood. The trunk was less than a foot in diameter. She could do this, she told herself with her arms already aching.

It took half the night and hands covered in blisters and a close call when the tilting trunk nearly crushed her, but before dawn rose over the eastern sky, Ava's tree was on the ground.

Twenty-One

She woke to a quiet house. The heater rumbled through the vents, and her down comforter pressed upon her with a cozy warmth that she fought not to leave. She rolled to her side and felt achy all over. A glance at the clock told her it was after ten already, which shocked her, yet she didn't feel compelled to get up. As she tucked her hands under her chin, she cried out at the sting in her palms.

Sitting up, she opened achy hands to see them covered in dried blood and blisters.

The tree. She'd cut it down. Reminders were everywhere. Her cashmere pajamas and slippers that cost more than her first car were stained with blood and dirt. Muddy footprints made a trail from her bedroom door to the bed. She touched her face and head and tugged out leaves stuck in her tangled hair.

One glance in the mirror depicted her face as it had been decades ago. The tangles, the tear stains, the expression of loss . . . Ava felt as if she'd morphed back into the child she'd been.

She showered, opening her hands beneath the searing hot

water, and scrubbed her fingernails, trying to get at the dirt. She wrapped herself in her robe, padding down the stairs. She'd never escape that little girl she'd been, no matter how often she shopped at Neiman Marcus or which Versace bag she bought. She was playing dress up, and now, finally, the game was over.

As she put Band-Aids on her blisters, Ava had a sense of relief that she didn't need to run from that girl any longer.

She made coffee and let her eyes sweep over the kitchen. It was as spotless as she'd left it yesterday, with only the mud-prints across the floor as evidence of the night before. She suddenly felt like she could be Alice in Wonderland.

Ava picked up the house phone where she'd left it on the counter and considered calling Dane. They'd be out on the river or climbing through the smooth rock canyons. She felt like she had so much to talk to Dane about, but the words would have to wait.

"Are you doing anything fun with your friends?" Dane had asked her before leaving with Jason.

"I don't have any money, what can I do?" Ava couldn't keep the bite of accusation from her tone. Usually, she would have taken this weekend with the girls—they'd drop in at the spa and return to her house exclaiming over how great they felt after massages, pedicures, facials, body wraps. They'd lounge around the pool, drink wine, and maybe catch a movie or local show.

"I have some money in the safe." His voice remained full of optimism and hope, and that bugged her. Everything about him bothered her lately. Even his new habit of praying aloud irritated her. She was the spiritual one, and now he was telling her they should seek God more.

"We keep spending money. I wouldn't enjoy myself knowing it's going to be gone soon."

"Yeah. But get some rest and do something fun. We're going to be all right."

"I know," Ava said. Why was his confidence so annoying? Was it a brave front? If so, she should be standing beside him, not joining ranks to make it all harder for him.

Self-pity—Ava was wallowing in it; she knew it and didn't care. A few days of feeling sorry for herself, under these circumstances . . . wasn't that acceptable?

She'd been in that shameful state when Dane drove away.

The coffee pot filled the house with a rich aroma. Ava opened her schedule to plot out her day, then realized she had nothing to plot after canceling everything. Maybe she'd stay in her pajamas the entire day. It was only Friday—she could stay in her pajamas the whole weekend if she wanted.

A screen appeared, showing that her laptop was trying to connect to the Internet but it wasn't working. A page appeared asking for a payment. Dane hadn't paid the bill and their Internet was turned off. Ava closed her laptop and went for her phone. She typed a message to Dane, then stopped herself from sending it.

Instead Ava carried her Bible from her desk and chose one of the coffee mugs from the set she and Dane had bought in Hawaii one year. They were handmade with a deep forest pottery and etched with palms and hibiscus flowers. They'd planned another trip to Maui, but the wedding plans had changed that. Now there'd be neither.

A hard knock on the door disrupted her thoughts, followed by several rings to the doorbell. The chimes echoed through the house again and again.

No, Ava groaned. This was not a morning to be sociable.

Perhaps it was simply a troop of Girl Scouts selling their cookies. But no, not on a school morning. Or a Jehovah's Witness. Ava could take a pamphlet and be alone again. It might be UPS, but she hadn't heard the rumble of the brown van coming up the road.

Usually Ava could distinguish a warped shape through the stained glass double doors, but nothing moved as she padded quietly toward the front door. She peeked through a square of clear glass, but no one was there. Just as she turned away, something on the cobblestone walkway caught her eye.

What was that? Perhaps a package after all.

Pushing the door open a crack, she suddenly flung it fully open while it felt as if the blood froze in her veins.

She stared at the sight.

Resting neatly on the doormat that read "Welcome To Our Home" sat a car seat with a pink blanket stretched over the carry bar. The seat sat on a base, the kind you keep in the car to easily snap the seat in and out.

Two tiny, sock-covered feet stuck out from under the blanket.

Ava looked down the driveway and then up and down her street. There was no one in sight.

She took several steps forward, half expecting some prankster to jump out and start laughing, then bent low to peer beneath the blanket.

Lifting a corner, she gasped, dropped the blanket, and took several steps backward, banging her back against the door frame.

"What in the world?"

A bird chirped and Ava heard the sound of cars down at the main intersection. Then a slight breeze touched the edge of the blanket, drawing her back for another look inside.

She peered in again. A baby slept with her head resting against the side of the car seat. As Ava watched her, the baby's mouth moved, making a sucking sound as if she dreamt of milk. The pink car seat, frilly dress, and headband made it obvious that the baby was a girl.

Then Ava saw the note.

A white envelope stood upright, resting near the baby's feet. It had her name written on the front.

"What?" she muttered, picking up the envelope and hoping the baby wouldn't wake up.

Dear Aunt Ava,

I've been glad that we've been talking. It's been real nice. I kind of guessed that you never heard that I got pregnant even, but I did. This is my baby girl, Emma Louise Sterling. I call her Emma. She was born June 22nd. She was a small little thing, maybe cause I sometimes sneaked a cigarette when I was pregnant. I felt awfully bad about that, but I couldn't help myself. I've gotten in all kinds of trouble because of taking the easy road. That's what Grannie tells me. Everyone in the family says that you have everything. They say that you left your family behind because you've got it all and now you're too high and mighty with your fancy house and fancy husband and fancy life. But I'd leave our family behind too if I could have a good life, and especially if I could give Emma everything. So I decided if I can't give her all that she should have, I want you to take her and raise her right.

Ava hurried past the car seat and ran out to the road. She spotted someone sitting in an old car with a faded hood a few houses up. It was certainly not the type of car usually seen on these streets. Ava tried to get a better look and suddenly the engine roared to life. The car jerked forward as the driver put it into gear, then it raced past her house.

"Bethany, wait!" Ava called to the girl behind the wheel. She caught one panicked expression as the girl looked her way before zipping past and then around the corner down the street.

Ava still held the note in her hand.

It breaks my heart to do this. She might not believe that I love her as I do since I'm just leaving her here for you. But I do. My Emma is the most beautiful, miraculous thing I've ever seen in my lousy sixteen years. I hope she'll understand and forgive me for this some day.

You are family. I'm believing that you haven't forgotten that. So please, take good care of my Emma. Please give her the life she can't have with me.

Love,

Bethany

P.S. I wanted to bring some dahlias for you, but I couldn't find any at Kroger's. So I hope you like the orchid they had there.

Ava hadn't noticed the potted orchid sitting a few feet from the car seat. The letter fluttered out of her hand, landing in the hedges. She grabbed it back up, turning it over in search of a cell phone number or some way to contact the girl.

The baby stirred in her car seat, and a panic filled her.

Ava stared at the car seat, acutely aware that she was standing outside in her pajamas staring at a baby. She realized that the object beside it was a cheap diaper bag stuffed full and straining against its latch.

She didn't want to carry the baby into the house. Yet she couldn't leave it outside while she retrieved her phone. But if she brought the baby inside her house, it seemed some line was being crossed. She did not want to cross that line.

Ava saw the garage door rising across the street. Old Hal Johnston must be coming out to walk his dog like he did every morning. His dog walking was more about visiting any neighbor in sight than actual exercise. Ava was not prepared to explain an abandoned baby to him.

And then the baby opened her eyes.

Twenty-Two

AVA ROCKED THE CAR SEAT IN THE ENTRYWAY OF THE HOUSE. THE baby appeared fascinated by the scene around her—the sweeping wood stairway and especially how the sun caught the chandelier. Ava turned on the light, and the baby squealed and kicked her feet, arching her neck to try sitting up, then falling back to the view above.

"It's okay, you can just hang out there. It's cozy, right?"

The baby strained against the straps, staring at Ava with large brown eyes as if trying to communicate.

"I know I'm a stranger, but I won't hurt you. Your mama probably will be right back. She'll get a few miles down the road and turn around . . ."

Ava's house phone rang, making the baby jump. She glanced at the child, then down the hall toward the den, then made a sudden run for it while keeping her eye on the car seat the entire time.

She scooped up the phone sitting on its charger and pushed On while racing back toward the baby.

"Your cell phone is off and you are not going to believe my date last night," Kayanne said cheerily.

"Can you come over?" Ava sputtered in a near frantic tone.

Silence hung over the phone. "Wh-en?"

"Now?" Ava tried to keep her voice steady, but an unexpected emotion welled up, threatening to bring her to tears. Why couldn't she control herself?

"What's wrong? Are you okay? Did something happen?"

Ava swallowed back the emotion and mustered a weak, "Just come soon."

"I'm at work. But . . . okay. On my way!"

She riffled through the diaper bag. There were diapers— five of them, and how many did a baby use in a day, she couldn't remember.

The diaper bag was clean but unorganized. There were several rattles and a teething ring. Two bottles were empty with instructions on how to make a bottle taped on the outside. Formula was in a small container. At the very bottom, she found a pacifier.

This baby needed clothing, more formula and diapers, and most of all, her mother.

The baby let out an irritated cry, again straining against the car seat straps.

"Okay, okay," Ava said, bending down. She unlatched the straps and reached beneath the baby's arms to pull her out.

Her small body was lighter than she expected.

Ava wasn't sure how to hold her and tried cradling her in her arms. The baby strained again as if wanting to be up, so she moved her to her shoulder.

And she smelled like a baby, that wonderful scent that didn't compare to anything else. Her hair was downy soft and smelled of baby shampoo.

The baby rested her head against Ava's chest, then squirmed and let out a howl. She leaned back, staring at Ava with a confused expression. Her soft pink mouth dipped into a pout, then she cried again, turning to look around the room.

The baby grunted, arching her back as she squirmed in Ava's arms.

"It's okay."

Surely the baby sensed the panic building in her. The more panicky she felt, the more the baby squirmed and fussed. She rubbed her eyes and suddenly let out a howl. Ava bounced and paced back and forth across the living room and kept talking as the baby calmed. The moment Ava paused, the baby cried again.

"You like the sound of my voice? But I can't talk all day. What can I tell you about? You don't want to hear about the crazy family you were born into. But don't worry, I was too and I escaped . . ."

Then she remembered rocking Jason to sleep. Babies like rocking, she reminded herself, and sat in the chair. The baby kicked up with her feet and threw herself backward. Ava almost lost her, which made the baby howl.

"It's all right, baby, it's all right," she said, and started making a shushing sound as she rocked. The baby settled down as she patted her back. Before long, the baby was moving less and feeling heavier as her muscles loosened. The feel of the baby against Ava's chest soothed her as well, then panic washed over her again as the reality of a baby abandoned on her doorstep sunk in.

Outside, the sky darkened as rain clouds gathered together for an afternoon storm. Ava could see the terrible mess in the backyard through the living room window, the branches and leaves scattered around and the jagged top of the willow stump—an ugly sight in the light of day.

A knock sounded on the front door, but Ava didn't move to get it. A moment later, she heard Kayanne coming inside.

"Ava, where are you? The front door was open."

"Back here," she called from the living room. The baby stirred in her arms as she rose from the chair, but with a few bounces, she fell back to sleep.

"I'm here, sorry to take so long. I stopped for coffee and I bought an entire coconut cream pie at Bailey's Bakery. It sounded like we'd need the whole pie."

"For just the two of us?" Ava asked, walking into the kitchen.

Kayanne froze when she saw Ava with the baby. One coffee tilted to the side and for a moment Ava thought she'd lose everything onto the floor. Kayanne recovered with only one slosh of coffee hitting the tile.

"What is that?" she asked, unloading the cups and pie box onto the counter.

"What do you mean, what is it? It's a baby."

"I figured that part out, and why do you have it?"

Ava smiled and shrugged. "I found it."

Kayanne's eyebrows lowered as she studied Ava, then the baby, then Ava again.

"And what happened to you—you're all scratched up. You're a mess. Are you okay? Am I seeing things?"

Ava laughed out loud, making the baby jump.

"Oh no," Ava said, bouncing the baby in short, hurried jiggles until she settled back against Ava's chest. Her arms and back were aching from her overnight adventures with the willow tree, and holding the baby was making it worse.

"Maybe someone slipped me a rufie in my water last night."

"You aren't seeing things. This is real."

"This is why you wanted me to come over? I'm so confused. I thought Dane was seeing another woman."

"What? You thought Dane was having an affair?" This pricked at the fear she'd been toying with in the past months.

"You sounded . . . well, devastated. Thus the pie. This ain't nothing like what I expected, girlfriend."

"I don't know what to do."

"You better start at the beginning. Why are you all scraped up? Where did you *find* this baby? And what are you going to do with it?"

"I called you to help me figure that out."

"Oh boy. Let me get us a piece of pie, or better yet, forget cutting it. I'll just get some forks."

Twenty-Three

"LET'S TACKLE THE IMMEDIATE PROBLEM FIRST," AVA SAID, BOUNC-
ing the baby as Kayanne held the note Bethany had left behind.

"You sound like we're in a planning meeting. Okay, immediate problems first. Which are what?"

"Well, we don't know how long I'll have her. Bethany might
come back any minute, or it might be a few days."

"Got it. So diapers, formula, baby food—is she eating solids
yet?"

"I don't know," Ava said, lifting the baby to face her. Their
eyes met. "Are you eating baby food yet?" she asked and the baby
gave her a huge smile.

"That was seriously cute."

"Do you know how to make a bottle?"

"We both nursed our kids, and I don't know how to do any
of this anymore."

"First, we need to sterilize everything."

"Her name is Emma. I love that name," Kayanne said, and
Ava realized she hadn't fully processed the baby's name.

"I considered it when I was pregnant with Jason."

"Your favorite Jane Austen book," Kayanne said, with a quizzical expression.

"Why are you looking at me like that?"

She seemed to shake it off. "Nothing, I don't know. Time to sterilize!"

A little while later, the few baby items from the diaper bag were drying on the kitchen counter—everything they could sterilize had been dipped in boiling water. While they worked, Ava filled Kayanne in on the last twelve hours, from her battle with the willow tree to the knock on her front door.

Kayanne used her smart phone to find online instructions for the ratios of formula to purified water as she double-checked the handwritten directions. A mom who leaves her baby on the doorstep might not be the most reliable in such things, they surmised.

"Okay, I'm heading out for some baby shopping," Kayanne said. She held a list they'd made after taking inventory of the diaper bag and copying a checklist of baby needs from a parenting website.

Ava fed the baby a bottle while rocking her. Emma's eyes closed and opened as they went to and fro.

"Call if you think of anything. I put your phone on vibrate so it doesn't wake her," Kayanne whispered as she tiptoed toward the front door.

When the baby—Emma, she reminded herself—had fallen completely asleep, Ava laid her carefully on the sofa and propped some pillows around her so she couldn't roll off. Then she dug out her old address book from the file cabinet in the den. She flipped through the names of her old family members, wondering if they still had the same numbers.

She tried her cousin Jessie—Bethany's mother—but the number now belonged to someone else. Her grandmother's house where her family surely still lived had its number disconnected.

Ava called every number in the worn-out address book. It was as if the entire family had disappeared. Every number was disconnected or reassigned, except for her brother Clancy's, but his line just rang and rang.

Then she remembered that Bethany had called her. She found the number and called it.

"This is Bethany's phone, but I'm doing something other than being on my phone. Leave a message and I'll see what I can do. Ciao."

"Bethany. It's your Aunt Ava. We need to talk right away. Please call me back."

She slumped against the sofa with the baby asleep close against the cushions. It was getting dark out and she realized she was starving—the only thing she'd eaten all day was a few bites of Kayanne's coconut cream pie. She went to the kitchen and poured a bowl of cereal and brought it back to the sofa, watching Emma sleep while she ate.

Ava could help other people in crisis. But her own extended family, Ava couldn't even remain in contact with them. She wondered if that was sort of like pointing out the splinter in someone else's eye when she had a log in her own. The analogy didn't quite work since she wasn't being judgmental, but instead was trying to help people. And Ava couldn't help her own family.

She stared at the baby.

You can help this one.

Ava shook her head. She wondered who to call, what person would be able to help during their crisis. Mostly Ava wished she could keep it all a secret—their financial problems and now a baby dumped on her doorstep by another loser member of her family.

Ava's phone buzzed and she popped open the text message to a picture of a sheer orange wall of rock with a vivid blue sky above. The message read: *We rappelled down this!*

Jason had copied it to Sienna, who wrote: *I'm jealous, little bro!*

Ava tapped one letter at a time. *Fun, be careful!*

She wondered what they'd think if they could see her now and considered taking a picture to shock them. Ava never shocked her family, she realized with a frown.

Baby Emma stirred within twenty minutes of putting her down. Ava scooped her up and rocked her again, feeling her small body go limp against her chest.

Her cell phone buzzed again—her husband this time.

"Hey there. I saw a pretty exciting picture from Jason," she whispered, hoping Dane could hear her without her waking the baby.

"We had the best day!" Dane said as he launched into describing their day as they canoed and climbed through a canyon to some Native American ruins. She took in the excitement in her husband's tone more than the stories he was telling. Dane talked about the clearness of the night sky and how they'd talked about God and eternity. He sounded happier than she'd heard in years. It was a youthful, carefree excitement that twisted up her emotions. She wanted to be happy for him, happy for their son—this was the closeness she'd hoped to see rekindled. But she was envious of it as she felt the worries and fears pressing in on her from all sides.

Ava wondered when or how to bring her own news into this conversation. When Dane asked how she was doing, she dumped it on him without much ceremony or warning.

"A what?" Dane's voice rose with surprise. "Wait, what? Did you say you found a baby on our front doorstep?"

Ava gave the short version of her baby discovery.

"Should we call Child Services? I need to be there. I'll find a way to get back. Um, I think we're going into a town tomorrow, but I have my GPS and could get out of here tonight. I'll wake Jason."

Ava bit the edge of her lip as she thought of Dane with his GPS launching into the desert to find his way home to rescue her. She couldn't help feel a little better with that.

"No, wait. It's okay. I'm fine. The baby is fine, for now. I'm going to try finding Bethany. Kayanne is out buying supplies as we speak. But if I can't reach them, I was thinking I'd drive out there tomorrow."

Ava hadn't actually thought of that until she was speaking it.

"You might go out there? Alone?"

"Maybe." She could feel the panic bubbling up in her.

"I don't know if that's the best idea. But, honey, my battery is running down and is only on a solar charger. I'll call in the morning."

"Okay. She's sure cute, though."

"Who? Oh, the baby? A girl, huh?"

"Yes." Ava wanted to touch the soft pink on her eyelids and the tiny pucker of her lips as she sucked air in her sleep.

"I look forward to meeting her. But . . ." Ava waited for the rest of his words.

"What are you thinking?" he asked.

"I don't know what to think. What are you thinking?"

"I guess it's more what I'm not thinking."

"Not thinking?"

"I mean, it would be crazy for us to take on a baby. We didn't want any more children." *You didn't want more children*, Ava thought, but she had to agree, it was crazy to think of them raising a baby now. "But especially when we're losing everything. And Jason will be gone in a few years . . . never mind. We'll talk about it when I get home."

"Okay . . . and of course we aren't going to keep her. Hey, I was hoping to talk to Jason real fast too, tell him good night—"

"He's asleep already. I'll tell him to be careful and that you love him," Dane said with a chuckle, then his voice grew serious.

"Listen, Aves . . ."

"I'm listening."

"We're going to make it through this. We have one another, but more than that, we have God taking care of us. He loves us more than we can even know. You can count on that."

Ava closed her eyes as she rocked. These were the words she was supposed to be telling him. These were the words she'd told others to believe and that she should believe herself. She did believe it in her heart, but what about outside her heart in the real day-to-day?

Kayanne returned with enough bags and boxes that Ava thought she could open a small baby store. She knew Kayanne expected Ava to repay her, and normally that would be fine. Since her divorce, Kayanne struggled paycheck to paycheck, especially with her husband's refusal to pay alimony and claims that he had no income while living at their island bungalow.

But Kayanne didn't know they'd had their accounts frozen. Why hadn't she told her? Why didn't she think of these things until a predicament like this?

"Can I have the receipt?" Ava asked, thinking of Dane's claim that she veiled her heart from her family and friends.

"Sure, but I'll contribute to the cause. I know I sort of went crazy. It just seemed better to get everything we might need in case this turns into a longer stay than just overnight."

Ava's heart dropped at the final cost. Baby swing, diapers, wipes, bouncer, bottles, formula, toys, outfits, playpen, blankets, onesies, front pack . . .

"It looks like we had a baby shower," Ava said, feeling a sense of claustrophobia at the brightly colored packages littering the kitchen, dining, and living room.

"You should have seen people staring at me in the check-out line."

"I can only imagine."

"We still don't have a high chair, and I bought this book about making homemade baby food. You have that great blender after all. I'll need to get some organic veggies first; we don't want all the stuff with pesticides."

Ava's mind whirled at it all.

"Whatever you don't use, we'll take back. But it's better to be safe than sorry."

"Good idea," Ava said, knowing this would've been her exact philosophy just a few weeks earlier.

"Watch the baby, and I'll be right back," Ava said, going upstairs to the small safe. Dane had given her a wad of money when he'd left. She counted out the money and needed most of it to pay Kayanne back. She had three hundred dollars remaining of her cash, and Dane had yet to tell her how long that needed to last.

Ava gave Kayanne the cash in an envelope, brushing away her attempts to help pay for the objects. "The baby was left at my doorstep, this is my dysfunctional family, and now I have to pay for it. Literally."

They laughed and cut tags from the blankets while Emma entertained herself in her car seat, and then Ava put all the baby clothes into the washing machine, even those neatly folded in the baby bag that smelled slightly of cigarette smoke.

Kayanne's phone had been beeping continuously as they organized.

"Who is he?" Ava asked, picking up Emma.

"Not *him* or *him him*. Why is it that the ones I like don't like me that much? And the ones I don't like, like me a lot." Kayanne picked up her phone and smiled. "Oh, there's a text from one I sort of like. He got home early from a business trip and wonders if I want to meet for coffee. Spontaneous, I like it."

"So, are you going?" Ava said with a growing sense of panic. She didn't want to be left alone with this baby all night.

"Well, it's Friday night, after all. Do you think you could manage for a while? I don't have to go. Or I can come back and have a sleepover."

"Go on your date. I can handle a baby for one night, after all. I raised two of them already."

"You do have enough baby gadgets for a daycare center." Kayanne's phone beeped again. "Oh, he just wrote again. He wants to get coffee and watch the meteor shower at one in the morning."

"Sounds . . . cold," Ava said.

Kayanne gathered her bag and jacket.

"Be careful. Have you actually met this one in person?"

"Yes, this is Dirk, he's not an online match. He's an engineer or an architect or maybe he's the biologist. I'm getting these guys confused. We met on that singles hike I went on last August, but he was sort of still seeing someone. He's pretty cute too."

"Still. Be careful, and you know what that means."

Kayanne tossed her head back in a laugh. "Yes, I know. Be careful he's not a serial killer, be careful not to believe everything he says, and be careful not to let passion get the best of me. You don't have to worry about that last one."

With Kayanne's departure, the house grew hollow and large around them again. Ava stared at Emma and Emma stared at her. A moment later, the baby let out a howl.

cɐ૭ಲ

Ava woke on the couch with the softest of morning light coming through the eastern windows. She bent her neck to one side, stretching out a kink ever so carefully. The baby was nestled in the crook of her arm.

A half-drunk bottle sat on the coffee table beside her, and Ava realized it had been five hours since Emma had last eaten. She'd written the time on a Post-it Note she stuck to the table. Five hours was pretty good, she mused, though she knew she'd only slept in short intervals during that time. Instead, she watched infomercials and reruns of *Bonanza*. If they weren't broke and without credit cards, Ava would've ordered a towel that could soak up a bucket of water, a real estate get-rich-quick program, and an exercise gadget that toned your abs while you sat watching television.

Carefully she rose, trying not to disturb Emma. She slid the baby toward the back of the couch and rearranged the pillows around her. Emma stirred, stretching her arms and legs taut, and then relaxed back into sleep.

Turning from the couch, Ava was stunned by the mess. Sterilized bottles, wrappers from packages, two piles of laundry, a baby swing partially put together with the box and plastic strewn across the floor. The house looked worse than after Jason and his friends came through like a pack of locusts attacking everything in sight.

Emma sighed that perfect baby sigh and looked like a tiny angel stretched out on her couch.

"We did it," she whispered with the words barely sounding. The heater hummed through the vents of the house.

They'd survived their first night together.

Twenty-Four

Once the coffee was brewing, Ava returned to making phone calls. There was no way she could keep the baby for another night. Surely there were laws against this kind of abandonment; Ava might be breaking them by keeping the baby instead of calling Child Services or the police immediately.

After leaving another message on Bethany's voice mail and sending her a text, Ava opened her laptop—she wanted to search the Internet and Facebook for family members she'd nearly forgotten.

Ava had never created a Facebook page, though people were constantly trying to get her to do so. Being publicly available allowed her to be a target for old family members, classmates, or her father's old congregation who might want to reconnect with her. Her ministry had a Facebook page, but the church web guy and Kayanne kept it current. There were some techie things she just didn't do.

Her web browser wouldn't open, then she remembered why.

She checked to be sure her phone still worked, then wrote a text to Dane. *The Internet is down. What should I do?*

Ava stopped before she hit the Send button. She could live without the Internet for a few days, though she was surprised at how alone she felt without it. But she could do web searches on her phone.

She found a phone number Ava believed was that of Bethany's father. Ava remembered her cousin Jessie's wedding to Lars. It was the last family event she attended. She and Dane had been married less than a year. Jessie was pregnant with Bethany's older sister, Deb, yet she was nearly too drunk to stand through the wedding. She laughed her vows instead of saying them.

A man answered the call. Ava asked if he were Lars Bacon who'd been married to Jessie Grant.

"I'm trying to reach your daughter Bethany," Ava said, not wanting to reveal too much.

"You're Jess's cousin? I don't remember you," Lars said.

"I haven't lived down there since I was seventeen. We're in Dallas."

"Dallas? Wait, you're the rich, snobby cousin right? The one who took off and never looked back. Jess hated you, oh man, did she. Well, they all did." He laughed.

"Yeah, I know. But I've been communicating with Bethany, and I'm trying to reach her. Do you know where I can find her?"

"Can't help you there. Once Jessie and I split, my girls wouldn't have nothing to do with me. I tried, but after a while, I just gave up. If they don't want to see their father, there's nothing I can do about it."

Ava swallowed back the words she wanted to say to Lars. She knew he used to beat Jessie and maybe even his girls. Yet he was going to play it like he was the victim.

"I heard something about her having a kid. Girls these days watch those reality TV shows and think it's all great and exciting having a baby until they have to change diapers and make bottles in the night. I was watching this one new program about where they have the most unwed mothers, and it's in a state that doles out the cash to these girls and their deadbeat boyfriends."

"Do you have Jessie's number? I tried Grannie's old house, but the line was disconnected."

"Yeah, they're all on cell phones now. Last I heard Jess was moving in with her mom—that's your aunt, right? None of them has talked to me ever since I put Jess's butt in jail, that's what I did. You know her temper, well, this time she had to receive some consequences. Spent the weekend in jail, she did, before posting bond. It didn't do much to clean her up, but I hope it might have helped anyway."

"Jessie went to jail?"

"Wasn't the first time, doubt it'll be the last."

Ava walked to the couch and knelt beside Emma sleeping on her back with her arms stretched over her head. This man was Emma's grandfather.

"Lars, it's really important that I reach Bethany."

"Sorry, but I suspect she's been living with all the rest of them at your grannie's ole farm. What a rundown mess that place is. Best bet is drive on down there if you want to catch 'em."

Ava hit End on her phone and chewed on the inside of her

lip. She called Bethany's number again, but this time the line had been disconnected.

She glanced toward the couch and saw small arms and legs moving.

"Good morning," she whispered.

Emma stared up at Ava. Her mouth broke into a wide smile with a happy coo.

Emotion welled tears into her eyes as she stared into deep brown eyes and thought of the world this sweet girl was born into—a horrible place where babies were abandoned and families deserted one another.

Emma wiggled her hands in the air erratically and glanced at the ceiling, then back to Ava's face. Then the baby sucked her lower lip in, exactly the way Sienna had when she was a baby. Ava had forgotten that.

As she changed the baby's diaper on a towel spread out on the floor, Ava marveled at the feel of her chubby legs.

"Your skin is so soft," Ava muttered in amazement. Did all babies have such velvety skin? She couldn't remember. She touched the skin on her tummy and Emma arched her spine.

"Did that tickle?" Ava asked, amused by the frown that dropped Emma's thin dark eyebrows. The baby puckered her mouth again and Ava thought of a warm bottle by the sucking noise and way she rolled her tongue.

"I wonder if you were nursed at all." Ava realized she knew nothing about this child. What if Emma had been born on drugs?

The baby started to fuss, and Ava finished dressing her in one of the new pajama sets.

"It's okay, it's okay," she said in a singsong voice.

Emma mimicked her with a monotone hum that came from her chest.

"Are you singing?" Ava said with excitement, turning the baby's serious expression into a huge smile and squeal.

"So you like singing?"

The baby gave her an open-mouthed smile, revealing pink gums, and stuck her tongue out from her lips.

"You are the cutest thing I've ever seen," she muttered as she lifted Emma and stood, then added, "The cutest baby I've seen in a long time, since your cousins Jason and Sienna." The baby laughed as if she'd made a great joke.

"You like me talking to you, don't you?"

She'd made a breakthrough. Singing and talking. That's what every baby needed. She didn't have much else, but for now, she'd sing and talk and play music. It would soothe both of their hearts, the broken things that they were.

Ava went to the kitchen and placed the baby in the bouncer seat while she made a bottle, then brought her back to the living room and sat down to feed her.

Emma's eyes stayed locked into Ava's as her lips puckered with the suckling motion. She sighed and squirmed but drank heartily until the bottle was empty.

As Ava watched her, she suddenly knew what she had to do. But first she needed a few moments to talk to God.

Twenty-Five

AVA STOOD BEFORE THE REMNANT OF THE WILLOW TREE, EMMA cooing in her arms as she looked at the sky, the leaves, and the trees. There was more sky than usual and the emptiness around the willow made her shiver.

Ava picked up one weepy branch and a trail of leaves fell from it. The impulse came over her to pick them up and glue them back on, then to raise the tree up and glue the trunk back to the stump.

During her crafty stage when the kids were young, Ava had joked that everything could be fixed with a hot-glue gun.

A light breeze lifted some of the leaves from the ground.

Ava had the sudden impulse to cry or to beg the tree to come back to life. It was the strangest sensation, this panic over a tree.

She prayed then, feeling foolish even before God. "It was a tree. But, God, I feel like I needed it. And now it's gone."

The tree had tied her to the good pieces of her childhood.

Now it was dead and she was about to return to that place of childhood dread, to see the people who caused a lifetime of pain.

It seemed such a short time ago that the willow had been normal, healthy, full of life. She remembered that calm Sunday when Dane and Jason were both at home for breakfast. It had been a perfectly unspectacular morning, but it was the day she'd first noticed something was wrong with the tree. The beginning of autumn. Football season had just started.

September. Summer had just ended.

That reminded Ava of her niece's note. Emma had been born in the summer . . . when? June twenty-second, she recalled. Four months ago.

At age forty-eight, four months earlier was nothing. But that was the entirety of this little being's life. Ava tried to remember what they were doing in June. Jason had gone to football camp, or was that July?

Bethany had been in the maternity ward, seeing her daughter for the first time. Ava didn't know any details of the birth, what Emma had weighed, how long the labor was, whether it was natural or Caesarean.

No one in the family had contacted her, and why would they? Years ago, when her children were born, Ava might have included her aunts and cousins in the birth announcements, but she couldn't be sure. She had taken them off her Christmas card list after a cousin calling for a "loan" accused her of bragging by including their family photos.

Oh, little one. You have so much living to do.

A longing washed over her to protect this innocent little

being from all that living she had ahead of her. It was a living full of pain and disappointment, especially in their family. Maybe she could find Emma a good home. Just a few months earlier, she might have thought a good home was their home. But now their future was clouded.

Have faith in me.

Even after all those years, Ava had an immediate "was that God, or was that me?" debate whenever such words whispered through her heart. With the doubts she constantly contended with, it couldn't be her.

Have faith in what I am doing.

Ava looked down at Emma, resting her head on Ava's shoulder. Content, at ease, trusting that she was safe. Her cheeks had the lightest hue of pink and her long, dark eyelashes touched her cheeks. One fist gripped Ava's hair.

An old tree dying. A baby being born.

She stared at Emma, who had arrived on her doorstep the very morning after she'd chopped down the dead weeping willow.

"What does this mean?" she whispered with her eyes inclined toward heaven.

Believe was the lone word whispered back to her heart.

Twenty-Six

AVA STARED AT HER MERCEDES SEDAN SHINING BENEATH THE FLO-
rescent lights. Dane had washed and cleaned it inside and out
since he'd been off work. Usually he hired people to do it. In
the past months, he'd neglected their vehicles like everything
else. But one of his first projects since the company closed was
to detail the cars.

So there it sat, ready for a road trip all glimmering and
clean, except Ava had received a text from Dane that morning.

*Aves, real sorry about this. E-mail from lawyer today—keep
your car locked in garage, don't drive it. I'm torn between coming
home to work this out or being with Jason—he's really different since
we've been here.*

Ava's first reaction was anger—was he saying her car was
in danger of being repossessed? Then she wanted to burst into
tears. But after facing her self-pity again as Emma cooed and
kicked her feet happily, Ava laughed at the added challenge.

She also realized her plush Mercedes wasn't the best vehicle to drive up to her grandmother's farm. It might disappear into a local chop shop.

Ava typed back: *Stay there. Jason needs you, and I'm fine. Guess we have Old Dutch for something.*

Now she stared across the far end of the garage to where the old VW was hidden beneath a car cover.

"Old Dutch, don't fail me now," she muttered.

By the time Ava had loaded everything into the car, taking breaks every so often to check the baby in the portable crib, change her, feed her, and give her a pacifier, Ava was exhausted.

"How did I ever raise two children?" she muttered. Emma smiled, and Ava saw a tiny lone tooth just barely protruding from her bottom gum.

"And now the car seat," she said with a sigh.

Getting the base properly secured by the seat belt was an even bigger challenge. She'd never been good at assembling things or figuring them out—another one of Dane's jobs. She got it strapped in, but then something niggled at her. Wasn't the baby supposed to be rear-facing? She took out the base and started over. After some trial and error, Ava was confident she had a safe ride for Emma.

Ava ran back in the house and rifled through the baby things Kayanne had bought. There! A mirror she could attach to the backseat so she could see Emma's little face while she was driving. She sent God a silent thank-you for Kayanne and ran back out to attach the mirror.

It was late Saturday afternoon, but the road beckoned. She locked the house, strapped Emma into her seat, and turned the key, hoping it would start.

The engine rumbled and sputtered, then sprang to life. Ava checked the gauges, trying to figure them out, found the lights for when it became dark and the wipers in case of rain, then she backed out of the driveway.

Emma started crying.

"Oh no, not one of those," she said, remembering how Sienna had hated the car, crying every moment they were driving. Jason, on the other hand, seemed to fall asleep on cue in the car, except he'd become carsick on winding roads. It had taken several excursions to figure out that he didn't have the flu every time they went on a trip. Emma cried louder.

The late afternoon sun cast long shadows across the driveway, making Ava wonder how late it had become.

"Oh, you must be hungry!" she exclaimed to the screaming baby.

Ava pulled back inside the garage, then hurried to get Emma free from the car seat. The baby let out a few remaining protests and babbled as if trying to chastise her for forgetting such essential needs. She scooped up the baby bag and headed inside.

The call of the road—thwarted by the hunger of a baby.

⚬⊚⚬

An hour later, Ava was back in the VW, Emma safely strapped in once again.

I'm going on my own little adventure. I'll be home before you and Jason are, she typed into her phone before heading off.

Old Dutch rolled along nicely—not quite the ride she'd become accustomed to, but Ava found the high humming of the VW engine to be like a soundtrack to her adventure. She and a baby in a VW were heading south out of Dallas toward her hometown—it sounded like a Lifetime movie, which amused her to no end. Emma chewed on her teething ring in the middle seat behind her.

But as she rounded the turn from the smaller highway to the interstate, her lukewarm coffee toppled over, spilling across the seat and over her leg.

She pulled into a parking lot where she saw a sign for a dollar store and decided to look for some paper towels. After wiping off her leg with some baby wipes, Ava started thinking of more things she'd forgotten on this ill-planned excursion.

Ava carried Emma in her car seat and set her in the small shopping cart, nearly filling it. Emma kicked her legs in and out at the bright lights and Thanksgiving and Christmas decorations covering the wall near the entrance. As a child, Ava had been used to the five-and-dime, but she hadn't been in a discount store in decades. She pushed down an aisle of ornaments, decorations for parties, cosmetics, and cleaners with a number of well-known brands. Some of the items looks like they'd been packaged in the '60s, but other things—the majority—were fresh and useable. There was even food—Ava had no idea that dollar stores sold food, though since her organic kick had started several years earlier, she wouldn't be serving up dollar TV dinners to her family anytime soon. But what a deal, she thought as she wheeled around a woman with a basket full of items.

With her dwindling funds, Ava had to conserve. Dollars added up quickly . . . surprisingly so, she realized, as she counted the items filling up the small spaces around Emma's car seat.

She'd picked out some snacks, cups, a few candy bars, and diaper wipes that smelled a bit like ammonia, but they were a brand she recognized.

As Ava rounded a corner with her cart, she nearly bumped into Corrine Bledshoe.

"Well, Ava," Corrine said with surprise.

"What are you doing here?" Ava asked, as if accusing her of a crime.

"I'm buying some canned goods for the food bank. What are you—" Corrine broke off as her eyes drifted to Ava's shopping cart with Emma chewing on her bare toes.

"Who is that?"

"What?" Ava said, retrieving Emma's discarded sock from atop a package of thank-you cards.

"You have a baby in your cart."

Ava bit her lip and couldn't help chuckle. Of course she would run into Corrine at a moment like this. The irony tickled her funny bone.

"Why are you laughing?" the woman asked, frowning.

"I'm sorry, it's just . . . here you are and here I am."

"And why is that funny? Are you babysitting for someone?"

"I'm shopping. And no, I'm not babysitting."

"Is she yours?" Corrine appeared more than a little confused, and Ava could practically see the math going on in Corrine's mind as she tried to estimate if it were possible for Ava to conceive a child. This made Ava laugh even further.

"No, she's not mine, but in a way . . . I have to go. Sorry."

"Wait!" Corrine said, but Ava sped away toward the entrance of the store. She scooped up the car seat from the shopping cart, leaving everything inside and rushing out the door. Oh, how Corrine was going to have a field day with this one.

The thought turned her back around. She wasn't going to let anyone get the better of her. Lugging the car seat back through the entrance, she reached her shopping cart just as someone was about to take it.

"Sorry, that's mine."

Corrine was pushing her cart around the corner of a display of canned corn with her ear leaned against her phone. Ava zipped up to her.

"Corrine, I just have to ask you. Have you ever had anything go wrong in your life?"

"Hang on, it's her," she whispered and set the phone against her chest. "What did you say?"

"I asked if you have had anything go wrong in your life."

Corrine shrugged. "Of course."

Ava had heard about Corrine's husband's alcoholism and her recent estrangement from her son, but in Bible study and planning events, Corrine never let on that there was a problem.

"Do you think it's your fault every time something bad happens?"

"I examine my life and spirit and seek to find anything that God wouldn't approve of in me."

"And does everything get better then?"

"Some things are out of our control. I'm not saying that you have sin in your life, but someone in your house obviously must. It's the same with my house."

Ava felt a sudden sadness for Corrine and her entire family. They lived with the sense that God came at them constantly searching for ways to harm them. Ava couldn't change that.

"Oh, Corrine. God's grace is offered so that we don't have to live in fear that any mistake or any struggle will produce some awful circumstance."

"God's grace is for our salvation. We still have consequences for our actions." She glanced down at the baby as if to bring home the point.

Ava sighed, knowing that some people couldn't escape the prison cell despite how Christ had opened the door. She'd grown up with such fear, and she'd been allowing her grandmother's beliefs to infuse her life, blotting out what Christ had done for each of them. The prison door was open. She needed to stop walking back inside and acting as if it were locked again.

"Have a nice night."

"But—" Corrine called after her. Ava headed toward the register.

Okay, Father, I surrender everything. Show me what you want me to face that I've been trying to escape.

❦

Emma cooed contentedly as Ava drove onto the highway heading south out of the suburbs and into the vast, open Texas prairie.

The sun was dipping low in the sky, but Ava was prodded forward by the need to face both the past and her future. She hadn't planned anything—this was her being spontaneous, she thought with a mustered-up sense of adventure.

She called Kayanne to fill her in on their location and route. Luckily Kayanne was getting ready for a date and didn't have much time to grill her but extracted a promise that Ava would call tomorrow.

Emma's noises softened, and Ava glanced back. In the mirror she could see Emma's head resting against the side of the car seat, unmoving in sleep. The ticking of the VW and the open road at twilight filled Ava with a sense of nervous excitement. She'd never taken off without another adult—her aunt, a friend, or Dane was always with her. Night dropped like a stage curtain over the plains, and small towns stepped up and fell back from the country highway.

Eventually Emma stirred and began suckling at the air, grunting as she did, cueing Ava that the hours had passed between feeding times. She pulled into a Dairy Queen parking lot to prepare a bottle from the warm distilled water she'd packed in a thermos. She picked up Emma and settled herself into the front passenger seat with the baby in her arms.

Emma put her hands around the bottle, staring at Ava with round, dark eyes. She drank anxiously at first, then settled into a gentle rhythm. She paused to reach up with a chubby hand for Ava's face. Her soft fingers brushed Ava's cheek, then returned to grasp awkwardly at the bottle.

"It's just you and me, little one," Ava whispered with a growing awe at the little life in her arms. She was so small and beautiful. In the great big world, this one child could become lost in the shuffle. Fear suddenly crept toward the windows of the VW. Ava clicked the door locks and prayed for God's protection and guidance, which brought the strength of peace encapsulating them.

Across the road, Ava saw a billboard for a familiar hotel with luxury beds. They'd need a place to stay tonight, but their funds had dwindled far below the rate of her usual hotel choices. How much did a decent motel cost these days? She thought of the comfort of home only several hours back. Ava chastised herself for venturing out so unprepared.

Her cell phone rang and she saw Dane's face appear on the screen.

"Hello?" she whispered as Emma's eyes fluttered open and then her lashes dropped like a butterfly's wings back closed, open and closed again.

Dane's voice crackled with static. "Hello . . . where . . . you . . . thing . . . all right?"

"I can't hear you," she whispered again.

"Try . . . ter . . ." and the line went dead. Ava was relieved she didn't have to confess to her husband that she was sitting in a parking lot in the middle of Texas with an infant in the car.

Dane didn't call again as she waited, and Emma's body grew

heavy and limp. She shifted the baby onto her chest as she considered what to do and adjusted the seat back down. She closed her eyes . . . for just a few minutes.

A sound she didn't recognize stirred her. Ava jumped at the face staring at her, only inches away. Emma pushed herself up with her hand and let out a protesting grunt, then chewed on her fist hungrily.

"Where, what?"

Dawn softened the bleak horizon. The inside of the VW was cold, as were the baby's cheeks and hands.

"No way, we slept here!" Ava's eyes bounced around the fast-food parking lot as she pulled Emma's blanket back over her. She'd slept for hours with Emma on her chest. Anything could've happened.

Her heart pounded and her face burned with heat, but all thoughts of what could have happened were interrupted as Emma released a wail, letting Ava know exactly what she expected.

They'd been cooped up in the van for long enough, so Ava made use of the bathroom inside Dairy Queen to change the baby. Then she ordered herself a breakfast sandwich, made a bottle, and somehow got both of them fed inside the restaurant.

After getting Emma strapped back into the car seat, Ava searched for her phone. It had fallen beneath the seat and it beeped as the battery was dying. Dane had called back and left a voice mail saying he was worried. Sienna had called, stunned by the news of Bethany's baby at their doorstep and the vanishing act of her predictable mother.

"I'm both excited and worried about you. Giving me a taste of my own medicine, huh? Call!"

Corrine's message said, "Ava, I gathered with a few gals from the church. We prayed together for you. We are in agreement in our concern for you. Please return my call so that we can join you in prayer and seeking what God is trying to show you. I called Kayanne and she said you were on a road trip. But you can't run from your troubles. God will find you. Now I know you don't like me, but I want to be there for you. I am here for you."

Ava smiled at the message as she got back on the road, unwilling to let any more aggravation inch its way inside of her. Corrine was trying to help her. She didn't know that Ava had been running from a portion of her life and self since she was seventeen. This was the first journey back to that place.

What do I believe? What is true?

There was a difference between the two. What she believed and what Corrine believed were quite different despite their joint professed love of Christ. But what was true had no bearing on what was believed. Truth was truth, and she prayed as she drove that what she believed was in line with Truth.

I have hidden Your word in my heart, so that I won't sin against You, Lord.

That was the best she could do. Pray, infuse her life with God's word, and trust Him to guide her in the ultimate Truth.

They rumbled along the rural highways with Ava feeling less and less equipped for the journey. Emma slept or rode along agreeably, and they stopped every few hours for snacks and restroom visits. The wind whipped dust devils across the open fields and occasionally tumbleweeds rolled along the highway, so big that she had to swerve out of the way.

God, what am I doing? Tell me to go back or go forward. Show me the way.

There was no answer. No still, soft voice in her head, only loud doubts crowding each other out to be heard. There was no bulletin board on the highway that gave some direction like, "This Way! You've Almost Made It."

God, am I doing the right thing?

The engine light on the old VW fluttered on and off on the dashboard, and the gas gauge had made a sudden plunge toward E. The baby would need food soon and a diaper change. It was Sunday afternoon and only small towns dotted the landscape with long intervals between, and most shops closed down for the day.

Glancing back at the baby, Ava could see that Emma's eyes were still closed. Ahead, Ava could see a tall flashing sign.

"Please let us make it," she whispered. The engine light was on continuously now, and there was a distinct sound in the engine that didn't sound right at all.

She stopped at an intersection. The traffic light rocked on the line, and a dreary fog permeated the surroundings, casting a hazy shroud around a gas station, diner, and motel.

Ava pulled into the deserted gas station and auto shop. A few lights were on, but there was no one around. She kept the engine running and stepped out, feeling the bite in the wind at the edges of her clothing. Through the window, Ava could see Emma stir in her car seat. She wouldn't leave the car with Emma inside, yet she didn't want to wake her if no one was here. Finally Ava saw a young dingy-looking man sauntering slowly toward her.

"Can I help you, ma'am?"

"Are you open?"

"For gas is all."

"Is there another mechanic's shop somewhere in town?"

The guy spit out a wad of chew, sending a line of black juice across the dirt. Ava raised her eyebrows and he looked apologetic.

"Sorry 'bout that," he muttered and wiped his hands on a grease-stained rag he pulled from the back pocket of his blue dungarees. "None's open on Sunday. Charlie is our best man, but he's gone fishing in Alaska for a week. I got a bit of an eye when it comes to fixing cars or knowing when they've gone to the happy home."

Ava wiped the cold sweat that gathered at the back of her neck, shivering in the chilly weather. At least it wasn't a Texas summer with her off on this odyssey. For that, she could thank God. The rest of her situation didn't fill her with gratitude.

"Would you have time this afternoon?"

"It'll cost you."

Ava bit the edge of her lip. "I don't have a lot."

He studied her a moment, then stuck out his hand.

"M' name's Duffy, and we'll figure somethun out."

"All right," Ava said, glancing back at Emma. She caught a neon sign flickering against the dusk.

Lonesome Café and Motel.

"That place any good?" she asked Duffy, slipping into a stronger accent without meaning to.

"It's all we've got, so guess it be good enough."

Ava nodded and opened the door to the backseat, where Emma was moving her head from side to side.

Duffy peered into the engine, making enough noises as he perused the parts to make Ava wonder if he'd ever seen a VW before.

She told him she needed an estimate before he fixed anything. He frowned, looking her over, before she hurried to the motel with Emma in the car seat and her purse, baby bag, and overnight bag weighing down her shoulders. Ava got a key and room number, and after dumping the things in the motel room, her grumbling stomach led her to the café.

——

The café was nearly as empty as the town.

The muscles in her back, neck, and arms seemed to moan in protest as she stood at the front counter waiting to be seated. Her hands stung beneath the Band-Aids from the blisters. Driving all day and carrying the car seat hadn't hastened her healing.

"Sit wherever you like," a woman's voice called. Emma blinked in the lights and yawned with her pink mouth making a large oval.

"You've got your pick of the place," the friendly voice called from the back. Ava noticed the empty seats.

"Thank you," she called back, moving between a row of red vinyl booths and the counter bar. She found a booth away from the draft of the front door and set Emma down. The baby gave her a large smile and kicked her feet as Ava sat down next to her.

Ava folded her manicured nails together and noticed how they were well past the time for a fill. She'd never gone this long, not even when she'd given birth to her children. Ava didn't look the menu over—she wanted a grilled cheese sandwich, fries, and a Diet Coke. Anyone could make that.

Outside the window, the vacancy sign shown in neon against the gray early-evening sky. The letter C fluttered off and on as if ready to blink out at any moment, making it read "Ya ancy." Ava wondered about the people who slept in the rooms in the two-story building with a parking lot as a front yard. Probably mostly people passing through. The name Lonesome made it all the more depressing.

The highway stretched out across the desolate plains like an endless ribbon cast off an opened gift. Someone had taken that gift and left the ribbon as trash, just like the shabby little towns in this part of the state.

Ava knew these kinds of towns and these kinds of people. Many of them were honest and hard working. Then there were the others—the meth cookers, the deep-seated racists, and probably some who were hiding from the law.

Ava's uncle was as racist as they came. He showed it through his jokes and his bar fights when drunk. Uncle Stan would narrow in on any person he could guess had some Hispanic blood, and would walk up unprovoked, with barrel-chest stuck out and fist clenched. Most Texans had their own way of thinking, their own ideals, and their own way. They were Texans first, and then Americans.

"Well, what a cutie," a woman called as she carried a menu and glass of water to the table.

"Yes, she is," Ava replied as she unlatched Emma from the seat and gave her a rattle.

The waitress leaned close to Emma, cooing to her, and Ava felt a protective instinct to pull her away.

"You are a beautiful little girl," the waitress said, and Emma responded with a huge smile.

"What can I get you?"

"I'll just take a grilled cheese and fries . . . and I see your special today is chili. Do you recommend it?"

"Best chili around," the waitress said. "And to drink?"

"Diet Coke?" Ava glanced at the car seat where Emma grabbed at her feet, trying to pull them toward her mouth.

"Got it. You aren't from around here." The waitress said it as a statement instead of a question.

"No, not really." Ava wasn't about to explain her history to this woman. She was close enough to home that Ava didn't want to chance someone knowing her father or some other friend or family member.

"Let me guess. Dallas-Fort Worth or Austin . . . probably Dallas."

Ava chuckled. "Why do you say that?"

"It don't take Sherlock Holmes to figure it out. Accent, hair, accessories, nails. The car nearly threw a wrench in my guess."

The woman looked like she'd worked the diner for decades. Her buttons were undone low enough to show an aging bosom that was most likely her pride as a younger woman—perhaps it still was.

"It also don't take Sherlock to know that there baby isn't yours."

"You think I'm too old?"

"Nope, not at all. In fact, I gots me a kid who just started kindergarten, so you ain't too old for that there baby. All the movie stars are having kids in their forties now, so you're just in vogue if you do. But you aren't real comfortable with that baby. She's not even your grandbaby, is she?"

"No, she isn't."

"You didn't steal her, did you? I'd really hate to see you in prison . . . you seem nice enough."

Ava laughed, surprising Emma, who burst into tears.

"Oh, sweetie, I'm sorry." She pulled the baby up, cradling her against her chest, rocking and patting her back. The feel of Emma's small warm body coursed through her with a soothing energy and melted her heart.

"That looks a bit more natural," the waitress said.

"She's my cousin's baby, so I guess she's my cousin as well. I'm taking care of her for a while."

The woman studied her thoughtfully.

"Let me see that little muffin." She set down her pad and pen on the table and reached for Emma. Ava immediately wanted her back, not in the arms of a stranger, though the waitress quieted Emma down with her bouncing and cooing noises that caused the baby to pull back and study her face.

"I'm Jackie," she said.

"Ava. Nice to meet you."

"Let me get your order in." Jackie moved around to the counter, bouncing Emma as she did. She stuck the order into a metal rack that the cook spun around. He nodded Ava's way as he pulled it off and disappeared into the kitchen.

"We're slow tonight. Big rodeo drains the town out until near midnight, then we'll see things hopping as everyone comes back to town with their stomachs aching for some grub after that drive home."

"Sounds exhausting." Ava reached out her hands for Emma. The baby stared at her, then seemed to lean toward her.

"Looky there, she's reaching for you," the waitress said, but hung on to Emma. "You staying at the motel tonight?"

"Yep."

"Watch out for this little one. Keep her close to you."

"Why?"

"Just saying. I'm sure it ain't as clean as you're used to."

Ava held a teething ring out for Emma to grasp. "Beggars can't be choosers."

"Why are you a beggar? Don't seem like it should be so."

"Circumstances. And I'm bringing the baby back to her mama."

"Does her mama want her back?"

Ava thought about lying and keeping this from getting too personal. But then she thought, what the heck.

"Not sure. You've lived around here a long time?" she asked Jackie.

"'Bout twenty-three years, I guess. Raised my kids in this town, though the first three got out as fast as they could say *eighteen*. My second husband dragged me out here. He's buried down the road, next to my third husband. Guess I should've learned to marry younger, not older."

Ava wasn't sure how to respond to that.

A ding on the counter sounded and Jackie handed Emma back to Ava. "Your order's up."

Ava pulled a bottle out from the baby bag. She still worried that she was doing the formula thing all wrong. Her babies had nursed their entire first year with food coming along at five months. She felt completely inept at this formula feeding.

Jackie reappeared and placed the food on the table. "You got kids of your own?"

Ava nodded. "Two." She nibbled on her grilled cheese, enjoying the soft crunch of butter on the bread and gooey cheese that stretched into long strings with every bite.

"I better get back to work before I get fired . . . Isn't that right, Barney!" Jackie called to the cook behind the small window. He stuck out his head and cupped his ear.

"What?" he yelled over the sound of the fryer.

"Nothing, nothing," Jackie said with a laugh, waving him away. She cleared the dishes from the table in the next booth, and Ava focused on getting herself and Emma fed.

"It was nice meeting you," Ava said after she'd paid the bill. "If you need anything, you give me a holler."

"I just might do that," Ava tossed out as she carried bags, car seat, and baby out of the diner.

❧

Ava stripped back the bedspreads right away. Even in the five-star hotels where they usually stayed, she was meticulous about the bedspread habit. She'd seen one too many news investigation programs were they took a black light to the bedspreads, floors, and walls.

Next Ava checked the sheets, which passed her inspection, though who knew what frightful things were hidden from the human eye. At this moment, she cared less than usual. They had a room, that's what mattered. Her exhaustion and relief that they weren't stranded somewhere in the car or sleeping in it once again outweighed her germ phobia, which normally would've been heightened with the baby in tow. She laid Emma down in the middle of the sheets.

Emma wiggled around, putting her feet in the air and rolling over to one side. Then she tried rolling to her stomach, grunting and struggling with one arm stuck beneath her.

"You can do it," Ava said, kneeling next to the bed. She laughed at the determination, and finally gave Emma a little nudge to help her over.

"You did it!"

Emma's focused expressions transformed into a huge smile

and a giggle that filled Ava's heart with a joy she hadn't felt in years. She'd forgotten the maternal delight of tiny accomplishments like this and wondered why it was suddenly so strong for this little one.

After feeding Emma and rocking her to sleep with her back muscles burning, she placed Emma back on the bed, ever so carefully. The baby opened her eyes a moment, then she settled back to sleep. Ava felt like doing a cheer as she lined the pillows along the edge of the bed.

"We're getting the hang of this," she whispered with a yawn.

Ava fell back upon the bed with her arms outstretched across the width of it. She closed her eyes and could visualize the road stretched in front of her. Her nerves longed for a luxurious bath with bubbles, a glass of Pinot, and the thick down comforter of her favorite hotel. Instead they had a dank motel with suspicious carpeting, crooked curtains, and a neon light flickering outside.

"We'll be back home tomorrow night," Ava muttered to herself and to Emma, who made a soft sigh in her sleep.

Ava wondered what tomorrow would hold. The goal was clear. Find Bethany. Could that be accomplished without seeing too much of her family? Should she take time to visit her brother while she was in town?

She drifted in and out of sleep as she went over different scenarios. Then she heard it. Not noise from the other rooms or big rigs on the highway or a clock ticking obnoxiously keeping her awake. No, this was much more detrimental to her chances of getting a good night's sleep.

Ava smiled wearily as Emma giggled beside her.

Despite her exhaustion, it wasn't that late, so Ava called Dane again. The call went directly into voice mail. He was obviously out of a service area. Loneliness swept over her, as if she were much too small to be alone in this dank motel room with a little baby to care for. She longed for Dane and the strength he always offered her.

She called Kayanne.

"My phone is going to die pretty soon, and I can't find my charger. I'd forgotten how frazzled I get with a baby. And I can't reach Dane either, so if you have a chance, will you call and tell him that I'm all right and what's going on?"

"Of course, but go get a new phone charger," Kayanne said.

"I'll look for a store, but there's not much out here."

"Everyone has a cell phone. And by the way, I really hate praying aloud," Kayanne said with a grumble that made Ava laugh.

"That was random. And using *hate* and *prayer* in the same sentence might be sacrilegious, so be careful. But I'll admit, I don't like it either."

"You don't? But you pray out loud at Bible study every week."

"Doesn't mean I like it. It's my responsibility."

"I think Corrine enjoys it. I think she practices her prayer during the week before Bible study so that she'll sound pious. Don't you notice how she volunteers every week?"

"You are so bad," Ava said, sitting in a chair near the bed. She'd had the same thought herself, especially since she'd seen Corrine with a small cheat sheet in hand.

"Why don't you like praying aloud?"

"I have to organize my words and thoughts for the benefit of others. When I pray at home, to myself, it's more like me dumping everything on God."

"Yeah, sometimes it's more like pummeling God with prayer."

"I think He can take it."

The baby stirred. "Why are we discussing this?"

"So you know how much I love you."

Ava was about to say how random that was as well, when Kayanne launched into a prayer over the phone.

"Father God, I pray much better in my head, but I need you to be with my friend Ava while she's in some seedy motel in the middle of nowhere with a baby that isn't hers and while she goes to see people who have never been very good to her. Let her feel your peace and go before her in everything she faces in the days ahead and even tonight in that dark, scary motel room. Keep her safe. Be with her."

Ava found herself looking around the room as if some specter might rise from the closet or under the bed.

"Amen."

"That was actually quite wonderful—thank you. Want me to pray for you? Your man issues?"

"That sounded lovely—my man issues. And don't you already pray for me to find the love of my life?"

"I do, but maybe not as often as I should."

"Then by all means, please do so now. And aloud so I can hear it."

Ava prayed for Kayanne, her life, her dating, and her future.

She disliked praying aloud because of the need for cohesiveness, whereas within her head, it could be a jumbled outpouring that she knew God could unweave. Yet the peace that settled over her during Kayanne's prayer and now her own made it worth it.

"Where two or more are gathered in Your name, Lord, there you said you will be also . . ." And Ava could feel God with them in the midst of their uncomfortable, aloud prayers.

Emma slept soundly after a final bottle. Ava muttered the Lord's prayer several times, and she too collapsed into the warm arms of sleep.

ເ∙ອⓅ∙ɔ

She woke in the deep of the night with Emma stirring restlessly beside her. She'd want a bottle soon.

After piling pillows around her little form, Ava forced herself from bed. As she plugged in the portable teapot she'd brought along and poured in some bottled water, Ava realized she'd been dreaming, or perhaps she had been reminiscing about her aunt and their days in the San Francisco Bay Area.

They'd been talking about God in the dream or the memory. The question was whether God was orchestrating every detail that occurred in their lives. Or was He more distant, caring for the bigger things, reaching out when people prayed? Prayer did something divine; Ava had no doubt about that. She didn't fully understand it, why God said to pray, why or how it all worked. But that part didn't worry her—after all, she could watch the stars in the sky or see a jet fly overhead and be okay with knowing nothing about how it all worked. And the Bible had countless stories of God doing something because His people prayed.

As a child, Ava wanted to think of God as with her always. Sometimes her heart filled to overflowing with the sense of God . . . His greatness, His majesty, the wonder of someone she couldn't fully grasp or comprehend.

And God loved her. She knew this as she knew nothing else. Throughout the pain, especially in the pain, God was there. She had crumbled beneath the willow trees along the Black Rock River and found God there. Even when she thought He was distant, so far away that she almost stopped believing in His existence, if she sought Him again, He never failed to be found.

"How do I find Him?" Ava had asked her aunt in a tone that didn't veil her resentment. She was in her late teens by that time and had moved to California. Aunt Jenny was her cool aunt, not someone bound by church rules. She wore designer clothes, ate sushi, and went to the opera. Business trips had taken her around the world where she disappeared with her neatly packed suitcases and briefcase in hand.

"Seek Him," Aunt Jenny said, and it reminded Ava of her younger days beneath the willow trees.

Seek and you will find Me.

Ava ignored the words in her head. "How do I seek Him?"

"Look for Him as you would something very valuable."

Where your treasure is, there is also your heart.

"Like a treasure? God is a treasure?"

"Yes," Aunt Jenny said with a smile.

"But He isn't a treasure to be found. I hate words like that. They're such pat little Christian answers."

"But they're true sometimes. What would be better in this life to find than God?"

She'd felt so bitter about all of this. About anything that hinted of church, Christianity, faith, or religion.

"I know why you are so hurt." Ava was surprised by the tears in her aunt's eyes. She looked away. "I was raised in the same church," Aunt Jenny said.

Ava studied her then. She'd forgotten that. Aunt Jenny had already moved to California by the time Ava was old enough to know her. She never visited the church when she came to town, never stayed out at Grannie's farm either.

"My dad wasn't the pastor when you went, right?"

"No. Your dad is a few years older than I, but we were in the same youth group together."

"What was it like back then?"

"Strict. We were happy kids, but there was a rule for every-thing, and it seemed anything wrong we did—which was most everything—was sure to damn us to hell. It kept us in line, sort of."

"My daddy is a hypocrite."

"No, your daddy is human." Ava bit her lip at that. "He's also your daddy. But more than that, he isn't God."

"Well, I know that, obviously. God wouldn't get arrested, kicked out of church, shame the entire family, and end up in prison."

"Well, Jesus did some similar things, but He wasn't guilty."

Ava laughed at that, though there was an element that definitely wasn't funny at all.

"You have to always remember that although we think of God as a Father, He isn't at all like our earthly fathers, thankfully."

"Then what is He like?" she'd asked.

"He's like God."

⌒◉⌒

Monday morning, Ava was trying to figure out the best way to take a shower with Emma sleeping in the bed when a gentle knock sounded on her door. She crept to the peephole and saw Jackie, the waitress from the diner, waiting on the other side.

"I brought you some grub and caffeine," Jackie said through the door.

Ava studied the woman a moment through the distorted view that made her head and hair appear huge and her body small.

Ava grabbed the pepper spray from her purse and slid it into her pocket, just in case. Then she moved the chair from beneath the doorknob and slid the chain open. Jackie carried a cardboard box with a dishtowel over the top.

"Good morning," Jackie said, walking around her and straight to the dresser before Ava responded. She wore tight, sparkling jeans and a low-cut shirt that showed off her bulging chest.

"Good morning," Ava said, her stomach growling at the sight of eggs, bacon, pancakes, fruit, and a carafe of coffee.

"Hope you aren't a vegetarian—I just don't get them people, no offense if you are."

"I never could let go of bacon and steak. This looks great. I really appreciate it."

Jackie pulled out silverware, a plate, and a coffee cup from the box and set them on the small table.

"I kept thinking about you and that little sweet pea. I did some praying last night. I may not look like much of a God-fearing woman, but I'm that exactly."

"Thank you. I'm in need of coffee in a bad way."

"Let's get you plugged in then." She poured Ava a cup of coffee and unwrapped the food, setting it on the table.

"You're eating as well, I hope."

"Nope, I'm two weeks into Weight Watchers. Gotta drop me a few pounds before my sister's wedding in two months. I'll be seeing my ex."

Ava nodded as if she understood completely. She was making herself a plate when they heard noises from the bed.

"Kids always do that, as if they know you're about to eat without them."

Emma rubbed her eyes as Ava picked her up.

"Good morning, little peanut," Ava whispered as Emma touched her face.

"I can hold her while you eat . . . and if you need to shower too."

Ava didn't mean to blatantly frown, but Jackie let out such a laugh that she knew her thought that Jackie might steal Emma while she was in the shower was written all over her face.

"Leave the bathroom door open, and I'll sit with her where you can see me."

"I'm not above running after you in my birthday suit, and that sight alone will scare you into giving the baby back."

Jackie roared with laughter. "I think I like you even better than I expected."

Ava ate breakfast while Jackie gave Emma a bottle. Then Ava showered quickly, with the door open so she could hear Jackie talking and singing to the baby.

After the shower, Jackie remained in the room while Ava got ready and packed their belongings.

"Another set of hands is more helpful than I realized," Ava said, wishing she'd brought Kayanne after all.

"Of course. Takes a bunch of hands to care for one little sweet pea, doesn't it?" Jackie bounced Emma in her arms. "By the way, I told Duffy to cut you a deal on the repair. He'd try to pad the price, seeing that honking stone on your finger. But he knows better than to mess with me."

"Oh! He was supposed to give me a price before fixing it." She'd counted her money that morning—it was getting low and she still needed gas and food for the rest of the trip.

"Why for?"

"Well, how much do you think it will be? I don't have much money with me."

"Oh, no problem, he takes plastic."

"Yeah, well . . ." Ava's mind whirled. She glanced down at the "honking stone" on her finger, but she'd never part with her wedding ring. She touched her ears and felt the diamond posts there. They weren't a gift, just something she'd bought at Tiffany's while on a trip to New York.

"Let's see what we can do. You are quite a little mystery, but I know this to be true: God's gonna take care of you and that baby. Do you believe that?"

"Yes, I do believe it." The words filled her with strength, and she saw how God was caring for them even in that moment, preparing them for what lay ahead.

An hour later, Ava waved toward Jackie standing with one hand on her hip and the other waving. The woman turned back toward Duffy, obviously giving him a few of her thoughts. It was only the engine light and Duffy had fixed it and checked the fluids, charging her first sixty dollars, then lowering it to thirty-five after getting an evil eye from Jackie.

Ava could see Jackie in the rearview mirror as she pulled onto the narrow highway and she couldn't help but laugh. An angel in a waitress uniform—who would've guessed?

Twenty-Seven

FOR THE NEXT HOUR AVA SANG WORSHIP SONGS AND EMMA MADE baby noises as if singing along before falling silent into sleep.

The open plains had turned to farmland and scattered lakes. Storm clouds gathered and Ava knew there'd be rain before long. This part of Texas was far to the south, almost to the Mexican border, and felt distinct from the rest of the state. She felt her roots stirring as she got closer—roots she'd tried to keep tucked away from even her own memory.

At the crossing into the Rio Grande Valley, Ava's contented faith was attacked with the realness of her return.

The highway was like an old friend she'd cut ties with, and now it came to her with such familiarity that she couldn't believe she'd forgotten it. It had been nearly two decades. Despite her family's dysfunction, Ava's brother lived here too, and he'd done nothing to deserve her neglect.

It didn't seem possible that so much time had passed without her making the trip. Her children had never visited her hometown, her grandmother's farm, or the old farm where she'd grown up and their Uncle Clancy still lived. They had never met their grandfather in prison either. Ava wanted to protect them, and as she considered whether to ever bring them to meet her family, the years passed.

The last time she'd driven on this road Dane was in the passenger side after a knee surgery that ended his college football career. She'd needed her birth certificate for their marriage license and a few other documents left behind after her mother's death and father's incarceration. She was the oldest child, so it seemed right that she stop running from the family and get what she needed to move on.

She hadn't been to the farm in three years, and she'd nearly forgotten who her family was after her time in California.

"This land doesn't belong to you, and we're not leaving," Aunt Lorena had said as soon as she'd opened the door to Ava. Behind her, children and cousins craned their necks to see. Ava saw a shotgun sitting on the coffee table with a small child asleep on the couch beside it.

"I'm not here to take the land."

"You better not be. 'Cause we'll burn it all before we give it over. Your mama had no right getting it from Papa, and she had no right saying it was yours once she died. It's the family's, and you ain't been part of this family for years now."

"I'm just here to get the box of papers Mama left me."

While Aunt Lorena grilled her, Aunt Lara had stood at the front window, drapes clenched in her hands and glaring out at Dane. "Your man's too good for your folk, that it? Don't get out of the car and has his woman driving him around. Men drive the cars where I come from."

"I told him to wait in the car." Ava didn't defend him, didn't explain that he'd had surgery on his knee and was still hobbling around on crutches.

Lorena laughed. "Got him whipped, eh? Your grandma would love that one."

"Where is she?"

Chills ran up Ava's back at the thought that her grandmother might appear from one of the bedrooms. The last time she'd seen the woman was when Ava told her she was moving to California to live with Aunt Jenny. Grannie had been drinking and knocked Ava down, clawing her face. She still had a slight scar near her eye.

"In a old folks' home."

Ava shuddered at the thought. She'd sung Christmas carols at a few of the low-income homes for the elderly during her few months in Girl Scouts. "Can I please just have the box? That's all I want—you can have the rest."

"I burned it," Aunt Lorena said with a look of defiance.

Ava turned and walked off the porch without another word, too afraid of what those words might be and how she'd regret them. She wasn't afraid of the aunts or of Grannie any longer—they couldn't hurt her—but Ava sometimes feared she'd hurt them and follow the family heritage of uncontrolled anger.

Dane had studied Ava's face as she tore down the driveway. "I should have come with you. It's rude of me, sitting out here like this. I should've met them properly."

Ava shook her head. "They aren't proper people. She would have found something to say about you. Like the way you hopped on your crutches was condescending to them. She's so much like my grandmother."

"I do get that quite often—about my condescending hopping." That made Ava smile.

"So where are the papers?" Dane asked.

"Burned up."

Dane upheld an innocent expression as if really concerned. "Did they run out of firewood?"

Before long they were laughing again as the miles fell away behind them.

Dane had been good at making her laugh her way through the stress of her family. Whenever she brooded over them, once he found out the subject of her moodiness, he found a way of lightening it up.

As Ava approached her hometown, a flurry of mixed emotions filled her. Outside of town, a massive Walmart rose from what had been bramble woods and countryside. A gas station with a mini-mart sat at the corner intersection, and a strip of stores and shops lined the edges of the parking lot that was full of cars and buzzing with people. A few miles later, the town welcome sign ushered her back home. She felt a wave of nostalgia as well as a shiver of dread. Ava glanced behind her to where Emma slept on, safe and contented in her slumber.

The town had a dingy, rundown feel, exactly as Ava remembered it. Many of the buildings were familiar with minor changes—an old Italian restaurant was now a sandwich shop, a small grocery was a used furniture store now, and Jem's Frosty, behind which she'd smoked that first cigarette, was completely gone and only a cracked parking area remained. Ava drove slowly, taking it all in. She passed the elementary school she'd attended from kindergarten to fourth grade. Its trees appeared taller than she remembered, but the steps up to the entrance seemed shorter. Beyond the school, a subdivision rose up an incline where a popular dirt bike track had once been. The houses were small and many needed paint and a lawn mower— many had For Sale signs stabbed into their lawns.

The town had relocated closer to Walmart, Ava realized, the downtown aging with neglect. An old gas station was closed down with the gas sign saying $1.27 a gallon.

I don't hate this place anymore, Ava realized.

And she suddenly wasn't angry with her family anymore either. Long ago, she'd worked hard at forgiving them, but a deep resentment had buried itself deep and hardened like a tiny stone.

But as she crossed the Black Rock River where they'd once picnicked under a hot Texas sun and where Daddy held his baptism services, Ava knew that the years had softened the bitterness. This place and her family had no hold on her, and it hadn't for a long while. Yet Ava hadn't recognized her own freedom.

They were getting close now, Ava realized as she turned

down a smaller country road with farms and thickets interspersed between the rolling hills and valleys. Her grandmother's farm was only miles ahead. Ava knew every inch of that road, having walked it with her brother and cousins countless times.

Behind her Emma made sucking noises in her sleep, reminding Ava that this wasn't her journey alone. This was little Emma's heritage and her own children's as well. Just as she'd done with her babies, Ava suddenly wanted this child far away from the pain of such a history.

Emma.

Suddenly Ava pulled off the road at a turnout. An open hay field stretched out, half plowed with rich earth churned up and the other half covered in rebel grasses that pocked the field between the harvest and planting time.

Emma remained asleep, but she shifted restlessly now that they were stopped. Ava didn't have long before she woke unless they kept driving. But Ava didn't want to go forward suddenly. Forward meant taking this child back to the world she had escaped. Turning around . . . what did that mean exactly? She and Dane would have a new child? Dane didn't want another child, and she didn't either. That stage was behind them. They would soon have an empty house, adult children, and later grandchildren.

Ava needed Dane. He'd have something witty to say, as well as a direction to go—either forward or back. He'd know exactly what to do.

She couldn't keep going down this road.

Emma rested peacefully, oblivious to everything going on

around her. Before Ava could put the van in gear again, an old Chevy pickup approached and slowed to a stop beside her.

"No," she muttered as the passenger cranked down the window. Ava reluctantly rolled her window down as well.

"Take a wrong turn, ma'am?" the driver asked, leaning this way and that to see around the passenger who studied her suspiciously.

"No." She waited for one of her cousins to recognize her.

"Well, so as you know, this here is private property. Probably should turn back around."

Ava wondered if she could turn around and escape before they realized who she was, but Frankie's frown was already turning into a look of recognition.

"Hey, Franks and Beans," she said, smiling. Benny's mouth dropped and Franks started laughing as he slapped the steering wheel.

"Well, I'll be thunderstruck," Franks said. "It's the Aviator herself."

"That's right," she said, nearly falling fully into her old thick accent that most everyone in the family used with vigor.

"What the heck are you doing out here?" Benny asked, folding his arms onto the window frame and leaning out.

"I was just in the neighborhood," she said, glancing in the mirror to check on Emma.

"I didn't recognize you in your fanciness, though that car be about ole as this Bessy." He slapped the outside of the door.

"Lean back, I can't see through your head, numbskull!" Frankie grabbed Benny and pulled him away from the window.

"You're a numbskull," Benny said, punching Frankie's arm.

Ava half expected a brawl to break out between them. Some things didn't change. Her cousins' hair had turned from brown to nearly gray, deep lines baked into their faces, and still they acted like they were ten years old.

"So do you have that baby in there with you?" Frankie said, leaning on the steering wheel.

"What baby?" Benny asked, looking to Frankie and back to Ava. His one eye drifted left as it always did, then he blinked and it returned to normal. "Did you go and have another baby? Ain't you too old to have a baby?"

"That's not polite, Beans. And women have babies into their sixties now."

"They do? That's sick," Benny said with a horrified expression.

Ava laughed, waking Emma. She broke into an immediate cry.

Benny's face lit up in surprise. "You do have a baby. I'm sorry if I off-ended you."

"No, it's okay. She's not . . . mine, not really." Ava hopped out and around the van to open the back door and reached for Emma, pulling off her thick baby blanket and unbuckling her straps.

The back of Emma's head was wet with sweat, but she stopped crying and arched her neck as Ava walked back around toward the two men gawking at her from the truck.

"I'm sorry, little sweetie," Ava said, worried that the cool afternoon would give her the chills. She wrapped the blanket around her.

"You sure looking good, cousin. Hardly aged at all compared to ole gruffy there and me," Benny said with some embarrassment. He opened the truck door and brushed at his pants as if the stains might actually come off.

"Thank you," Ava said with a smile as she hugged him. She caught a whiff of tobacco and straw. "I guess we're certainly aging, though."

"So you adopt a kid? I'm a little corn-fused, if you know what I mean."

Frankie walked up next, slamming his truck door shut after shutting off the engine. A plume of gray exhaust drifted lazily into the afternoon.

"That's Bethany's kid, Stupid Beans." He hugged Ava and pinched her cheek as he always had when she was a kid.

"It is?" Benny asked, completely unfazed by the insult. "How'd you get Bethany's kid?"

"You didn't hear about her going off and leaving her baby with Ava and her husband?"

"Nobody tells me nothin', that's what I always say because it be true."

"So you're bringing her back?" Frankie took a pinch of tobacco from a box and stuffed it behind his bottom lip.

The question hung in the air.

"I'm not sure. I'm trying to find out what's going on, and why Bethany left her."

"It don't take a rocket scientist to understand what's going on. Bethany got a new beau who don't want some screaming brat around—sorry, little baby—I know you aren't a brat." He leaned toward her and wiggled his finger at Emma. She stared at him with large eyes.

Ava sighed. "I didn't know that was it."

"I thought Bethany was going to become the next Taylor Swift," Beans interjected.

"As if it's that easy." Frankie shook his head at his younger brother.

"Anyway, you come on up to the house. You've got to meet Beetle."

"Beetle?" Ava glanced at Frankie for an explanation.

"You'll see," Frankie said with a grin.

Ava was searching for some excuse to turn back around when another truck came down the road. It pulled up beside them. The window came down and an older woman with a scowl shouted toward Franks and Beans.

"Quit flirting with that woman and get home like I told you both to. The hay ain't gonna bale itself." Ava was stunned to see how much her aunt had aged.

"That ain't no woman, Ma! That's Ava Lynn!" Benny laughed like he'd just told the funniest joke ever.

"Who? Say what? Ava Lynn?" Aunt Lorena stared at her with narrowed ice-blue eyes. Ava gave a small wave as she bounced the baby.

"Oh, of course. That'll bring you out here. Well, get your-selves all up to the house then."

Ava glanced longingly down the road she'd come up, but Frankie backed up, waiting for her to follow where Aunt Lorena sped toward the old farm. If she'd had her Mercedes,

Ava could've whipped around and easily put distance between Franks and Beans and herself.

What am I doing? What if they take Emma away from me now?

A panic came over her—what a terrible idea this had been. She'd jumped into the car, driving without any plan, without anyone with her. No one was coming to help if this situation became tense. It was Ava against a family who didn't answer to typical reasoning. Ava had walked straight into their territory without an ally on her side.

God, help me, she whispered.

"God is taking care of you and that baby," Jackie had said earlier that morning.

She gripped the steering wheel and pulled onto the road toward the old family farm.

Believe. Hadn't that been the word she'd been given?

I guess this is what it means to put action to faith, she thought, wishing such words were as easy as they sounded inside the walls of the church or at the table of her Bible study group.

Belief had a lot more to do with courage than she'd ever known before.

Twenty-Eight

THE HOUSE STOOD STRAIGHT AND OMINOUS ON A RISE OF HILL-side. The roof with its different colors and one section covered in a blue tarp reminded her of the old overalls she'd worn as a kid with patches covering the knees. The blue-painted clapboard siding had faded and peeled beneath the hot Texas summers. A chimney puffed out wood smoke into the already-gray sky.

Aunt Lorena's truck chugged up the last rise ahead of her, and she felt the push of Frankie's truck behind her. This was where Ava and Clancy had lived with their grandmother when their father went out evangelizing across the country every summer. Not having parents of his own, he figured his former mother-in-law owed it to him to help out. The summers at Grannie's were her worst childhood memories.

Ava's grandmother had raised five daughters on the farm after her husband was killed in a machine "accident" on the land. The girls had been given L names: Aunt Lara, Aunt Lorena, Aunt Lynne, Aunt Liza, and Ava's mother, Leanne.

Then there was Aunt Jenny. Not until Ava was living with her aunt in California did she discover why Jenny didn't have an L name. She'd been dropped off with Grannie by a woman she didn't know, unlike Grandpa. Before his suspicious accident, Grandpa was known to have a cheating heart.

Grannie's daughters all had various marriages and boyfriends that produced Ava and her generation of cousins. The cousins were now in their thirties and forties with children of their own—Bethany, Sienna, and Jason's age group. With Emma, the youngest generation was born.

Ava thought of the dozens of children who had run these grounds, playing hide-and-seek, tag, and king of the mountain.

Looking in the rearview mirror, Ava saw Emma's small face in the infant mirror on the backseat. Her eyes were turned downward in concentration and Ava heard the sound of her rattle.

Grannie had died when Jason was only two, and Aunt Lara had died several years earlier. Clancy had called with the news both times. Ava had considered making the trip out for the funerals, but she found some excuse to stay away. They were good excuses—Jason had the flu and something else she couldn't remember—but in the end, she hadn't gone. That's all her family would remember.

Aunt Lorena waited on the cracked cement walkway. The yard had been mowed and a flower bed grew wildly up the front porch, but it looked almost cute close up like this, as long as she didn't look toward the barn where the yard was littered with broken farm equipment, old cars, washing machines, and other appliances wrapped in tall grass and vagrant weeds.

She stopped behind her aunt's truck and waited a moment for the dust to settle before hopping out of the VW. The house was spitting out people and animals from the doorway.

With a whispered prayer, Ava pulled Emma from her car seat and walked toward her family. Children of all sizes, at least eight of them, stared at her curiously, and several dogs barked, racing toward her until one of the children shouted and threatened to hit them with a stick.

"Yes indeed, yes indeed," a woman said, emerging from the house. For a moment Ava thought Aunt Lara had returned from the dead. Then she recognized Aunt Lara's daughter Jessie—Bethany's mother and Emma's grandma—who stared at her from the door and walked forward clucking her tongue as if she'd expected Ava's arrival. Jessie had not aged well. She wore stained bunny slippers, sweats, and an oversized T-shirt.

"The prodigal cousin returns, and with my own granddaughter to boot."

Frankie and Benny came up from behind.

"Doesn't Ava Lynn look great?" Benny said, getting a hard punch to the arm from Frankie and a scowl from Aunt Lorena.

"She oughtta when she can afford to pay for good doctors and expensive clothing and enormous jewelry," Aunt Lorena said.

Ava almost laughed at how expected this greeting was. Some things didn't change, and that was a sad fact when it came to her family. She realized her bitterness was truly gone, replaced with sadness over their lives. There'd be no reconciliation with these people who shared her blood.

Emma wrenched her body around to take in the view as a young boy raced up and wrapped his arms around Benny's legs. He tugged at his sleeve until Benny bent down to catch the whisper.

"This is your cousin. Her name is Ava and she lives in the big city of Dallas."

"And who are you?" Ava asked the boy as he stared up at her with large blue eyes. His cheeks were smudged with dirt and his clothes were worn thin.

"This is my boy, Beau Jackson, but I call him Beetle. Did you know I had a kid?"

"I didn't. Clancy usually gives me all the family news, but he didn't tell me this."

"He might not know. I ain't talked to Clancy in a bit. And I didn't know I had a boy until his mama brought him last winter. We got shared custody now, and I gotta work to pay some child support. But he's a good boy, aren't you, Beetle?"

The boy hid behind Benny's leg when Ava smiled at him.

"How old are you?" Ava asked, but Jessie came forward abruptly, interrupting them.

"Enough of all that. I suppose I'll have to take the kid, if Bethany's gonna desert her on someone's doorstep." Jessie reached for Emma.

"I only came to talk," Ava said, pulling Emma closer against her chest instead of handing the baby over.

Jessie frowned and set her hands on her hips.

"Let's get out of this cold and do some talking then. Boys, this is women business, you two get about with the evening chores," Aunt Lorena said, and Ava realized she'd taken over for her grandmother as the matriarch of the house. She wondered just how many people were living here. Ava retrieved the baby bag, then followed them inside with Jessie tailing her every move.

Ava peered into a house that was messier than she remembered with piles of dirty dishes, napkins, and pizza boxes covering most every surface. The television flickered in the living room and the dogs took up barking from some back room.

"Let me at least hold her for a minute. She is my grandkid."

Ava reluctantly passed Emma over to Jessie. There was a surprising sense of loss in Ava's arms, and she watched carefully as Jessie carried Emma to the old couch that was piled with laundry—hopefully clean laundry.

"Have you seen your father?" Aunt Lorena asked, motioning Ava to sit down at the dining room table.

The question surprised her. "My father?"

"Yeah, your father, did you forget you had one? He's the one in prison."

The floor was littered with stray socks, crushed leaves, and yellow potato chips.

"Not yet," Ava muttered.

"So you're gonna see him?" Jessie pressed in a sarcastic tone as she bounced Emma.

"Maybe. I came out here for another reason."

Jessie laughed and looked her over. "I knew you wouldn't want the kid. Told that stupid daughter of mine when she hatched this plan."

The baby lifted her face upward, watching Jessie, and Ava considered scooping her up to leave then and there.

A boy who looked about ten walked out from down the hallway carrying a bag of chips and crunching on a mouthful.

"That's Amber Lee's second one."

The boy stared at her without much expression, continuing to crunch on his chips.

"Hi, I'm your cousin Ava," she said, smiling at the boy. He stared back without any change in expression.

"Tell her your name," Aunt Lorena said sternly. When he didn't respond, she slammed her hand on the kitchen table. "Manners!"

"Jarrod," the boy muttered with a mouthful.

"This family is going to hell," Aunt Lorena muttered. "These kids keep having kids and dropping them off with us 'cause they're on drugs or in jail or have some far-fetched ideas in their head. What happened to raising your own kids?"

"If they'd keep their legs together, we wouldn't have this problem," Jessie said, bouncing Emma on her leg. Ava suddenly felt sick to her stomach.

"So Miz Dallas-High-and-Mighty, we know why you're here. Why don't you head back to your fancy life?"

Ava stood and rushed over to Jessie. "I'll take her."

"You have no rights to her." Jessie held her away from Ava with a mean smile on her face.

"Bethany left her with me. I'll talk to her about what we should do with Emma."

"Emma, huh? Is that what she named her? Poor kid didn't

have a name for the first few months. I don't know what they put on the birth certificate."

"I should get over to my brother's house anyway. I came here looking for Bethany."

"She's not here, as you can see. But I'm her grandmother, so the baby should stay with me."

Aunt Lorena watched the scene as if amused. The dogs started barking, and Ava noticed the children gathered on the stairs watching as well.

"Mama, give Auntie Ava the baby."

Bethany stood in the doorway to the kitchen.

"Sneaking in the back now? I thought you was gone," Jessie said with a snarl.

Bethany stood with her long legs in a "just try me" stance that Ava thought was part of every woman's DNA at one time or another. Ava took the chance to grab the baby from Jessie. Emma smiled her wide grin, showing off her pink gums.

"Isn't this convenient timing?" Aunt Lorena said, leaning back in the old dining room chair. "That Benny should mind his own business."

"Uncle Beans cares more for me and that baby than you do, Aunt Lorena."

A sense of déjà vu swept over Ava as if she'd been in this conversation with her family over and over again.

"Is that one out there the father?" Aunt Lorena asked, motioning toward the front window. A guy stood smoking a cigarette on the porch, gazing out across the land.

"No," Bethany muttered with her arms crossed.

"She won't tell us who the father is. She don't know who the father is."

Bethany glared at Jessie. "You just hush it. You don't know what you're talking about. I know who it is, but it ain't none of your business. When my daughter is old enough to ask me who her daddy is, then I'll tell her. Until then, I don't want my baby daddy around and neither do any of you. It's best left as it is."

Jessie made a huffing noise and plopped back onto the couch.

"Do you want my kid or not?" Bethany asked Ava.

Ava felt the weight of Emma in her arms. "I do . . . but . . ."

"That's fine by me. You take her, or you can leave her while you decide. It's up to you. I'm gonna find her a good home. I won't let her live in this pit I grew up in, that you grew up in too. My baby isn't gonna have this life. I'm making sure of that."

Ava nodded. "I need to know how to reach you. There are legal avenues we have to follow no matter what happens. You might change your mind too. But I'll take her while my husband and I decide what to do."

Bethany glanced at Emma with a pained expression as she swallowed hard. "Deal. Let's shake on it."

Ava grabbed the hand the girl offered. Had they just made some kind of family pact over Emma?

"Leaving just like that? Back to Dallas?" Aunt Lorena said.

"I'm going to see my brother."

"I bet you don't go see your daddy."

Ava frowned at that. What did they care if she saw her father or not? He wasn't related to this side of the family, though they'd all attended Daddy's church when they were growing up.

"No, I probably won't," she said, staring back at her aunt.

"I'm gonna walk you out," Bethany said.

Several children followed, until Aunt Lorena screeched at them to come inside. Ava realized that she hadn't met all of them and had no idea who they were.

The shadow of the house was long and narrow across the ground as they walked toward the cars.

Frankie and Benny had disappeared, and Ava caught a stench of something she didn't want to recognize. The family had always supplemented their income with some kind of illegal activity, and cooking drugs had been their most profitable.

"I wish I could take them all," Ava said, glancing back at the house.

Bethany nodded, her eyes studying Emma. The baby seemed to finally notice her and perked up, kicking her feet as she smiled.

"Can I hold her?" Bethany asked meekly.

"Of course," Ava said, passing Emma into her mother's arm. Tears fell quickly down the girl's cheek.

"I never guessed that I'd love something so much."

"There are ways to keep her. We could help, at least as much as we can."

Bethany touched Emma's head and seemed to breathe her in. Ava could see the resolve in her eyes.

"Can't do it. I'm too messed up right now to be her mama. I'm as bad as this place," she said, motioning toward the house. "I appreciate you talking to me on the phone, though. Made me feel like I could get out, do something, clean my life up, and make something of myself. Then I'll have babies that I can raise. Maybe Ems will forgive me when she grows up. She'll see what a better life she had and that her mama loved her enough to get better."

Bethany wiped at her eyes and cradled Emma against her.

"I never knew a baby could feel so good. I'd do anything for her."

"So how are you going to change your life?" Ava wanted this girl to succeed, to make her plans really happen. They'd both seen enough failed dreams in this family. She glanced up at the house and knew that as little kids, none of Ava's aunts or cousins wanted their lives to become this.

Bethany shrugged as she looked at the guy who walked by them, offering Ava a nod before he hopped in the driver's seat of an old Trans Am. His hand moved in and out of the window as he took drags from the second cigarette Ava had seen him smoking since she'd arrived.

"I like him. We might have a chance. He's a decent guy."

"You need to get out of here, at least for a while." Ava had a memory of Bethany as a child with long blond hair, always wearing her mama's high-heeled shoes.

"I'm trying. My guy thinks I've got some talent. I sang at a talent show at the fair last summer. Got runner-up. But I don't know. I'm stuck here in the valley, don't ask me why. I went to Vegas with some girlfriends for a bachelorette party, and one time I went to Disneyland after my daddy got his settlement for that tractor accident. It's all right going places like that for a time. But I think this is where I belong."

Ava saw a slight dip in her chin that reminded her of Sienna. The girls were only a few years apart.

"It doesn't have to be like that, Bethany. I'm sorry that I haven't been here for you while you were growing up."

"Oh, I don't blame you. You had to do what you had to do. I don't blame you one bit. Just like I'm doing with Emma. We do what we must to survive, right?"

They were words of someone who'd seen too much in her young life. Bethany kissed Emma's forehead and held her against her for a moment longer.

"Take her now, will you?" Bethany passed the baby into Ava's arms.

"I can't make any promises, except that she's not growing up here," Ava said, feeling a sudden burden for the other children she was leaving behind. Then she remembered all that was happening at home. They were broke, losing everything. She and Dane didn't want to raise another child. How could they even consider it? But Ava couldn't speak one word of this as Emma held on to her arm and laid her head against her shoulder.

"Tell her I love her."

"I'll tell her," Ava said as she watched Bethany hurry toward the Trans Am. The engine roared to life before Bethany had hopped inside. A moment later, they were turning around and Bethany leaned forward, her hands covering her face, her shoulders shaking with sobs. The guy put one hand over her back and gave Ava a sad look as he drove by.

From the corner of her eye, Ava saw faces peering through the window of the house. She wished to load up all of the children, but she couldn't save them all. She didn't know if she could save this one, or even how she'd hold up herself. But that was God's job, she reminded herself.

Benny came out from the barn as Ava buckled Emma into her seat. They hugged and she saw the tears in his eyes.

"Bye, Beans. And thank you."

He nodded and said good-bye to Emma as she fussed in her car seat.

"I better get to driving before the baby gets too fussy."

"Come see us more often, Ava Lynn."

"I'll try. Or you come to Dallas. And tell Franks good-bye."

Ava took another look at the farmhouse and wondered if she'd ever see this place again.

Aunt Lorena appeared on the porch, put her hands together over her mouth, and shouted, "Go see your daddy!"

Ava just waved and turned on the engine. It was definitely time to leave. But as Grannie's old farm grew smaller behind her, Ava knew for sure that the place she'd dreaded and avoided for all these years had no more hold on her life. God had brought her back to reveal how He'd set her free long ago.

Twenty-Nine

"WE'RE SURPRISING YOUR UNCLE CLANCY," AVA TOLD EMMA AS SHE fed her a bottle in a fast-food parking lot by the Walmart in town.

After feeding Emma and changing her diaper, Ava drove the thirty minutes toward the house where she'd spent most of her years as a child.

Her parents had bought the land when she was a toddler. When Daddy was sent to prison, he offered the place to the kids. Ava gave her half of the deed to Clancy. It was not land she cared to own.

Ava turned down the driveway, the gravel crunching beneath the tires. The road branched into a Y with the house in one direction and the barns and mechanic's garage in the other. The trees had grown higher and blocked out much of the darkening sky, even with branches empty of leaves.

She followed the trail of abandoned cars that she could see in a field along the left. Ava guessed where she'd find Clancy.

With a glance in the rearview mirror, Ava could see Emma's

eyes closed. The long gravel road had lulled her back to sleep. How grateful she was for such an easy traveler.

The huge workshop came into view with a circle driveway around it. A sign sat on the ground, leaning against the outside of the workshop, that read Grub's Auto Repair. Clancy had told her this sign had hung over the garage of his auto shop in town until he shut it down. He had more business than he could handle. Expanding wasn't in Clancy's blood, and he didn't need the headaches of two garages, so he moved back to the workshop on his property. *Simplify* was Clancy's motto.

The workshop appeared freshly painted but the metal roof showed its age with long, rusted streams along the grooves where the winter rains had stained it. A newer truck was parked to the side with shiny rims and gleaming red paint.

Ava turned off the engine and stepped from the car, zipping up her jacket. The cold came quickly with the autumn shadows. She tucked a blanket around Emma, leaving her in the car seat, and then left the door ajar while she walked toward the open garage where two cars and a small tractor were in the process of repair.

The air smelled of grease, gasoline, and burning leaves. Ava noticed the smoldering pile of leaves at the corner of the garage as she approached. If it weren't for a light bulb dangling from the ceiling and the low sound of a radio playing from a stereo on the floor, Ava would've guessed the workshop was abandoned.

"Anyone know a good mechanic around here?" she called into the open garage, not wanting to move far from the baby.

Ava heard a tool clang onto the concrete floor and the slide of a floor dolly. Large work boots emerged first from beneath a sedan, then the rest of her brother on his back on the dolly. Clancy pulled off glasses and a headlamp, squinting his eyes as he stared at her.

"You have got to be kidding me," Clancy said, breaking into a wide grin.

"You didn't answer the phone. It just rang and rang."

"I only have my cell now, haven't had the chance to call everyone with it. That's on my list, you know. But what a shocker—I can't believe my big sister is here, in the flesh," he said, grabbing her into a strong bear hug.

Clancy's full head of thick hair had that messy look so many young people used gel and a blow dryer to get. He was well over six feet tall, towering over her. His bright blue eyes seemed to twinkle like Santa's.

"I didn't realize just how much I missed you until right now," Ava said, overcome with such emotion that she looked toward the baby to keep from bursting into tears.

"I know what you mean, exactly," he said sincerely. "Did you come down to see Daddy?"

Ava frowned. "No, why?"

Clancy shrugged, uncomfortable suddenly. "Just thought that was why you were showing up."

Ava didn't understand the connection. Rare as it was when they talked, Clancy never brought up their father. "When did you speak to him last?"

"First Saturday of every month."

Ava tried taking that in for a moment. "You mean, *every* first Saturday of *every* month?"

Clancy shrugged. "I missed one in 2004 when we had a bad ice storm and again in 2006 'cause I had the flu."

"That's incredible . . . I think. Or else something is wrong with you."

They laughed at that. Ava glanced toward the open car door where Emma slept.

Clancy walked to a tube of disinfecting wipes and pulled one out, cleaning his hands and forearms. "We both know something's wrong with me. But you know, I don't have kids and nothing much better to do but work and hunt. Dad needs someone."

Ava felt the stab of guilt. "I haven't seen him in thirty years, actually thirty-one."

"Yeah, I know. I haven't wanted to bring it up. But that was another reason I was going to call you soon."

"Aunt Lorena wouldn't let it go that I see him."

Clancy's mouth dropped dramatically. "What the heck? You braved that looney circus? Sister, what are you doing here?"

Ava motioned toward her car. "Come see."

It dawned on Ava as they walked up the front porch of Clancy's house—their childhood home—that there was a reason behind her brother and aunt's questions.

"Something's wrong with Daddy." Ava stopped suddenly.

Clancy didn't respond as he held open the door with the

baby bag on his shoulder and waited for Ava to enter the house. Her brother had kept the place clean and maintained. The front door had been painted a shiny black, and the white of the house appeared crisp and clean.

Emma rubbed her eyes and whimpered before dropping back to sleep over Ava's shoulder. Ava's back ached from holding the baby for the past few days, but she savored the feel of the little life pressed against her chest with head tucked near her chin and neck.

The inside had the décor of a practical man with a Western style. There were pictures of cowboys and wild horses, and horseshoes were recycled and welded together for use throughout the house as coat hooks, towel racks, a fireplace grate, even an entire bench near the back door.

"Did you make that?" Ava asked, inspecting the welds that held the shoes together.

"I have a little too much time on my hands," Clancy said with a chuckle.

The furniture was distressed wood, and giant rugs covered clean wood laminate floors. Ava smelled stew cooking and saw a large kettle simmering on the kitchen stove.

"It's usually a tad cleaner than this, but you caught me unawares, sister."

Ava looked around with admiration, though a knot had formed in her stomach as she realized how much of her brother's life she'd been missing. Questions about their father kept rising to her thoughts, but she squelched them for the moment.

"The old place looks great. You've made some changes. And new appliances too. It hardly looks like the same house." Clancy showed her how he'd knocked out the wall between the living and dining room and put in a large window and sliding door out toward the backyard where a brick barbecue and long rock bar replaced the dried grass where the Doughboy pool had been. She felt relieved to see that her brother hadn't kept the house like a memorial to a tragedy.

"I've gotten quite handy. Have you eaten? I'm cooking a stew. I make a big one when I cook, then freeze the leftovers."

"My domesticated brother. Smells great, and I'm starving."

Over giant bowls of stew and store-bought corn bread, Ava finally returned to the topic she dreaded.

"Tell me what's wrong with Daddy. What is it?"

"The cancer."

"What kind? How bad? How long has he had it? What are they doing to treat it?"

"Pancreas and it's pretty bad. Stage four. He found out last month. They aren't treating him, he don't want it anyway."

Ava leaned back in her chair, trying to take it in. She stared toward the living room where Emma played on a blanket with her teething ring.

"So that's why Aunt Lorena kept asking me if I'd seen him."

"Yeah, I'm sure. She still is one of his ardent followers."

"Really? Since the days he was a preacher?"

"Guess before that too. She had a thing for him when they were younger, but he only had eyes for Mama."

"I had no idea." Ava shook her head in dismay. Perhaps that was the reason Aunt Lorena had always seemed to hate their mother.

"She's been visiting him for quite a few years now. This hit her pretty hard."

Ava watched Emma trying to turn over on her blanket from her back to her stomach. She got stuck on her side again and finally gave up, flopping onto her back.

"I guess I should see him," she muttered more to herself than to Clancy. She rose from the table to turn Emma over for some tummy time. She kicked her arms and legs excitedly and grabbed the teething ring.

"Seems there are a few reasons for your trip out here," Clancy said in a matter-of-fact tone. "I haven't had a house guest for quite some time, and tonight I get two."

They stayed up late talking. Clancy hadn't visited them in Dallas in a number of years, and he'd never been much good on the phone. Ava was surprised to hear that he'd nearly married and that he'd become a golfer of all things.

"Golf? You?"

"I dated myself a photographer from Austin for a while. She was out here taking pictures when we met. She liked to golf— her father was really good and taught her. She bought me some irons for Christmas one year, and I got hooked."

"So the girlfriend ended but the golfing didn't?"

"You got it."

"And no girlfriend now?" Ava asked, her eye sweeping the place for any sign of a feminine touch.

"Not at the moment. And with work and visiting Dad more often, I don't see time to look for one."

"How often do you visit him now?"

"Coming on to every few days now. He don't have much time, so I figured might as well make it good."

"Why didn't you tell me, Clancy?"

He chewed the edge of his lip and rubbed his forehead.

"Daddy told me not to, but I was going to anyway, Aves. Just I wasn't ready to break his request quite yet."

Ava pursed her lips. Was this the real purpose of Emma coming into her life, so that she'd come back home and find out about her dad? If so, what did God want her to do with the baby?

"So we'll see him in the morning then," Ava said with a dread that sent shivers through her body.

Clancy set Ava up in his guest room. He moved the bed against the wall to keep Emma with one safe edge and Ava would be the border of the other. After getting Emma to sleep, she crawled into bed with her muscles aching and head full of the day's events.

With the house settled down for the night, Clancy's dog bounded inside and straight for her brother's room. She heard him talking to Danner and the hound's tail knocking against something in the room. The woodstove popped with a fresh oak log stuffed inside, and off in the distance, a chorus of coyotes yelped in an otherwise silent world. She stared at the ceiling and was glad to be sleeping in Clancy's old room and not her own.

She couldn't sleep, and Emma seemed to sense Ava's unrest as she squirmed, frowned, and then stirred again.

Today was Monday and she hadn't talked to her husband since Friday. It felt like a month. They kept missing each other's call or their service was bad. Ava hadn't talked to Kayanne, Sienna, or anyone from church, but her in-box was filling up.

Ava typed a text to Dane: *I know you won't get this till you're on your way home or on top of some mountain somewhere. But I'm thinking of you tonight. Of us, our family, and our life together.*

As unstable as their life was at the moment, more than it had ever been, their marriage was home and she was filled with a longing she hadn't felt since their early years together. *I'm home-sick for the things that matter,* Ava thought with bittersweet joy.

Tomorrow she was going to see her father. Her mind drifted to the prison, to that awful confined existence. She remembered the initial shock of seeing her father there many years earlier. He came into the visitation room wearing an orange jumpsuit and sat at a table across from her. Her father, Reverend Daniel Henderson, had gotten himself a tattoo. Ava could see the bottom of it sticking out from his orange sleeve, and though she wished to know what it was or said, she resisted showing interest and kept her eyes averted with quick glances at his face and then around the room.

She'd never asked him or Clancy about it. Ava expected her father to have a great story. "Prison does things to a man" would've been his likely words. After everything, Daddy was still the best excuse-artist she'd ever seen. It was a gift Ava hadn't inherited. Even when her excuse was valid, she couldn't say it right and she sounded false doing so. But to weave sympathy out of any kind of sin was a talent, like that princess who could weave gold from straw.

"I'm so happy my firefly finally came to see me," Daddy had said as he reached across the table with two hands because they were bound together in handcuffs. Ava had pulled her hands away into her lap, leaned back, and blew a bubble with her chewing gum. She'd dyed her hair platinum blond for the occasion. When he'd seen her last during the trial, it was raven black.

"How are you?" he said with less confidence than usual.

"I'm doing drugs," she'd said, trying to express boldness with her words. "And having sex. Lots of both." She'd never said the word *sex* in front of him before in her life, and she was proud of herself for doing it.

Daddy stared at her with those deep brown eyes, and there it was, the look of sadness that made her feel guilty for hurting *him*! Ridiculous.

"Firefly, oh, my little firefly." He rubbed his ears as if to rid them of what she'd said. So he'd believed her? Ava had said it to hurt him. He deserved it after the way he destroyed their lives with his lies and deceits. But not long after his prison sentence, Ava had decided that what she did with her life was her choice. She wouldn't rebel because she was angry at him. She would live her life on her terms, not in retaliation, because then he'd have a hold on her again.

You don't own me now, Daddy. You don't mean anything to me.

She'd practiced saying it but the words caught in her throat. Instead she chewed on her nails and pretended she was sitting through the most boring of Baptist preachers.

"I've been ministering to the men here. For this next season of my life, this is my calling. My lawyer hopes I'll get a new trial or early release. Then I'll be home, and we'll make amends." He spoke in a low tone as if more to himself than to her.

"This is your calling? No, Daddy, you stole money, you got drunk, and you killed somebody. All the while you were a preacher and that should've made you get punished all the more."

"Yes," he agreed, "but God can use everything for good."

Ava looked away from her father then, and she saw a tiny girl coloring a picture beside a huge dark-skinned man. Every inch of the man's skin was covered with tattoos, including his face and smooth, bald head. The little girl glanced up at him with that admiration and love only very young girls have for their daddies. She probably had no clue she was visiting her father in prison. If only Ava could switch places with that little girl and look at her father with the utter devotion she'd once had. She wondered how many years it would be until that little girl arrived for a visit with dyed hair and black nail polish. Two years earlier, Ava had looked like the perfect ultraconservative Christian with no makeup, wearing dresses instead of jeans, and able to recite scripture in a single bound.

"I'm moving to California," she'd told him.

He paled instantly. She was his firefly leaving the cage and flying away. He hated that, she knew. Him stuck inside that prison was less terrifying than being out in the world. The world was where evil resided and the devil waited to snatch us all away.

The devil was right inside our church, Daddy.

Then he cried. Ava tried to ignore the tears, telling herself they were his act, his on-cue display of false remorse. She recalled the tears her father could present on demand from behind the pulpit. They were well timed and set to the tempo of his message. But these didn't seem the tears of a charismatic minister. These were messy tears, and they crushed her heart.

His head hit the table with a thud, and his bony shoulders shook.

Her arms refused to reach across the table to comfort him. Her mouth refused to work as it jammed with words of both hate and love. She didn't apologize. Instead she stood abruptly.

"Gotta go, I don't feel well."

Ava looked back once as the correctional officer opened the door with a buzz of the locks. Daddy was wiping his eyes, slumped low in his seat, looking small and frail. Her father was a shadow of the man who lifted his fist to the sky in triumph, who would jump in the air rejoicing as a new convert was ushered into the family of God.

The word that came to mind made Ava finally believe he was sorry. Even if he didn't say it the way she wanted him to say it. Her father was broken.

Now, thirty years later, Ava feared learning what that broken man had become.

~⊙~

She pushed the porch swing with her feet as she cradled a cup of steaming coffee between her hands. The chains creaked back and forth as she moved. Clancy peered through the window at Emma sleeping in her car seat before he sat in a patio chair near her.

"I can't believe I'm really here," Ava said, taking in the landscape.

"I need to do some remodeling on the old place."

She had a thousand memories on that porch. She'd played with Barbie dolls here during the winter months, read her library books here escaping the summer heat, and sketched images she loved into her long sketch pad. Clancy and Ava had taken care of themselves here for over a week when they'd run away from their grandmother's farm and before Daddy returned from the road. The house had been locked up, so they made the covered porch their house. She'd been hiding supplies under a broken board, so they were fed well enough.

"I'm surprised you never left here," Ava said as a rooster crowed from a distant ranch.

"Where would I have gone?" Clancy said, looking out across the green yard toward the fields.

Ava shrugged. "Somewhere else in Texas? You could have come to California with Aunt Jenny."

"Me in California? Imagine that." Clancy chuckled as he took a sip of coffee.

"There are a lot of ranches and farmland out there. It's not all surfers, palm trees, and tech companies."

Clancy snickered. "I could've worn my cowboy boots and Wrangler jeans."

"Most anything goes in California, but that might be taking it too far," Ava teased.

"So why haven't you come back?" Clancy leaned back, placing his feet on the porch railing. His boots were worn but surprisingly clean.

Ava shrugged, unable to articulate an answer.

"I should have," she said, and realized how true that statement was. Here she'd thought it was about protecting her kids. But Ava hadn't needed to pull back from the entire family, Clancy included, to do so. She'd been protecting herself all these years, turning her back to the past and its pain, trying to blot it all out and forgetting the good parts.

"I understand. Must be pretty hard once you get outta here," Clancy said with sadness in his tone.

Ava pulled her feet onto the swing, sitting cross-legged like how she'd sat as a girl.

"I really should have," she whispered. "You are my brother, after all."

"That road goes both ways," he said.

But Ava knew he'd needed her, and she'd been in the best position to reach out. She spearheaded a ministry for broken people, after all. Yet the years clicked by, and she marveled that so many had disappeared. Sitting here with her brother and their childhood all around her, it seemed impossible they were in their late forties now. Perhaps this was all part of God's plan to bring her back so they could finally move forward.

"What's he like now?" Ava asked. She could see their daddy walking in from the barn, practicing his sermon as he walked. The country life didn't sit well with him, and the farm fell into disrepair until they leased most of it out. Daddy took an apartment in town where he stayed sometimes for whole weeks.

Clancy sipped his coffee again.

"Daddy is Daddy. He'll be crazy-chimp happy that you're in the house."

Ava laughed out loud at that. "Crazy-chimp happy—I forgot that one. I remember you jumping around that Christmas when Aunt Jenny brought us all those gifts."

Clancy chuckled. "You just stared in awe."

Ava pushed off from the swing to peer in the window at Emma still sleeping soundly.

"Daddy would've been out in another few years. Aunt Lorena is broken up about it. She had her heart set on them finally being together."

Ava shivered at the thought, wrapping her coat tighter around her.

"I wouldn't have ever guessed it of Daddy."

"Between us, he told me that's why the cancer got him— to save him from Aunt Lorena and her house of inmates."

"I can almost believe it," Ava said, thinking of those sweet children trapped in that life.

Clancy rose from the bench, his knees popping as he

stretched. "We're going to visit Mama on the way. So we better get moving."

"We are?" Ava hadn't been to her mother's grave since the visits with her father as a child.

"We are," Clancy said, and she knew that this was his tone that meant no negotiating.

⋘⋙

They walked the green manicured lawn dotted with gray headstones that seemed to grow right out of the grass. Ava followed Clancy's lead as he carried Emma in one arm and held a bouquet of flowers they'd picked up at the supermarket on the way. Emma stared at Clancy, scrunching up her eyebrows as she studied him suspiciously.

Mama was down a long row of flat headstones. Ava would have never found it without Clancy, but then there it was.

Leanne Rosalie Henderson.

Only twenty-five years separated her birth and death dates. She wasn't much older than Sienna, Ava realized with a sense of sadness and horror. Such a short life.

"I barely remember her," Ava said just above a whisper.

She'd been beautiful, and she loved putting on makeup, though it was a secret from Daddy. Ava remembered watching her apply bright red lipstick to her lips and then she'd kiss the air, saying, *"Bonjour, mon cheri."* She'd wipe away all the evidence before Daddy came home from the church. Aunt Jenny later told her that a few months after she left them, Daddy found the tube of lipstick hidden under Ava's pillow. But Mama was mostly a void in her memories.

"Ava's here with me today," Clancy said to the green space her mother occupied. Ava watched her brother chew on a long straw weed. He chuckled out of the side of his mouth. "No, Ma, this baby isn't mine."

"Do you think she hears you?"

Clancy winked. "No."

"Really, you don't? Then why talk to her?"

"It's nice to talk to someone, even if that someone isn't actually there. If I did that other places, I'd get looked at oddly. But at the cemetery I can talk all I want, no matter who else is there, and they understand."

"Brother, you are starting to worry me."

He laughed so loud it echoed across the cemetery grounds. Emma jumped at his laugh, then cooed and smiled at Clancy.

"I'm just messing with you. Don't worry, I don't spend my days hanging out with our mama in the grave and Daddy in the pen. For a while I did. For another while I hung out at the bars, doing that scene. I still can't get myself back to church, though you forgiving church folk make me think it's possible."

Ava took the flowers from Clancy, unwrapping the plastic and rubber band.

"It took me awhile, and I think getting away from all this helped. God wasn't the problem. He's always here, faithful, loving, unfailing, and true. Unlike His people. Unlike Daddy and Grannie."

"Praise Him for that," Clancy said.

Ava bent down, cleaning out old leaves and dirt from the metal vase beside the headstone. She arranged the flowers inside, then she brushed her hands together as she stood.

"How often do you come then?"

"I stop in to see Mama maybe once a year or so. I like to put some flowers on her grave so as she's not all the way forgotten. You know, I don't have one memory of her, being so young as I was. Seems like a good son should do a little something to take care of his mama, so this is what I do."

Ava threaded her arm through her brother's, bending her head against his shoulder. "You are a wonderful man, Clancy Henderson."

Thirty

ANY WORDS THEY MIGHT HAVE SPOKEN SETTLED DOWN INTO thoughtful silence as they drove between the cemetery and the prison.

They rode in Clancy's old Chevelle as the heater rumbled, fighting the outside chill that rode in on the autumn breeze. Emma fussed in the back, and Ava climbed over the seat and gave her a pacifier, leaning close as she talked to the baby. Emma looked up at Ava with those chocolate brown eyes and smiled through the pacifier.

They came into a town and suddenly Clancy turned right onto a street and she saw boxy buildings surrounded by fencing topped with razor wire. A guard tower came into view, cutting into the cold blue sky.

Ava wondered if they'd allow a baby inside. She stared at Emma as the baby squeezed her finger within her tiny hand, and she suddenly regretted this idea. She shouldn't bring a baby into such an environment. Prison was a place that housed evil and sorrow—how could that not affect them all?

It was one of many reasons she'd never brought her children to see her father. Her father's choices sent him to prison, while her children were innocent and needed protection. This was her reasoning. And so she'd stayed away.

Dane had come a few times. First to ask her father's permission to marry Ava, and then again within the first year after both Sienna and Jason were born. He brought pictures and shared the details, giving excuses as to why Ava couldn't come herself.

And so quickly the years had passed. Ava hadn't planned to stay away. She sent him a box of goodies every Christmas and on his birthdays. For several years she'd helped his prison get new books in their library. Yet now more than thirty years stretched out since she'd seen her father face-to-face.

Clancy pulled into the parking lot, and Ava stared at the same towering building that hadn't changed in the years between. Her mouth went dry, and she couldn't quite process the reality that her father had been right here all this time while she'd been out in the world, going to college, meeting Dane and getting married, having her children, watching them grow up, traveling on vacations, celebrating holidays and birthdays. He'd been in this prison since she was seventeen years old.

"I'll keep the little one here," Clancy said as he turned off the engine.

"You're not coming with me?" Ava said, her heart rate rising.

"Can, but seems best not to take the baby."

Ava nodded, relieved and panicked at the same time.

"Tell him I'll see him Saturday. It'd be better for you to talk to Daddy that way."

Ava nodded, staring up at the ominous razor wire that surrounded the prison. "I won't be long."

"Take your time. I can manage. You've got the thermos to make formula in there, and I'm good with kids apparently."

Ava forced a smile. "Okay. Here I go."

She went through the security checks, filling out papers, checking in her purse, walking through the X-ray machine. She joined a few other women and an elderly man separated from the other visitors who were going to the main visitation area. They were going to the prison hospital area. Ten minutes later, a buzzer sounded and they were escorted into the visitation room.

I can do this, she told herself again and again. She tasted blood from biting her lip. Then she prayed, *God, help me to do this right. I want to run out of here, but you brought me to this doorway. Guide me through it.*

Ava didn't recognize him, and she was already assuming he'd be considerably changed. It was something in his walk that returned her attention to the small silver-headed man who gazed around the room searching for someone other than her.

The Reverend Daniel Henderson was an old man.

His age wasn't just in his hair and wrinkles as he squinted, searching the room for his visitor. It was in his movements and the defeat in his shoulders.

He met her eyes and recognition lit his face. Ava walked toward him. They were nearly the same size now.

"I can't believe my eyes. I would not have guessed this,"

he said, pressing down his stick gray hair. He didn't try to hug her, and Ava wondered if that was because of prison rules or choice or respect for her.

He stood with several feet between them. "You look so . . ."

"Old?" she said with a laugh.

He took her in, as if trying to memorize every detail. "Beautiful."

Ava took a surprised step back. She couldn't remember her father ever saying she was beautiful. He was good at instructing and giving approval for accomplishments, a verse memorized, or a song sung at church. But approval was different from a genuine compliment. She knew he believed this was protecting her from vanity, never understanding that a girl didn't grow vain from her daddy's love.

The look in his eyes and that singular word from her father—*beautiful*—shook her emotions from unsteady to critical instability.

She cleared her throat. "Um, it's good to see you."

He laughed and she noticed his teeth, or rather the lack of several. They were black gaping holes that made him appear even older than he was.

"Can't say that I look beautiful, that's for sure. So your brother told you." He pulled out a chair with a loud screech along the floor, motioning her to sit down before he sat in the chair beside her.

"Yes," she said, settling uncomfortably in the hard plastic chair.

"And you came to wish me good-bye and good blessings

on the journey over?" he said with a wink and set both hands palms down on the table in a gesture so familiar that it took her back to his preaching days.

"No, that's not it." Ava wanted to explain everything in a nice, clean package. But the truth was, she had come because he was dying. "I suppose, in a way."

"All right then. Before all that good-bye nonsense, lemme hear about you and yours. I have many years to get caught up on. Your brother tells me you do a lot of ministry work in your church. Your Christmas letters don't tell me squat really."

She nodded, but couldn't get any words out. How did she fill in all the spaces between them?

"You're part of one of those mega-churches?" he prodded as if helping her grasp something to steady her emotions.

"No, it's large. But not as large as a lot of the churches in Dallas."

"Anything over a few hundred is pretty mega to me."

Ava didn't know what to say to that. He'd been a preacher with a rabid following. Now he was a felon preparing to die.

"What ministering do you do?" he asked.

Ava inhaled deeply. "I teach a Bible study on Thursdays. And I'm part of a ministry that helps people in tragic or crisis situations."

"That must be a busy ministry."

Ava breathed in and out again, feeling her head clear and the sense of being overwhelmed soften. "Getting busier and busier."

"And my grandson plays football, I'd love to have seen that. And my granddaughter is getting married?"

"No, she's now going to travel in Asia." Ava wondered how he'd take that.

He frowned a moment, staring at his hands. Then nodded slowly. "Asia? She's got to be careful. But good for her. I should have traveled more away from Texas."

"Where would you have gone?" Ava never considered that her father had dreams outside of his congregation, though he'd had an entire life she knew nothing about.

"Israel would have been first choice. To see where the Lord Jesus walked and everything else way back to Moses, and Joshua's days. But other places too. I once read a book about those Terra Cotta Warriors they dug up in China. I'd have liked to seen that and could've ministered there as well."

Ava felt a sense of bewilderment that through everything her daddy still had a passion for God.

"You don't come see me. I ain't never seen my grandbabies. But I guess I understand. Prolly would've done the same."

When had her father start using *ain't?* In their other life, he would have whipped them for using slang like that, saying it was akin to profanity.

"Profanity of the English language," Ava muttered without meaning to.

"That'd be correct. Too many years inside. I've lived a third of my life in here now, did you know that?"

Ava counted the years and realized he was close to her age when he was arrested.

"I'll bring your grandchildren to see you. They're grown now, and it should have happened before. I know that now."

"I'd 'preciate that. Gotta protect kids from places like this when they're young. This is a very bad place. For a long while I thought I was like Joseph. Kept expectin' to start understanding dreams or what not. But now I'll be freed, though not in the way I expected."

"Daddy, I'm sorry I didn't come see you." Ava knew her excuses had some validity. Without putting the past behind her, she might not have been the functioning adult she'd been. She could've easily turned out like the rest of the family, stuffed in together at her grandmother's farm. It had taken hard work to not settle for what she'd grown up with.

"If we let it, life can easily get measured by what we should have done, instead of what good we did. I hope you can remember some good memories."

Ava nodded and reached for hands worn thin by age and illness. "I remember, Daddy. I really do." Then Ava realized he might need to hear some of it.

"I remember picnics down at the river beneath the willow trees. In fact, I had a willow tree in my backyard in Dallas just to remember the good times. I love the Bible because of your Bible, and I'll always listen to the sound of people turning the pages. I memorize Scripture even today because of that habit you gave me, and those verses come to mind when I need them, which is all the time. I'll always remember you baptizing people, how happy they were rising from the water all fresh and new."

Daddy covered his face with his hands as tears streamed down his cheeks.

"Thank you, Father God," he murmured.

Ava felt tears on her cheeks as well as she continued, "When Sienna was little, I couldn't fix her hair without thinking of how hard you tried to get the tangles out of my hair and make me look presentable. She was just like me, fighting against the hairbrush, and I thought I was getting my due after all the grief I gave you."

He wiped his face as he chuckled.

"You were a little hellion when it came to getting your hair fixed."

Ava smiled and cleared the teardrops from her cheeks. Daddy sighed deeply and reached for her hands once again.

"My little firefly, it makes my heart glad to know I gave you something good for all the pain. I hope you will forgive me. I did lots more sins than I let myself see for a long while. Joseph fled from temptation, but I didn't have the strength. And all the while, I loved Jesus. I hope you know that. The Bible is full of fallen men, so maybe that helped me excuse myself, or I thought it didn't count when I did it. It caught up to me all right."

Ava squeezed his hands, aware of their fragility.

"But you done well for yourself and your children. I'm proud of that. Anyway, I made that whole cancer thing up to get you here," he said with a chuckle, and for a second she nearly believed him.

"Clancy said you didn't want me to know about it. Why not?"

He pursed his lips as if considering what to say. "Guess part of me wanted you to remember how I was, looking all young and dapper. I've been writing down some things for him to give you. Seems nowadays I'm better with a pen than my words. My mouth has gotten me in a heap of trouble over the years."

Ava nearly agreed, but remained silent.

"I still minister to people here and through letters outside. But time in here has softened an old codger like me into a real kind of humility. Not the humility I thought I had back in the day."

Ava understood what he meant. He'd been a showman, shouting and pointing his finger about the dangers of pride, talking about humility as if he owned it, working with the poor and "people of color" as his acts of helping the less fortunate. But in all of that humility was his pride.

"Your mama really loved you."

Ava released his hands, surprised that he'd brought up Mama.

"You were her joy for a really long time," he said, and she waited, holding her breath. He sighed and rubbed his eyes, "But I'm getting tired now. I think it's time I return to the infirmary."

"Of course. Are you getting good care?"

"Yes, very good care. And it's almost worth the cancer to be staying in the infirmary," he said with a chuckle. He pushed himself up to stand, stopping partway to study her again. "You look like her. In the eyes and that little chin. Your mama believed in happy endings. I always believed in God's judgment."

"What do you believe now?"

He chuckled as if she'd told a joke. "I guess somethun' in between the two. Most people don't have a happy ending here on this ole earth, but we can get us one on the other side. At least, that's what I'm hoping. Then yer mama, and me, too, I suppose, could have our happy ending."

"I do believe it, Daddy. I love you," she whispered, reaching out to hug him. He sighed as if he'd longed for such words. Ava could feel the outline of his bones beneath his jumpsuit. He didn't smell of aftershave like he always had, but of age and sickness. And yet Ava treasured the feel of his arms around her, patting her back and whispering his love back to her.

"My firefly," he said, kissing her cheek. "You know, God is much more than I realized before."

Ava considered the words. She knew what he meant, but it had always hung off the edges of her busy life. The past week opened this up like clouds parting to rays of sunlight. She taught Bible study every week, quoted Scripture, and lived a Christian life. Yet God was more, much more than she could grasp, and her father knew it too.

Outside the visitation room Ava leaned her forehead against the wall, trying to breathe, trying not to succumb to the sobs as tears dropped to the gray tile floor between her feet.

Thirty-One

CLANCY SAT ON THE HOOD OF THE OLD CHEVELLE, LOOKING LIKE
James Dean except with a baby instead of a cigarette in hand.
He lifted his head and frowned.

"That bad, huh?" he said.

Ava closed the distance between them, still unable to speak.

"Please tell me you didn't shock the old man again by telling
him you're doing drugs and having sex all the time," Clancy said
as he opened the car door with Emma in one arm. Ava wiped
the tears from her eyes and laughed as she scooped up the baby
and received a welcoming squeal.

"I was a little more subtle this time," she said, kissing Emma's
cheek.

"That's a good thing. Remember how you wrote him that
you'd become a vegetarian and were considering converting to
Buddhism?"

"I was angry. And I thought he needed to know there were
consequences for what he'd done."

"Yeah, and a life sentence in prison wasn't enough."

"All right, all right. I apologized later for that."

Clancy laughed long and hard at the memory. "I admired you for it, wished I could tell him a thing or two. Anyone else and I'd have done more than said a few words. But Daddy, well, I just never could."

Clancy turned on the key to the Chevelle and the engine roared to life.

Ava remembered the last time they'd driven away—it had been with the windows down and music blaring.

"It saved you a lot of guilt and a fortune spent on a therapist," she said, leaning in to buckle Emma.

"This fine specimen of a man wouldn't be here today if it weren't for my own load of guilt and my AA sponsor."

As they drove, Ava turned back to check on Emma and watched the prison falling away behind them. Daddy was in his box, folded up and put away.

"Want to stay another night?" Clancy asked after a while.

A longing for home came over her. Not her house, the swimming pool, or the stump of a tree, but she longed for Dane and her children and the sweet yearning that they brought of a home beyond this one.

"It's time for me to get heading back home. I need to make some headway tonight."

She made a mental tabulation of her money. With her remaining stash, she had just enough for gas, a little food, and a stay at the Lonesome Motel again. Perhaps she'd see the waitress, Jackie, and tell the older woman all the ways God had taken care of them in the past few days.

They arrived back at Clancy's with it still early afternoon. Ava packed up from the night before. She'd been wearing the same jeans since Saturday and it was now Tuesday. Thankfully she'd been smart enough to toss in extra underwear, though she'd only planned on being gone one or two nights. Somehow one or two had grown into three or four.

Ava made Emma's bottle, then remembered one last thing she wanted to do.

"Would do you mind watching Emma for me? I want to see something one more time."

"'Course. I might just keep the little peanut if you aren't careful."

"It won't take me long."

"The willows?" he asked, taking the baby from her arms.

Ava bit the edge of her lip. Her brother knew her better than she realized.

"Yeah. They still there? No subdivision moved in when I was away?"

"Not with me holding the deed. How about I drive you down there with the little peanut? The road's gotten pretty rough. Emma and I'll take a walk in the great outdoors, give you some time."

Clancy put Emma in her car seat in the middle section of his work truck, leaning over to entertain her as they went. He made funny faces and airplane noises, which brought smiles and squeals of joy in response.

"I like this kid," Clancy said, meeting Ava's eyes.

For a split second, Ava nearly said *Want her?* But she vetoed the joke before it slipped from her lips. She'd grown quite attached to the little sweetie herself.

"It doesn't take long for this baby to attach herself to your heart," Ava said, looking down at Emma.

"You call her *the baby* or *this baby* pretty often."

Ava was aware of that. "I know. I must be afraid to call her anything else."

"You don't want to fall all the way in love with her."

Ava looked at the road ahead, surprised again at her brother's insightfulness. He was wasting his life out here all alone without a woman to love or a larger purpose for his many gifts.

"You know, Thanksgiving is coming in a few weeks," Ava said.

"I wondered if I'd get an invitation this year."

"Hmm, I don't know." She laughed. "You have one every year. You're always welcome. Now the rest of our family, not so much."

"I've eaten many Thanksgivings alone instead of going to the family circus."

"The kids haven't seen you in a while, why not come?"

Clancy nodded. "Just might do that."

"We may be losing everything," she stated without ceremony. "The company, the house, our retirement . . ."

Clancy turned quickly as if to see if she was serious. "It's been happening a lot, and to unexpected people."

"Funny how in the last few days it's been the least of my concerns." She gazed out at familiar fields, bouncing along the road nearly covered in brush and grass.

"You've got a place to come to you, if you need it," Clancy said, navigating around a large Manzanita.

"You'd be up for us all moving in with you?"

"Sure. I'm ready for a big change myself. And I have job security. Everybody needs their car fixed at some point, though I may be getting trades of eggs and beef with how things are going."

Ava laughed picturing it. Dane in a flannel shirt out plowing the fields. Jason under a car with his uncle learning the ins and outs of an engine. Baby Emma climbing into a tree fort in the backyard . . .

"You're going to be okay. *Mi casa es su casa*, quite literally." Clancy laughed. "I don't see that as your future, but it's an alternative if you need it. In any case, I'd love to see my family out here more often."

"So why haven't you settled down, found someone? You're no spring chicken, you know."

"Yeah, but I haven't met the right woman yet. I got me some high expectations," he said with a laugh.

Ava wondered how many single women there were in her old hometown. She wondered what kind of a girl would make a good match. Her mind stopped suddenly on Kayanne. They'd met years earlier before Kayanne's husband had left her. They'd joked amicably about Clancy sitting at the kid table. But she'd never considered setting the two up. Her brother lived out in the sticks, and Kayanne was a city girl. But stranger things had happened.

Clancy stopped at the edge of an overgrown meadow. The

path to the river was only a faint trail of dual tire tracks with dry, wheat-colored weeds bent and broken above the new green grass that had only just appeared underneath.

Clancy motioned with his head for her to go on, and Ava suddenly felt like running barefoot and free as she once had as a child.

Instead she walked slowly, running her hand over the tops of straw-colored grass just as she'd done as a child and then a young woman.

There along the river's edge, the five willow trees remained and had grown, though not as much as she expected. Then she realized that her perspective had grown with the years faster than the tree branches. Many things that were grand and exciting as a child were now seen with new eyes—adult eyes—and often found lacking.

The leaves dripped liquid sunshine toward the earth. She bent low and stood beneath the umbrella of leaves and branches. Beyond the trees the gray-blue water of the Black Rock River moved at its laziest pace of the year before the winter rains filled it up again.

Ava thought of her journey here. Less than two months earlier, she was planning a wedding and believed things were darn near perfect. She'd been comfortable in her life, confident in her relationship with God, and proud of the family they'd become.

In such a short time frame, all that she found secure had been shaken. And Ava had taken Emma on a five-hundred-mile road trip. The sweet baby didn't know where she was going, what was happening around her, or who she'd meet along the way. Yet she knew her needs would be met. She cried out and expected someone to hear her.

"I guess we can't all live life like an infant," she muttered to the air where a breeze stirred up the branches.

After all these years seeking God, it amazed her to realize just how vaguely she could see Him. Emma had such a limited vision of what was happening around her, and still she trusted. Wasn't that exactly how they were supposed to live their lives—with the faith of a child?

She remembered a verse in Job that she'd recited with confidence as if she fully understood it. But the verse held a meaning she'd never known before.

"I had only heard about you before, but now I have seen you with my own eyes. I take back everything I said, and I sit in dust and ashes to show my repentance." — Job 42:5–6

Thirty-Two

THE SIGN TO HER MOTEL GLOWED WITH A HALOED LIGHT THROUGH misty night. Drizzling rain came down in long angled sheets and an occasional gust of wind rocked the car.

The old Lonesome Motel was a welcome sight as the weariness of the past few days settled over her on the drive from Clancy's house.

As she pulled into the parking lot, her lights flashed across the front of the hotel lobby. A man rose from a couch and peered out the window, bending to look toward the car. Ava knew that shape, the way he leaned forward, the mannerism.

What was he doing here, she wondered, with a great sense of relief flooding her.

Ava pulled into a parking space and watched Dane run through the rain toward her. She opened her door.

"Hello," he said with a slight smile on his face, still a few feet away. Ava felt love well up within her in a way she hadn't felt in decades. A shy excitement washed over her. Her tongue felt tied.

"You're getting wet," she said, biting her lip and feeling the longing to touch him. "What are you doing here? How did you find me?"

"I've missed you." He took her in his arms and spun her around.

"How did you know where I was?"

"I'm kind of smart that way," he said in a thick Southern accent that made her laugh.

"I have no choice but to agree."

"It helps that your brother actually answered his phone. But what I can't believe is that you took Old Dutch out," he said with a laugh. They were both getting wet, and Ava took a quick peek at Emma asleep in her car seat.

"It seemed like a good idea at the time."

"You need me, and more than you care to admit. But then, I most certainly need you. I need you, and I want you."

She actually blushed as he pulled her tighter against him. His body sent shivers through her own.

"We have a baby with us," she muttered.

"That didn't stop us when the kids were small. And I got us a room with two queen-sized beds."

"Aren't you proactive? What if I wasn't a sure thing?"

"You aren't a sure thing. But you can't blame a guy for trying."

"Well, that guy might just get everything he's hoping for, and much more." She laughed at herself. She was shamelessly flirting with her husband.

"Let's get inside. First thing I want to do is meet that little baby."

Ava beamed with a pride that could only be found in a mother's love.

⌘

The streetlight streamed through the curtains. Emma slept soundly on her back on the bed across from them. Their legs were woven together with the sheet and blanket from the bed.

"You want to sleep with her, don't you?" Dane said. Ava's head rested on his chest.

"Why would you say that? I'm in perfect bliss right now. Why don't we get away more often together?"

"I don't know. I guess we get caught up in everything else and forget that we actually like one another." Dane tightened his arms around her.

"I didn't forget," she said, leaning up to kiss his neck.

"I didn't either, but it feels different right now."

"Different how?"

"I guess God has worked in me in ways that only God can. He's made me see everything in a new way when all the while I thought I had it right."

Ava propped her chin on his solid chest. "That's quite a true statement—and I can relate. We have some stories to swap."

Ava glanced again toward Emma sleeping with her arms stretched out, surrounded by pillows.

"What are we going to do with her?" Ava asked with a lump forming in her chest.

"What do you want to do with her?"

"I want her to have a good family and a good life."

"She can have that with us."

Ava stiffened and leaned up on one elbow to see Dane's face. He'd said for years that he only wanted two children. Ava had long since moved beyond the question. She'd agreed that two was perfect—one girl and one boy.

She tucked the sheet beneath her arm. A forty-eight-year-old body wasn't the same as it once was.

Dane tugged it down.

"Stop," she said with a tease in her tone, pulling the covers back up. "But seriously, I am concerned that Jessie would try to get her if we found her someone outside the family."

"Seems to me she's supposed to be ours."

Emma puckered her lips together and moaned sweetly in her sleep.

"She's all alone over there," Dane said.

"She might be cold." Ava gazed up at Dane with a smile.

"Do we bring her here or go there?"

"Let's go there so she doesn't wake up."

They untangled from the sheets and got up. Ava snuck off to the bathroom with her pajamas and toothbrush. When she returned Dane rested on his side, gazing down at Emma.

"What will the kids think of this?"

"Think of what?"

"Having another sibling, of course."

Ava laughed and the baby jumped. Dane placed his palm against Emma's chest and one finger into her open palm. Her fingers wrapped around his as she settled back to sleep.

Was there anything more attractive than a man curled up next to a baby?

"We might need to sneak back to the other bed if you don't stop that," Ava said, sitting on the edge.

"What do you mean?" Dane said innocently with his most mischievous grin.

"I'm giving you all of myself. All that a human can give another human."

Dane's face grew serious, touched by her words, and she was glad he understood what she was saying.

"You have my heart, soul, and body as well." Now she smiled, and again felt her face flush.

He leaned down and kissed Emma's cheek. "We'll be back in a while."

Thirty-Three

AVA OPENED THE DOOR TO SOMEONE HOLDING A PILE OF GIFTS. She recognized his hands and the "Ho, ho, ho."

"You made it! Everyone is already here," she said, taking several presents to reveal her brother's face.

Ava ushered Clancy inside with her eye catching on the For Sale sign stuck into their front lawn. They were downsizing, and Ava had reached the point of letting go of anything that came between her family and peace.

She set the gifts under the tree, announcing Clancy's arrival to a host of subdued cheers since Emma was taking her afternoon nap in the playpen in the den. Cheerful Christmas music played in the background.

With a sly expression, Sienna motioned to Ava toward the scene of Kayanne and Clancy chatting as if they were old friends . . . or perhaps as if they were something more. Ava studied her best friend, then her brother, and her best friend again. There was certainly something there—she could see it on both faces. She hadn't dared really hope it might work out.

After Thanksgiving dinner, Clancy and Kayanne had been talking, but Kayanne wasn't saying much about it. It sparked Ava's curiosity, especially since Kayanne was taking a break from her online dating sites.

The timer on the stove sounded and Kayanne pulled herself away from Clancy, following Ava to the kitchen.

"Did I tell you that Corrine Bledshoe is leaving the church?" Kayanne asked as she opened the oven and removed a tray of stuffed potatoes.

"Why?" Ava asked, strangely saddened by the news. Corrine had removed herself from the Bible study Ava led and her involvement with Broken Hearts. Ava guessed Corrine may have decided that her strange behavior was proof she wasn't on Corrine's list of approved acquaintances.

"She told Pastor Randy that she's looking for a more old-school church."

"That's too bad," Ava said, and meant it. She wondered what kind of a path Corrine had ahead of her.

"Mom, you have to come out here," Jason said, bursting into the living room from the backyard, the French door slamming against the jamb and back open.

Emma's frightened wail sounded from the den down the hall and over the baby monitor.

"Sorry, I forgot again," Jason said, standing awkwardly with the door open behind him.

Dane strode down the hall and returned a moment later with an already subdued Emma bouncing on his shoulder.

"What is it?"

"Out by the willow tree."

"You mean where the willow tree once stood before my mountain woman hacked it down with an ax?" Dane had teased her to no end about that. He'd laughed till he nearly turned blue when he saw the jagged cuts she'd made all over the tree trunk and the healing blisters that covered her hand.

"Can you show us after we eat?" Ava asked, but Jason immediately shook his head.

"You just need to come out here. I'm not saying more. You have to see for yourself."

Ava was about to insist she'd go see whatever it was after they ate Christmas dinner, but the earnest expression on her son's face changed her mind.

"All right, what it is?"

"Everyone should come too," Jason said, leading the way.

They gathered around the stump of the willow tree. Rising out of the white wood was a sprig growing straight toward the sky.

"Is that . . . It can't be. It's winter. Nothing sprouts in the dead of winter."

"Apparently this does," Dane said, holding Emma wrapped in a blanket.

"It's not dead, even after I chopped it down?" Ava said in amazement.

"It came back—remember how the nursery guy said it might? Something in the old tree made this one grow." Jason bent down next to the sprig of willow tree.

They all headed back inside, but Ava stayed behind. She

couldn't believe it. The willow tree would grow again. As Jason had said, something in the old had given life to something new.

Ava was filled with an overwhelming sense of God's hand working through all of it. Faces scrolled through her mind, from Bethany and her father to Corrine and the families she helped through Broken Hearts. Faces of grief and faces of loss, faces of pain . . . all of them had broken hearts.

But something beautiful grew from there.

Ava could see her family through the windows of the house as she walked to join them. Her daughter peered into the oven, checking the pies, and seemed more radiant than she could remember seeing her. Clancy was surely teasing his niece and Kayanne as he tiptoed around the kitchen bar stealing bites of food. Jason and Dane played with Emma, her teenage son reduced to a boy as he made silly faces and laughed at the baby's exuberant response.

They were the new, grown up from the loss.

Ava thought of Bethany and the children being raised out at Grannie's old place. What kind of Christmas were they having, she wondered. She'd find a way to help them—she wasn't sure how, but in whatever ways God opened up.

As Ava went to join them inside, Jason opened the door, her phone in his hand.

"I think the woman is crying," Jason said with a concerned look.

Ava took the phone, glancing at the number, an area code she didn't recognize. She moved inside and down the hallway away from the cheerful banter and Emma's happy squeals.

"I'm so glad you're there. This is Nancy Branson—something just awful has happened, on today of all days."

Ava recognized the voice of a woman from her favorite boutique in town.

"What's going on?"

"It's my best friend. Her son." Nancy covered the phone, but Ava could hear her sobs. "Her son overdosed last night. I would be there, but I'm visiting my sister in Maine, and I can't get a flight out until this storm passes. You told me about that service or volunteer work or whatever it is you do that helps people. I know it's Christmas, but if someone could be there for her. She's divorced and her family is all far away . . ."

Ava bit the edge of her lip, running through her mind's list of the women who might be able to help today. "We'll get someone out there right away. Give me the information, and your friend's number."

Ava turned and met Jason with a pen and paper in his hand. The rest of the family had crowded near to hear what the urgent call was about.

"I'll go," Kayanne said as Ava ended the call.

"Why don't you and I go together?" Dane said to Ava.

"We can't," she said, glancing at the faces around her, but feeling the tug of the woman's grief in her heart.

"The baby and I will watch a Christmas video and maybe sneak a peek at the gifts," Sienna said, taking Emma from Dane's arms.

"We'll wrap up dinner and have a late one when you get back," Clancy said with a wink.

"Go, Mom. It's important, and we'll be together when you get back," Jason said.

Ava and Dane quickly gathered up their coats, and Ava asked everyone again if they didn't mind.

"It kind of seems like this is what Christmas should be like," Jason said, and Ava kissed him good-bye.

As they drove away from the house, Ava glanced back at the cars on the driveway and the blinking Christmas lights on the eaves of the house. She didn't know what the future held, but God knew and He was carrying them along in His arms, healing their broken places and taking them on new adventures.

"Do you have the directions?" Dane asked.

Ava smiled to herself as she answered, "I sure do."

Reading Group Guide

1. In the novel, Ava's comfortable life suddenly spins out of control. How have you experienced such times, and what did it feel like?

2. Though Ava built a new life separate from her past, she reaches a time when the past returned to her. If there are painful places from your past that continue to bubble to the surface, do you think God is trying to heal you or something else?

3. When bad things happen, do you tend to blame God or draw closer to Him? How does your reaction affect you and the people in your life?

4. Does every person experience brokenness of some kind at some point in his or her life journey? Why or why not?

5. In the novel, Ava constantly tried to "keep all her ducks in a row." Do you think a person can try controlling too

much of their life and of their families? Too little? What is the balance between making life our own and living in faith?

6. Do you think the church should do more to care for the brokenhearted? What can they do to provide such care?

7. Ava had learned through her ministry that when people are hurting, there are times to talk and times to be silent, times to quietly help in the background and times to step up and actively contribute. Discuss times that you experienced this or when someone hurt you because of their good intended words and actions.

8. Though God can heal our lives, why can't we fully out-run the past?

9. Do you believe God is the source of suffering in the world?

10. Can God heal every broken heart?

11. Do you think God is ever brokenhearted?

12. How can God transform our broken hearts into something of beauty?

13. Write down five ways God has helped bring healing to your life (directly, through surprising circumstances, or from other people in your life).

14. How has God shocked you by opening a door that you never expected?

Acknowledgments

SHEILA WOULD LIKE TO THANK
THE FOLLOWING PEOPLE:

The Nelson Fiction team who intentionally pursue excellence
in everything they do.
 Huge thanks to Cindy who is creative and kind, a true soul-
sister.

CINDY WOULD LIKE TO THANK
THE FOLLOWING PEOPLE:

I have been blessed with an amazing group of people who have
been a song to my broken heart and who bring me renewed joy
every day.
    My parents, Richard and Gail McCormick—parenting
never ends, does it? Thank you for the constant little things

you both do to be such great parents. And Mom, thank you for "Grandma Wednesdays" with Lily so I can keep putting down words.

Ruby Duvall—your laughter and joy are infectious; I'm blessed to have a grandmother who is a great woman of strength and heart.

Amanda Darrah—our friendship spans the best and worst of times, and in both, it's amazing to know you are always there (and THANK YOU for Hawaii!).

My sister, Jennifer Harman—sister power! No other words needed, right?

"My Kate" Martinusen—third grade and onward! Thank you for faithful friendship and prayers.

My sons, Cody and Weston Martinusen, bring daily laughter and life to my world. I'm glad God let me be your mom.

Madelyn Martinusen—it's amazing to have a daughter grow up and become such a wonderful, close friend. I truly cherish you.

My sweet Lily Jane—since your birth, you've brought enormous joy to my every moment and to our entire family.

Nieldon Coloma—the joining of our lives provided healing and newness, and I'm excited for all that stretches before us. It's wonderful to share life with you.

And to so many other people, I hope you know how much you mean to me.

ANGELS EAGERLY WATCH OVER ANNE FLETCHER'S EVERY MOVE. SHE JUST DOESN'T KNOW IT YET.

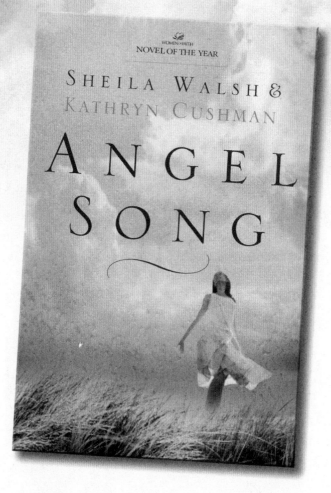

WOMEN OF FAITH
NOVEL OF THE YEAR

SHEILA WALSH &
KATHRYN CUSHMAN

ANGEL
SONG

THOMAS NELSON
Since 1798

AVAILABLE IN PRINT AND E-BOOK

WREN HAS TRIED TO SHELTER HER ONLY SON from the tumult of the world. Now she's about to find sanctuary . . . in the last place she ever expected.

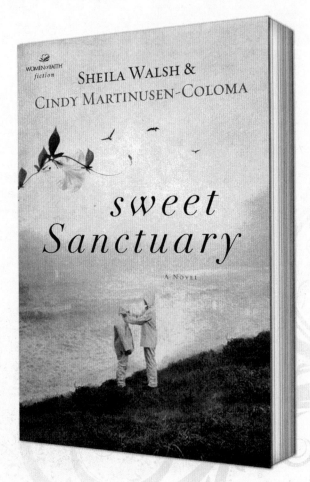

THOMAS NELSON
Since 1798

AVAILABLE IN PRINT AND E-BOOK

DON'T MISS THESE NOVELS FROM CINDY MARTINUSEN COLOMA

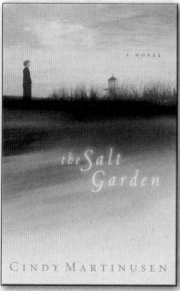

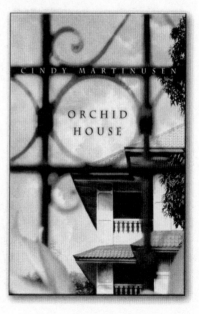

FOR THE YOUNG
ADULT READERS
IN YOUR LIFE
FROM CINDY
MARTINUSEN
COLOMA

About the Authors

SHEILA WALSH, Women of Faith® speaker, is the author of the award-winning Gigi, God's Little Princess® series, *The Shelter of God's Promises*, and the novel *Sweet Sanctuary*. Sheila lives in Texas with her husband, Barry, and son, Christian.

CINDY MARTINUSEN COLOMA is the bestselling author of several novels including *The Salt Garden*, *Beautiful*, and *Orchid House*.